The Fuller Creek Series

Holiday Blizzard: The Moment of Truth!
&
The Search for Rosemary Pullman

(Episodes Three & Four)

David C. Reyes

The Fuller Creek Series
Holiday Blizzard: The Moment of Truth!
&
The Search for Rosemary Pullman

Copyright, © 2013 David C. Reyes

All rights reserved. This book or any portion thereof
may not be reproduced or used in any manner whatsoever
without the express written permission of the publisher (author)
except for the use of brief quotations in a book review.

This is a work of fiction. The names, characters, places and incidents
are products of the author's imagination or are used fictitiously. Any
resemblance to actual events, locales or persons, living or dead, is
entirely coincidental.

REYES, DAVID C
ISBN: **978-1494363987**

Printed in the United States of America.
All rights reserved under the International Copyright Law.

Unless otherwise indicated. All scripture references are
taken from the Holy Bible, King James Version, Cambridge, 1769

CONTENTS

INTRODUCTION

CHAPTER ONE – FIRST KISS

CHAPTER TWO – THE FIELD TRIP

CHAPTER THREE – THE THIRD FLOOR

CHAPTER FOUR – REPERCUSSIONS

CHAPTER FIVE – HOLIDAY VACATION

CHAPTER SIX – THE BLIZZARD!

CHAPTER SEVEN – BIG MAN ON CAMPUS

CHAPTER EIGHT – THE ANSWER

CHAPTER NINE – THE MOMENT OF TRUTH!

CHAPTER TEN – THE CHRISTMAS DINNER

THE CONCLUSION

Holiday Blizzard: The Moment of Truth!
(Episode Three)

INTRODUCTION:

The fall season of our second year living in the town of Fuller Creek had arrived. One thing I have come to realize is that life can be one crazy rollercoaster. Sometimes it seems like things are looking up and you have reached a pinnacle in your life. But then it can all come crashing down, where you drop like a rock to the bottom of a pond. A lesson I am beginning to learn is a little thing called parental experience. Sometimes you think your parents are so outdated, but I guess they went through similar things when they were young. My mother helped me out with some good advice in dealing with Katie, and I really appreciated that. My friendship with Katie was kind of surprising, as I had never had a best friend that was a girl. Brian was my best "guy friend," and so it was kind of good to have friendships from two different perspectives.

Looking back at the strange and dangerous adventure Katie and I had at the Grand Canyon, I now looked forward to a nice calm year and starting the eighth-grade. My sister Tami had moved on to high school, which was basically across the street from the middle school. During the summer, Brian had introduced me to this girl named Melissa. She and her cousin Michelle would meet us at the mall, where we would hang-out. From what I knew of Melissa so far, she appeared to be nice and was very pretty too. I think Brian and Michelle wanted for us to "get together" as a couple, but every time I would think about doing that, something would always hold me back. I still hung-out with Katie once in a while, but she was busy with Becky, Marci, and all their other friends. The word going around was that this guy named Marc had a crush on Katie and I guess maybe Katie liked him too. Whenever Katie and I would do something together we never brought up the subject of liking other people. For the most part, we just stayed off of that subject.

Of course, being in middle school and beginning our teen years, you had to realize one thing… that gossip and stories were always flying around about somebody. Sometimes you heard stories which were pretty funny. But then other times, those stories were slanderous or hurtful to the person. Last year, Brian and I were the victims of some pretty bad rumors which almost messed up me and Katie's friendship. What I didn't realize was in the eighth-grade they can get even worse… to the very point of changing someone's life!

CHAPTER ONE – FIRST KISS

As we entered into the eighth-grade, Brian and I finally had a class together, Algebra. Although it wasn't my best subject, it was kind of cool to have a class with him, and of course we sat next to each other. Katie and I both took a drama class, as playing interesting characters fulfilled that adventurous side in us. Melissa and Michelle were also in our drama class, which caused me a bit of anxiety, knowing that all of us were in the same class. That particular day at lunchtime, Brian suggested the four of us do something this coming weekend.

"Hey Jess… do you want to go to the movies Friday night? That new movie E.T. is out—everyone says it's really good."

"That sounds cool. Who's going to drive us?"

"My dad said he would."

Brian turned to the girls sitting at the table. "Do you think you can go with us to the movies?"

"I'm pretty sure I can," Michelle said, as she looked to her cousin Melissa for her response.

Melissa flipped her long brown hair, and directed her gaze to me with a flirtatious smile. "It sounds like fun. It would be kind of like a double-date."

The way Melissa said that only confirmed what I had been thinking all last summer. That Melissa had a lot of ideas about the two of us being a couple and all.

"Then I guess it's a double-date," Brian added. "Do you girls want my dad to pick you up? Or will you just meet us there?"

"We'll meet you guys there," Michelle answered. "My dad will take us and pick us up afterwards. We kind of don't want my dad to know this is like a date or anything."

"Okay, sounds good," Brian said. "We'll see you girls there."

*****

On Friday, I began to get ready to go to the movies when my mother came into my room and sat the edge of my bed. From past experiences, whenever she did that it usually meant she was going to lecture me about something.

"Jesse…"

"Yeah, Mom?"

"You sure have been hanging around with this Melissa girl a lot?"

I grabbed my shoes from the closet and sat on my bed to put them on. "I wouldn't say a lot, but Brian wanted to go to the movies, so he invited Michelle and her cousin Melissa to go too."

"I know, but I saw the way this girl looked at you when I dropped you off at the mall. And to me, it's more than just a youthful crush. It's seems she has some serious ideas about you and her. What happened to Katie? It seems like the two of you are not hanging around as much as you used to. Katie is such a sweet girl."

I kept my focus on tying my shoe, because I knew where she was going with this, and I guess I didn't want to hear a lecture at the moment.

"Mom, Katie is too busy with her other friends right now."

"Well, just be careful with this Melissa."

I turned to her with a questioning stare. "What do you mean by that?"

"I mean this Melissa seems very mature for her age, and I'm a little wary of what her intentions are."

I got up and looked at myself in the closet-door mirror. "Intentions? All we intend on doing is watching a movie. That's all the intentions I know about."

I said it that way because I really didn't want my mom continuing to discuss the subject. All of this dating stuff kind of scared me, and at this point I was fine just getting to know different girls and see how they are. I didn't have any other "intentions."

Holiday Blizzard: The Moment of Truth!

After Brian's father picked me up, we drove out to the theater. Michelle and Melissa were waiting for us in front of the theater when we arrived. After we greeted each other, Melissa quickly stood by my side while we went to the counter to buy our tickets. When we got in the theater, we took our seats with Michelle sitting next to Brian of course, and Melissa sat down next to me. One thing I didn't like is they wanted to sit all the way in the back, whereas I liked to sit about halfway up in the middle of the theater. As the previews started, I could tell this was not going to be the same experience Katie and I had when watching movies. Even when the movie started, Melissa kept talking non-stop.

"What do you think of my new sweater?" she said, running her hand across her forearm to show me its softness.

"It's nice Melissa—a very pretty sweater."

I tried to keep my answers short and sweet, hoping maybe she would get the hint—unfortunately she didn't. She leaned into me once more.

"I got this sweater at the Totally Teens clothing shop in the mall last weekend. Michelle and I are going again next weekend. Maybe you and Brian can meet us there?"

I exhaled an impatient breath. "Maybe... but I'll have to ask Brian *after* we finish watching the movie." Hint-hint.

As she continued to talk all through the movie, it was starting to bug me. What made it worse was she didn't even comment about the movie itself. All she did was go on and on and on, about clothes and other stuff. At one point, she leaned into me, and laid her head on my shoulder. I know I probably should have liked that, with her being such a pretty girl and all; but I just didn't think our relationship was at that point yet. Since I felt a little uncomfortable about it, I made an excuse to leave.

"Melissa, I need to go to the restroom."

"Okay, but don't be long," she said with a flirtatious smile.

I rose from my seat and headed to the lobby. Brian quickly got up and followed me, finding me reading the poster for an upcoming movie.

"What's up, Jess? Why are you just standing here?"

"I don't know; I didn't know it was going to be like this."

"What do you mean?"

"I mean the four of us together—like we're couples or something. I never asked Melissa to be my girlfriend or anything like that."

"I know man, but you should. I mean just look at her. All the guys in our class think she's a total babe! If I didn't like Michelle, I would probably go for her myself." He punched me in the chest. "Na..., I'm just messing with you man, I wouldn't go for it. But seriously, do you know what kind of a rep you have now that you're with her? Guys from our school think you're 'The Man.'"

"The Man?"

"Yeah, they think you're going out with Melissa, and also have Katie on the side."

When he made that remark it really bugged me. I would never think of Katie that way. She meant so much more to me than that. Irritation rose in my voice as I answered.

"Brian, I don't have Katie on the side. That's not what our relationship is about."

"Alright, don't bust a vein. But seriously, you've now got a Rep as a ladies man since you started going out with Melissa."

I guess my ego got a little pumped-up with him saying that. Considering my sister is always calling me; squirt, twerp, and many other names. Plus I was always, "Tami's little brother" to all my teachers.

Hey, maybe I was "The Man." I thought. *"Maybe I do deserve some of this new-found popularity. And hey, if people want to think that, maybe I should let them.*

As I stood there thinking about that, Brian tapped me on the shoulder. "Let's go back in and finish the movie; okay Jess?"

"Alright, let's go back in."

After the movie ended, we had a little bit of time before Brian's dad was going to pick us up. As we walked outside of the theater, Melissa grabbed ahold of my hand.

"Come on Jess, I want to show you something."

She pulled me around the side of the theater, where there was like a back alley. As she stood staring deeply into my eyes, a weird feeling began to stir in my stomach.

Gee, I hope this feeling in my stomach is just nervousness being close to a pretty girl, and not that chili-dog coming back on me.

I looked to and fro down the alley. "So, what did you want to show me?"

Then without warning, she took the gum out of her mouth, pressed me up against the wall, and kissed me! We held the kiss for a few seconds, and then she pulled back.

"You know Jess, its better if you do your part," she said with a hint of sarcasm.

A look of shock ran across my face as the kiss totally caught me off-guard. I really didn't know how to react, and my head was spinning like a motorcycle in a motordrome. It was my first real kiss, so I was stunned by the whole thing. I had kissed this one girl in the sixth-grade while playing truth or dare, but that was just a peck. This was a *real kiss*, and so the experience was new to me. However, before I even had a chance to clear my head, she plunged forward and started to kiss me again. This time I decided to go along with it, and it actually felt pretty nice. When we released the kiss, she popped the gum back in her mouth.

"See Jess, it's much better when you do your part."

She confidently took hold of my hand, and we walked to where Brian and Michelle were standing. About that time, Michelle's dad pulled up to the curb. As Melissa headed towards the car, she turned and blew me a kiss.

"Bye Jess, see you Monday..." she said, with a flirtatious tone.

After they drove off, Brian turned to me with an inquisitive stare. "Dude, what was all that about?"

"I'm not sure; I'm still trying to figure it out myself. When she took me around the corner of the theater, she kissed me!"

"Really? Cool; how was it?"

"Well at first it was kind of like she was just *kissing me*. It took me off guard and at first I wasn't doing anything. Then the next time, I went along with it and actually it felt pretty good."

"So, are you guys going out—like a couple?"

"I don't know, I'm not sure what this means. The thing is… I'm not really sure how I feel about her. I mean part of me likes her because she's pretty and all. I also know she wants me to be her boyfriend, so that part of it is pretty exciting. But another part of me doesn't know if I really like her as a person. I'm not sure I like her personality, and we really don't have a lot in common."

"Dude… you just kissed a totally hot babe! How much more in common do you want?"

"I know, but I have way more fun and a lot more in common with Katie."

"Man, would you stop about Katie. Is Katie giving you any kisses like Melissa?"

"I don't know; I'll have to think about all this dating stuff."

*****

On Monday morning, the word got out about the four of us going on that date. And the story being told, was that Melissa and I we were now an official couple. In drama class, Katie and I were talking, when she brought up the subject.

Holiday Blizzard: The Moment of Truth!

"So Jess... I hear you and Melissa are now going-out. Congratulations, she's very pretty. You guys make a nice couple."

Before I could explain to her the reality of the situation, Marc Wilson came up and stood next to her side. He started talking with her about the upcoming skit we were going to be performing in class. When he finished, he turned my way as we stood staring at each other. What was weird about it was the type of stare down reminded me of those old western movies where two gunslingers are staring each other down, ready to draw their guns. Finally when our expressions softened, Katie realized we had never been formally introduced.

"Marc... this is a friend of mine, Jess. I wasn't sure if you guys had actually met."

He nodded his head in acknowledgment. "Hey man, how's it going? I hear you're going out with Melissa Stewart—she's smoking dude!"

Upon hearing his response, Katie looked the other way and acted like she really wasn't listening to our conversation. But I could tell by the way she glanced out the corner of her eye that she was. After we finished talking, she turned back around and tapped Marc on the shoulder.

"Come on Marc; let's go talk about that part for the upcoming skit."

As they walked-off, she placed her hand on his shoulder. I don't know if she did that because they were headed in same direction, or was it a sign to me that she and Marc were now a couple. Either way I wished we could have finished our conversation. I wanted to explain that Melissa and I were not an official couple. As I sat there in class, I thought maybe I would call her later that afternoon and try to talk to her about it. However in thinking it through, I wasn't sure how that was going to sound. Because then I would be assuming that Katie cared one way or the other about me and Melissa. In the end I just decided to let it go.

Later that afternoon at the McCullough residence, Becky gave Katie a call about all the happenings of the day.

"Hi Katie, are you busy?"

"No, I just finished with some homework—I can talk for a little while."

"So what did you think of Mr. Reed's new hairstyle today in math class?"

"Oh my God! He looked like Billy Idol with his hair spiked like that," Katie said, as they shared a laugh.

"For sure... that was one crazy hair-do."

Katie added. "I know; men can be so weird sometimes."

"Well speaking of men, or should I say boys... did you hear that Jess and Melissa are a couple?"

"Yes, I heard."

"So how do you feel about that?"

"I don't know, they make a cute couple. Why?"

"I'm just asking because you and Jess are close. And since he is apparently going out with Melissa, I was just wondering how you felt about it."

"I'm fine with it. I mean Jess has a right to go out with anyone he wants; and I can go out with whoever I want too."

"I know Katie, but there just seems to be something else going on there between you guys."

"What do you mean by that?"

"Well for example... you invited Jess on summer vacation and you have spent a lot of time going over to his house and hanging out. Then when two super-cute guys asked you to the winter formal dance, who did you end-up of going with—Jess. That's what I meant by 'something else' going on between you."

"I know, but Derek and Steve had other things in mind. Remember how I told you that Derek said he kind of liked me before he asked me to the dance. And then I think Steve might have liked me that way too. I just don't think I'm ready for all that yet. With Jess, it's safe; you know what I mean? And besides, anytime Jess and I get together, we always have so much fun. I also don't get nervous around him like when I'm around those other boys."

"Okay, I guess I kind of understand. But you still haven't actually answered my question. How you feel about Jess being with Melissa?"

"Like I told you before, I think they make a cute couple."

"Okay fine, I can see I'm not going to get a straight answer from you. So what about Marc? That boy has got a major crush on you."

"Marc seems nice and I know likes me, but like I said, I don't think I'm ready to be boyfriend and girlfriend yet. There are other things I have to consider when I think about starting that type of relationship."

"What do you mean? Like what kind of things?"

"Well for one, my religious beliefs. I want to know that anyone I might consider liking believes the same way I do."

"I know you have your strong beliefs, but I don't think it can hurt just see how different guys are. I mean it's not like you are going to marry them or something. Besides, a lot of these guys are awfully cute!"

"Yeah, I guess they are pretty cute, aren't they?" Katie said, as they laughed once more.

"Anyway Katie, I need to get off the phone, so I'll see you tomorrow."

"Okay, we'll talk then."

CHAPTER TWO - THE FIELD TRIP

Every year at the beginning of October, the eighth-grade class gets to go on a field trip. Sometimes they would go to a Mission or an Arboretum (plants, trees) or something like that. This year, we were going to the Museum of Natural History near Sacramento. You had to pay your own way to get into the museum, but the school would bus us there. They also provided the chaperones or teachers to watch over the groups of kids. As the event drew near, Katie gave me a call one afternoon to talk about it.

"Hey, Jess."

"Hi Katie, what are you doing?"

"Nothing much, I hadn't talked to you for a while, and I wanted to discuss the upcoming field trip to the museum. Are you going?"

"Yeah I plan to. How about you?"

"Yes, I think it will be pretty neat. Do you happen to know if Brian, Michelle and Melissa are going?"

"I think so. Almost everyone I have talked to said they are going. And why not, you get a free day away from school work. How about Becky and all of your other friends; are they going?"

"Most of the girls are going, but not Becky. Becky actually needed to go to the dentist, so she decided to do that instead. I don't think dinosaurs are really her thing anyways."

"Yeah, I don't see Becky getting into woolly mammoths."

After going back and forth on minor details regarding the trip, it seemed like neither of us would ask the other person who they were going to be with at the museum. It was then that I finally decided to put a stop to this "merry-go-round" we were on.

"Katie, do you want to hang around together at the museum? I have a little adventure in mind for the two of us."

"Really? What kind of adventure?" she asked, as I could hear the interest in her voice.

"I have a little mystery for us to solve while we're there."

"What kind of mystery?"

"Well, there's this story that has been passed down from all the eighth-grade classes that have gone to this museum. The story is; that there is a third floor or secret room hidden in the museum. It is said to have all kinds of dinosaur stuff and other artifacts they don't display to the public. They only show this room to special VIP type people—you know, like celebrities or rich people."

"Really? Are you sure that whoever told you this wasn't pulling your leg?"

"No, I don't think so. I saw this photo of the museum in the library, and the way it's built, it does look like there could be a third floor."

"So who told you about this?"

"I heard it from Brian's older brother, Tim. He went to the museum a couple of years ago. He and some friends of his friends tried to find it, but they never did."

"Has anyone ever found it?"

"No, some people have 'claimed' to have found it, but there has never been any proof. If there is a secret room in that museum, I want us to find it."

"Okay, I'm in!" she replied, without hesitation. "But how do you plan on getting away from the group we are supposed to be in?"

"Well, I was thinking about that. What we can do, is pick a group that has a teacher who doesn't know us very well. Then when the teacher isn't looking, we'll sneak off. I heard there are going to be a lot of other schools at the museum that day. There should be so many kids running all over the place, I'm hoping the teacher won't notice."

"This sounds so neat! I can't wait to go. But don't you think we should keep this to ourselves?"

"Oh yeah, definitely. I'm not even going to tell Brian about it."

"Do you know what this reminds me of? It reminds of when we went to the Winchester Mystery House. And how we tried to open that one door at the top of those stairs to that lead to nowhere."

"Oh yeah, how can I forget about that incident. Hopefully we won't get busted again."

"Yeah, let's hope not. You know, I just about had that door lock picked with my hair pin when that lady caught us."

"That was just so funny. Especially when the security lady shouted, 'Young lady; step away from the door!' Then when we started down the stairs; I still can't believe what you told her."

"Oh, you mean when I said, 'I'm the ghost of Sarah Winchester and I'm looking for my lost daughter,'" Katie said, in the same "haunting" voice she did that day.

"And then you tried to walk right past her with your arms stretched out like you were a zombie or a ghost."

Katie whimsically laughed. "Hey, I had to play the part!"

"What was even funnier was the security lady's response; do you remember? She looked at you, placed your arms down and said, 'Nice try kid... but they didn't have Calvin Klein jeans back in the late 1800s!'"

Katie and I shared a laugh thinking about that for a moment.

"Jess... why are we so crazy sometimes?"

"I don't know, sometimes I wonder about that myself. I know we both love a good adventure, but I would never think of doing some of these things with anyone else."

"No, me neither. You know, everyone looks at me like I'm 'Miss Church Girl,' and I guess maybe I am. But I think they would be surprised if they knew about some of the things I do."

"That's true, *you are* pretty crazy."

"You know they say that everyone has their own thing—you know, like a release. Maybe going on these adventures and investigating into things is *my* release."

"Speaking of releases… I just remembered I need to have one of my parents sign my release form so I can go. Before I forget, I think I'm going to get off the phone and go downstairs and ask my mom."

"Okay, I'll see you tomorrow."

"Okay, bye, Katie."

*****

The next day, right before drama class started, Melissa saw me and headed my way. For some reason every time she approached me I always seemed to get this weird anxiety that would creep into my gut. Once she brought up the subject of what she wanted to talk about, I realized my gut was right.

"Jesse… are you going on the field trip to the museum?"

"Yeah, I'm going," I replied, thinking to myself this was a subject I wanted to avoid.

"Well, I don't know if Brian told you, but he and Michelle broke-up and aren't going to be hanging around together at the museum. Michelle said it just wasn't working out. Anyway, I wanted to tell you, that you can still go in our group with me and Michelle if you like."

When she said that, I had to think fast knowing my plans with Katie.

"Well, I was planning on going in Brian's group. And seeing how they broke up, I don't think he would want to be in the same group as Michelle. Maybe we'll just play it by ear."

As Miss Simms gathered our attention to begin class, I knew what I had told Melissa wasn't exactly the truth, but I had to tell her something. I just hoped that it would all work out on the day of the field trip.

*****

On the day of our field trip, I woke up with a sense of excitement. Not only because I liked to see dinosaurs and science stuff, but because Katie and I were going on another adventure. In preparation, we made sure we picked a teacher who did not know us very well. We decided to go with, Miss St. John, who is the Home Economics teacher. Unfortunately, and I mean it in the sense that I wanted to be with Katie that day; Michelle and Melissa were going in the same group as us. Now don't get me wrong… it's not that I don't like Melissa, it's just that me and Katie have a special friendship and I have so much fun with her. We like to do certain things together; whereas I do other things with Melissa.

I arrived at school just about the time they were boarding the buses. Melissa saw me enter and signaled me over with a wave of her hand. I walked over to see what she wanted.

"Hi Jess… I didn't think you were going to be in our group. Why don't you come and sit with me."

Katie was already seated and saving a seat for me when she overheard what Melissa said. We glanced at each other with a telling look, and then Katie motioned for me to go ahead and sit with Melissa—so I did. Just then Marc Wilson and a few of his friends came onto the bus. Since the seat next to Katie was open, Marc asked if he could sit next to her, and she said it was fine. As the bus got on its way, Katie and I glanced at each other once more realizing that our little adventure was not starting out very good.

When we arrived at the museum, we gathered in our groups and began to tour the first floor. Melissa, Michelle and I were touring together, while Katie and Marc and a few of Marc's friends, were walking behind us. As we were looking at this one elephant exhibit, I looked up and saw something which piqued my interest. I stood waiting in front of the exhibit as if I was checking it out, so Katie's group would catch up. When she looked my way, I signaled her over.

"What is it, Jess?"

"Check it out. Lean over this rail and then look up. Behind the front wall of this exhibit, you can kind of see a window up there."

She leaned over the safety bar and looked up. "I see it!" she said, in a hushed tone. "That window looks way higher than the second floor."

"Yeah, that's exactly what I was thinking. Which means, there really is a third floor!"

"Yeah, but now that we might have found it, how are we going to do this? Marc is sticking to me like glue, and Melissa doesn't leave your side for a minute. Besides, I'm starting to worry that if we take off, it's going to cause a problem with you and Melissa. I mean; her being your girlfriend and all."

"She really isn't my girlfriend like most people think. To me we are more friends than anything else. Everyone else is making such a big deal about us being a couple, but I haven't officially asked her to be my girlfriend. Right now I just want to be with you, okay?"

She glanced over at where Melissa was and then back to me. "Okay, if you're sure it's not going to cause a problem with her."

"It won't. Now as far as sneaking off… I think we should continue to look for further clues on how to get up to that third floor. If one of us finds a clue on how to get up there, we can call the other person over."

"Okay, but at some point we're going to have to leave the group in order to go exploring."

Katie went back to her group with Marc, and I went back with Melissa and Michelle. When I came up to them, right away Melissa turned and gave me a suspicious look.

"So, what were you and Katie talking about all that time?"

21

"Oh, nothing much. I just wanted her to look at this one thing on that elephant exhibit. It was something we had talked about before."

I could tell by her expression, she wasn't too thrilled with me talking to Katie. That only added to my anxiety of us taking off on our little adventure.

As we continued on the tour, we came to an area with the big dinosaurs. Standing before us was this awesome display of a Stegosaurus and Tyrannosaurus Rex, which was so cool. I had seen dinosaurs in books before, but being up close and personal was something else. I began to read one of the plaques in front of the exhibits, which grabbed my attention. The information said that the dinosaurs ruled the earth millions of years ago. I guess I questioned that, because I remember seeing this religious program on TV that said that God created the earth in six days. According to Bible history; that would only make the earth to be in the thousands of years, not millions. I wanted to ask Katie about it, so I motioned her over. She walked over and stood next to me.

"Another clue, Jess?"

"No, actually I have a Christian belief question for you. What age do Christians think the earth is? I mean according to what science and people who believe in evolution say, they think that dinosaurs lived millions of years ago. But what do you believe?"

"That's kind of funny you asked that question, because about a year ago we had a special speaker come to our church, and one of the things he brought up was this very subject. I've heard a lot of arguments from both sides, but the way this guy explained it made sense to me. What he did was have one of the college-age guys from our church stand in front of the congregation. Then he said to the audience, 'I am God and this young man is Adam. I just created him in one day, just like the Bible says. Now I have a question for you... How old do you think he is?' Some people from the audience shouted,

19 years old! Others shouted, 21 years old! Then this lady from the back row stood up and shouted, 'He's 20 years old and I know because I gave birth to him!' Then the whole congregation started laughing because it was his mother. Then the speaker said, 'Now, if we brought in a doctor to examine Adam the very moment after he was created, how old do you think the doctor would say that Adam is?' Around the same age, the congregation said. 'That's right,' the speaker replied. 'A doctor examining Adam the very moment after he was created would say he is around 18-21 years old. Yet God created Adam in only one day. Now…let's say hypothetically that God asked scientists the very same question the moments after he created the earth. How old do you think they would say the earth is? Well scientists who believe in evolution would calculate how long it would have taken the earth to evolve to the current state, based on the Big-Bang theory of evolution. Yet God created the heavens and the earth in only six days. How is that possible? Because God creates things at a different speed and time frame than evolutionist theorize it would have taken it to evolve. An example to prove this is when Jesus turned water into wine. Most wine connoisseurs know from planting the vines to growing the grapes to their producing stage takes years. Then, after processing it takes time to age in order to make great tasting wine. Yet Jesus turned the water into wine in an instant. So in regards to the earth, God created it at a faster time frame than what man theorizes it would take for all the evolutionary stages to take place. You see, man is looking at the finished product with all those stages already built in."

"That's interesting Katie; I never heard it explained that way. If you look at it that way, then it just comes down to the speed in which you believe it was created. Was it was created in God's time frame, or in evolution's time frame. Yet the finished product is one and the same. That actually makes a lot of sense me—thanks."

"No problem, glad I could help."

"I didn't know you guys learned stuff like that in church."

"Yes, sometimes we have special speakers or we learn it in youth group. Speaking of youth group… I want to invite you to go with me. It can be really good and we have a lot of fun."

"Okay, sometime I'll go with you."

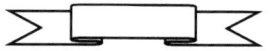

CHAPTER THREE – THE THIRD FLOOR

Katie and I went back to our group of friends. About that time, Brian's group entered the same exhibit room as he headed over to talk to us.

"Hey Jess, hi Michelle, hi Melissa. Do you guys like the museum?"

"Yeah it's pretty neat," we all chimed in.

"Well my group is totally boring. I have a bunch of brainiacs who are having these stupid debates as to who knows more about dinosaurs. If you don't mind, I'd rather hang around with you guys for a while. I asked Miss St. John if it would be alright. She said it was okay as long as I rode back home with my original group."

Michelle turned to Brian. "We don't mind Brian; we'd like to have you."

When Michelle said that, I could tell it made Brian feel good to know she at least still wanted to be friends after their breakup. However, a look of suspicion grew upon Melissa's face.

"Jesse… I thought you told me that you were going with Brian and his group?"

I swallowed the guilt in my throat. "Well, I was going to Melissa, but…"

"But what?" she snapped.

"Brian's group was all filled up, so at the last minute I had to switch groups."

As I said that, I thought to myself of that old saying of how you say one lie, then you have to keep on lying to cover up the first lie. With Brian joining our group, I thought this might be an opportunity for me and Katie to take off, as I could ask Brian to help us. Melissa then pulled Michelle aside to talk privately, so I saw it as an opportunity to talk to Brian. I quickly pulled him aside.

"Brian, come here; I need to talk to you."

"Sure, what is it?"

"I can't explain it right now, but I need for you to do me a big favor. If anyone asks where Katie and I have gone to, just tell them we went to the restroom and we will catch up to the group later. Tell them not to wait for us, okay? Also, I need for you to distract Marc and his friends for a minute. When I signal you, call them over, okay?"

"Okay man, I don't know what you guys are up to, but knowing the two of you, it's probably better *I don't know.*"

"Thanks Brian, you're a pal."

I motioned Katie over and told her my plan of action; saying that Brian was going to help us. When Melissa and Michelle were looking in another direction, I motioned for Brian to distract Marc and his friends. Marc headed over to talk to Brian when Katie and I made our move. We eased back, withdrawing from the group and used some other kids in the room to shield us from their line of sight. When we thought they couldn't see us, we bolted around the corner and over by the elevators. I pressed the elevator button, as we quickly scanned the hallway back and forth to make sure no one was watching us.

A look of concern grew upon her face. "Jess, I hope we don't get caught doing this."

"Not if Brian can help it. He's pretty clever about things like this. He'll come up with some good explanations."

She directed a wary eye towards me. "I certainly hope so."

When the elevator opened, we went in and headed up to the second floor. When we reached the second floor, the doors opened and we cautiously peered out.

"I think the coast is clear, Katie. Let's start looking around."

Immediately we went over to the windows to see where we were at in relation to the roof. She turned to me with her observation.

"I think you were right. There seems to be a lot of room above us to be a third floor."

"I know, let's look around and see if we can find a door or stairs that may provide an access to it."

We walked around the room, looking at all the exit doors and hallways, but there didn't seem to be anything that went upstairs. Katie tried one of the exit doors, but it was locked tight.

"Well, Jess, there doesn't appear to be an access from this floor, so let's go back to the elevator."

"Why you want to go back to the elevators?"

"I want to check on something."

"What do you want to check on?"

"Just something... I'll tell you my idea after we look in the elevator."

"Alright, let's go."

As we hurried over to the elevator, my mind was keeping a mental note of the time, as we were supposed to be in the restroom. Katie hit the "Stop" switch, which made the elevator come to a halt with a resounding clang!

"Why did you do that?"

"Because I need time to look for a special keyhole or something."

"A keyhole?"

"Yeah, I figure if there's a third floor there must be a special key that allows the elevator to go up there."

I placed my thumb and forefinger under my chin. "Hmmm..., I never thought of that."

She looked at me with a proud smile. "See Jess, aren't you glad you asked me to come along?"

I lightly pushed her shoulder. "Yeah, I guess. But we still haven't found anything yet."

Katie began to examine the elevator panel, but we didn't see anything except the buttons to the first and second floor; and of course the emergency stop button.

"Okay, maybe I was wrong about the keyhole, but I did see a service elevator next to the regular ones; we should go check it out."

We exited the elevator and waited for the coast to be clear once more. We walked over to the service elevator, got in and checked out the buttons. Basically the buttons were the same as the other elevator, however, it had an additional button to go down to the basement. When I saw the button to the basement, an idea flashed in my mind.

"Come-on Katie; let's go down to the basement."

"Do you think we should? Don't you I think there are probably a lot of workers down there."

"Hey, where's your spirit of adventure? Besides, if they ask us why we're down here, we will just tell them we got lost from our group. They have to figure that kids get lost in this museum all the time, right?"

Her eyes perked-up with interest. "Okay, let's go. Like you said, it will be a little adventure."

As the elevator went down to the basement, we waited with anticipation; wondering what we might encounter. I was just hoping we wouldn't run into any museum workers like Katie had said. When the doors opened, thankfully no one was nearby, so we began to look around. I pointed down a particular hallway.

"Let's go this way and see if there are any other elevators down here."

We went towards the left and down the hallway, when we came to another service elevator.

"Katie, I don't remember seeing two service elevators on the first and second floors?"

"I don't think there were," as we turned to each other with puzzled expressions.

"Wait a second," she said. "If that elevator does not go to the first and second floors, then it must go somewhere else—like the third floor!"

With heightened anticipation, we stood anxiously before the service elevator. First she tried the button so the door would open, but nothing happened—not even a sound. Then she pointed to a keyhole to the side of the elevator buttons.

"Look! There's a key hole on this elevator panel! See I told you..."

I smiled in admiration. "Wow, you're pretty smart."

"Hey, you didn't bring me along just for my good looks, did you?" she said, and directed a teasing smile.

"Well I don't know about the good looks part, but you sure have the brains!"

A look of shock ran across her face. "I can't believe you said that! I thought you said at the Winter Formal Dance that I looked pretty."

"You know I'm just kidding. You're pretty… pretty ugly!"

She shook her head and rolled her eyes. "Come on Jess; let's go back the other way; I'm not sure I can take much more of your compliments."

Just then we heard a whooshing sound coming from the main elevator, so we ran behind a bunch of stacked boxes and hid behind them. The bell sounded, indicating the doors were going to open so we ducked even further so no one would see us. Just then a group of people, who we assumed worked for the museum, got off the elevator. They made their way over to this back room and started working in there. As we peered around the boxes, we could see inside the room slightly and realized it was a kitchen. Katie focused her attention back to service elevator once more, and whispered so no one would hear us.

"Okay, let's think about this. If we think you need to have a key to go up that service elevator, then someone must have the key, right?"

"Yeah, but it must be with someone very important at the museum. I seriously doubt we would be able to get the key from them. Which means we're going to have to find another way up that elevator."

A few minutes later that same group of workers came out of the kitchen pushing these carts. They walked past us down that hallway, and over to where the service elevator was. We couldn't see because we were hiding behind the storage boxes, but we heard the elevator open and they got in. A couple of minutes later that same group of workers came back down and entered the kitchen once more. A few minutes later, they did the very same thing all over again. However this time, we noticed they were carting Champagne bottles and snack foods of all kinds. After a few minutes, they came back down and went into the kitchen again. When they came back out, this time they had some fancy sandwiches, and other foods on top of these carts.

"Katie, check it out...Do you think they are going up to the third floor to have like a party?"

Her eyes lit-up with excitement. "Well, there's only one way to find out!"

"Okay, I'm not sure I like that look of mischief in your eyes."

She smiled and then pointed to the carts which had long white table cloths covering over them. "I think I have an idea on how to get up the third floor."

"I hope you're not thinking, what I think you're thinking. Because if you are, then you're crazy!"

"I thought you said the other day, *I was crazy.* Besides, you're the one who wanted us to go on this adventure in the first place. Are you chickening out now?"

"I'm not chickening out! You're the one who's the chicken—you and your chicken legs!"

She shook her head. "Thanks a lot, Jess. That's just what every girl wants to hear. Anyway, back to the task at hand."

She peered around the boxes and headed towards the kitchen, as I followed close behind. With each step, the screech of my Vans tennis shoes seemed to get louder and louder, bringing on more anxiety of being caught. Finally, we were at the door's entrance as she peeked around the corner to see if anyone was there in the room.

"The coast is clear. And look... there's more carts with the tablecloths covering them—this is our chance!"

We began to take a step through the entrance of the door, when suddenly two big hands snatched the back of our shirt collars!

"Just what do you kids think you're doing down here?" came a deep and strong voice from behind us.

As we turned around, we saw this very large man dressed in a Tuxedo staring down at us with a piercing scowl. As I swallowed the lump in my throat, Katie answered his question in a soft and shaky voice.

"Well sir, we are here with Miss St. John's group."

"What's that?" he said, and leaned down so he could hear her better. "Did you say you're here with Mr. Johnson's group?"

Katie's eyes grew large, realizing the opportunity that presented itself. Suddenly she changed her voice to appear confident.

"Yes sir, you're exactly right. We're here with Mr. Johnson's Group."

His piercing scowl softened. "Well alright... but I don't know who told you to come down here by yourselves. You should have waited for your group to be escorted to the Executive Room."

"Yes sir," I quickly added. "We just thought we would have a quick peek at it first before the rest of our group came down."

"Well since the rest of your party should be here any minute, I guess it wouldn't hurt to take you up there myself. You can wait up there until the rest of your group arrives."

"Thank you, sir," we both said.

As we made our way to the service elevator, Katie and I glanced at one another with smiles etched across our faces. As this little misunderstanding was about to take us to the infamous third floor. We arrived at the service elevator, when the big man in the tuxedo pulled a key from his retractable key holder and inserted it into the keyhole. He then turned it towards the right, and at the same time, he pressed both the first and second floor buttons at the same time. Katie and I looked at each other realizing the secret method of pressing both buttons to get to the third floor. As the elevator rose, we looked at each other with growing excitement. We were about to become the first kids to discover the famous secret room. When the elevator door opened, we were awestruck at all the amazing displays in the room. The big man in the Tuxedo turned to us with some instructions.

"Now… you are free to have some snacks, but please don't touch any of the exhibits. I am sure they went over the protocol rules with you and your party."

"Yes sir," Katie said. "They went over the protocol stuff with us."

After the man got in the elevator and started down, we started to look around.

"Hey, Katie… do you know what the protocol stuff he was talking about?"

"No, I was just acting like I knew."

As we looked around this vast room, we saw massive amounts of food set up on fancy tables. It looked like they were preparing for a big banquet of some kind. As we continued to look around, we were amazed at the different exhibits. They even had some dinosaur exhibits and other fossils displayed throughout the room. It was like a miniature museum within the museum itself! Katie took her camera from her backpack and began to take some pictures. As we continued to look at the different displays, suddenly, we heard a whooshing sound and immediately panic set in—the elevator!

"Jess, what are we going to do? When the Johnson group get here, we'll be totally busted!"

Frantically we looked around the room to find another way out. Just as the elevator door opened, we ran behind this tall, free-standing cardboard figure of a Pterodactyl (flying dinosaur bird). I knew it was a Pterodactyl from a slide I saw on my talking ViewMaster. As the group of people came in, they began talking about the banquet and all the food choices. Katie peered around the edge of cardboard figure and exhaled a sigh of relief.

"Oh thank God," she whispered. "We got a break. It's not the man in the Tuxedo that escorted them in."

I leaned against the wall and wiped my forehead. "Whew, that was a close one!"

When I leaned back, I felt someone press hard on my lower back. The wall was covered with a type of black paper, but I could feel this hard object protruding from the wall, and it felt like a door knob.

"Check it out, Katie... I think there's a door behind here!"

We bent down to stay out of view, and made our way to the side of the wall. We removed a couple of staples that held the black paper in place. We pulled it apart just enough to be able to look behind the paper, when we saw it was, in fact, a door knob. Just then, we heard the elevator rise to our floor and the door opened. Suddenly, we heard that familiar booming voice of the big man in the Tuxedo; and he didn't sound very happy.

"Did you see any kids up here?" he asked the other museum worker. "I brought a boy and a girl up here a few minutes ago. Those two squirrels tricked me into believing they were a part of the Johnson Group!"

Katie and I glanced at one another in total panic! We knew right then and there we had to make our move. We ripped the black paper from the wall, flung the door open and scrambled through the door. As we started down a flight of stairs, we heard the big man yell in the distance. "They're over there, through the auxiliary door. Get them!"

We frantically ran down the stairs, not knowing where they would lead to. We came to the bottom of the stairwell and tried to open the door, but it was locked. We could hear someone open the door at the top of the staircase, so we bolted down the next set of stairs. When we came to the bottom of that stairwell, we tried the doorknob, but it was also locked. Katie quickly looked through the small rectangular window.

"That door leads to out the first floor of the museum," she glanced towards the next set of stairs. "Come-on, it must lead to the basement; that's our only hope!"

The weight of the big man coming down the stairs felt like earthquake tremors as he thundered down the stairs. With my heart pounding a mile-a-minute, we rushed down the last flight of stairs hoping it was a way out. When we got to bottom, we desperately tried the door, and thankfully it opened. We ran into a hallway and realized it was in fact the basement.

"Jess, I think I see that area where the elevators are at!"

With the sound of the big man's footsteps approaching quickly, we ran and hid behind the same boxes as before. Just then, the big man in the Tuxedo came busting through the door. At the same time, the other man who was with him, came out of the service elevator.

"Did you see them?" the man in the Tuxedo asked with urgency.

"No, but they couldn't have gone up the service elevator, because I just came down from there."

"Okay, you go check in the kitchen, and I'll check down the hall in the supply room. I know those two squirrels have to be in here somewhere!"

Katie and I waited for the coast to be clear; as our chests heaved; breathing heavily from the moment. When both men were out of sight, we rushed towards the main elevator and pressed the button. As we anxiously waited for the door to open, the big man in the Tuxedo came out the room and rushed towards us.

"Stop you two!"

We frantically pushed the button, as we waited for it to open. Finally, it opened with the chime of the door.

"Ah, saved by the bell!" I said, as we hurried in and hit first floor button.

"Come on, come on!" I said impatiently, as we waited for it to rise to the next floor. Finally the doors opened and we flew out the elevator and ran down the hall. As we slowed our pace near the museum entrance, we saw Brian and our group in the gift shop looking around for souvenirs. Bent over in exhaustion, we tried to catch our breath. She turned to me with a sense of urgency.

"Come-on, Jess, we need to get out of here. We can't let them see us in here."

"I know; we need to get to the bus."

We hurried out the door and over to where the buses were parked. When we found our bus, we jumped in, as the bus driver greeted us.

"Hi kids… Is the rest of your class coming soon?"

"Yes sir," Katie answered a bit out of breath. "They'll be here in a bit. They're in the gift shop buying souvenirs."

As we sat in the back of the bus catching our breath, we saw the big man in the tuxedo come out the front doors and look around. He began to head our way, so we quickly hid below the seats. I peeked over the top edge of the seat, when I saw him turn around and go back inside.

I slipped back down in my seat and wiped by brow.

"Man; that was a close one!"

"I know; I can't believe we actually found that secret room."

"That was so cool, and one crazy adventure."

"Yeah, thank God we made it out of there. That was a real close call."

As usual, I tried to be funny.

"Yeah, that is was what you might call… a 'Close Encounter of the Third Floor'."

CHAPTER FOUR – REPERCUSSIONS

After our little adventure at the museum, we were able to solve another mystery, however it didn't come without a price. The following Monday after the trip, believe me, Katie and I felt the aftermath from our actions.

When lunchtime arrived, Brian and I made our way to the cafeteria when the subject came up about the field trip. I told him how Katie and I had found the third floor and the secret room. I also told him we had taken photos, and as soon as they were developed I would show them to him. After I finished, he had a few comments of his own.

"Dude, I hope you and Katie had a good time. Because let me tell you, a few people were not very happy about you taking off—including me."

"What do you mean?"

"Not like it's a big deal, but I did join your group to hang around with you, then you took off and left me holding-the-bag lying to all these people. The worst thing was that I didn't know where you guys went, so that made it harder to come up with a believable excuse for you."

"Oh man, I didn't even think about that. I'm sorry Brian—really."

"It's cool, you know me, ancient history man. But in the future, could you tell me more details before you have me lie for you."

"Like I said, I'm really sorry."

"No problem, but I'm not the one you need to be worrying about."

"Why? Who do I need to worry about?"

"Melissa… Melissa was totally ticked-off."

"Why, what did she do?"

"Well after I distracted Marc and the other guys, I started to walk with Michelle and Melissa for a while. After a bit, they asked me where you were at and I told them you went to the restroom. Marc was standing nearby when he realized that Katie was gone too. Melissa went up to Marc and said, 'Guess what Marc? I think we have just been ditched!' I tried to tell them that the two of you would be right back, but I don't think they believed me. And then of course as time went on and you guys never came back, Melissa was getting madder by the minute."

"Really? What did she say?"

"Well, I can tell you one thing for sure… she doesn't like Katie at all. One time I overheard her tell Michelle, 'I have no idea what Jesse sees in that scrawny little girl. And Katie, she acts like she's 'Little Miss Angel.' I can't wait to see her fall from that heavenly cloud she thinks she's on!' Michelle then tried to tell Melissa that you and Katie are just friends, but I don't think she was buying it. And to tell you the truth, sometimes the way you two act together, I'm not so sure myself."

"We're just friends. People just don't understand our relationship and how much fun we have together."

"I don't know man, you and Katie can get carried away sometimes. Another thing, is I think you better decide which girl you want to hang out with. Because I think Melissa is about to dump you."

"Dump me? How can I be dumped when I'm not officially going out with Melissa in the first place? But you're right; I guess I do get carried away with Katie sometimes. I'll have a long talk with Melissa and straighten things out with her."

"Oh, and another thing…Miss St. John asked where you guys went when you took off?"

"No way!"

"Yep. I told her the restroom story, but then she sent Rick Stevens and Stacy into the restrooms to find you."

"Oh man; what happened after that?"

"Rick and Stacy came back and said you guys weren't in the restrooms. After hearing that, Miss St. John just shook her head, but didn't say or do anything after that."

"Well, she never said anything to us on the bus so I think were in the clear with her."

A few minutes later the bell rang to end our lunchtime. As we began walking to our next class, an announcement came over the loudspeakers in the hallways. And it wasn't long before I soon found out just how "free and clear" I was, as our names echoed in the hallways.

"Jesse Thompson, Katie McCullough...please report to the principal's office. Jesse Thompson, Katie McCullough...to the principal's office."

Brian placed his hand on my shoulder. "Oh dude, you are so busted!"

"Oh man; I guess we're not in the clear after all."

"Good luck man, I hope you don't get suspended."

"Thanks, so do I."

I walked over to the main building where the principal's office was located. With a guilt-ridden look on my face, I told the secretary I was called in to see Principal Hessman. The secretary escorted me down a hall and stood at the entrance to his office.

"Mr. Hessman...Jesse Thompson is here to see you."

He glanced up from his desk and motioned with his hand. "Yes, show him in."

I walked into his office and saw that Katie was already sitting in front of his desk with that same guilty expression as me.

Principal Hessman pointed to the chair next to her. "Have a seat Jesse—next to your partner in crime."

Katie glanced at me with fear-filled eyes and sat nervously biting on the end of her pen-cap. At first Principal Hessman just stared at us long and hard. To me that was worse, as I wished he would just start in with whatever he was going to say—the silence was killing me. Finally he spoke up.

"You know… when the two of you snuck-off campus to go to the new Burger King, I decided to let that one slide. Katie is a straight-A student, and you Jesse, you are a B+ student. So I figured this was an isolated incident and I happened to be in a good mood that day." He learned forward in his seat with a piercing scowl. "Well I'm not in a very good mood right now!"

We shrunk down in our seats, as I swallowed the lump in my throat.

"You knew about us going to Burger-King?"

"Jesse, I happened to use the drive-thru that day while the two of you ordered a couple of Whoppers and shakes!"

I glanced at Katie who was covering her face, which was blush red. Principal Hessman continued.

"Now… sneaking off to Burger King at lunch time is one thing. But ditching Miss St. John's group, having a friend lie for you, and tricking a museum employee into taking you to an unauthorized area of the museum is totally unacceptable. And if you're wondering how I know about that? It's because I got a little call from our district supervisor, who in turn received a call from the Sacramento Museum. He advised me that two kids, a boy and a girl, had snuck into an unauthorized area. We also had an anonymous person tell us that the two of you left Miss St. John's group and never returned. So I think we can put two-and-two together and figure out just who that boy and girl were who snuck into that unauthorized area."

I bit my lower lip nervously, knowing we were totally busted.

"So was that anonymous person who told you we left, Miss St. John?" I said, with the slightest bit of sarcasm.

Anger rose on Principal Hessman's face, as he raised his voice. "Jesse, I wouldn't worry about *who told me*. If I were you, I would be more worried of what is going to *happen to you*!"

I shrunk down in my seat. "Yes sir, I'm sorry, sir."

"I'm sorry too," Katie added.

"Not that it's any of your concern," he added. "But it wasn't Miss St. John who told me—she never said a word to me."

I glanced at Katie and wondered to myself who might have told on us.

"You know," he continued. "There is one thing I just don't understand about all of this. Both of you are such good students, so this kind of behavior makes no sense to me. I won't mention any names, but we have a few students here that I won't be surprised if they end up in Juvenile Hall. Yet I don't see them doing some of the crazy things the two of you pull sometimes. Like the stink-bomb incident in the ventilating ducts. I couldn't prove it, but I think the two of you probably had a hand in that too."

I quickly countered. "That wasn't us Principal Hessman."

Katie and I turned towards each other. "Katie, don't you think the stink-bomb incident was Chuck Buchannan?"

"I think it was. That sounds like something Chucky would do."

"Yeah and that was a good one too. When they turned the air-conditioning on, it stunk up the entire school!"

"I know, that was just too funny," she said, as we shared a laugh.

I turned in my seat, to give her my full attention. "Yeah, I just wish we had thought of that one, but I'm pretty sure it was the ole-Chuckster."

"I think you're right, that had Chucky written all over it!"

As we continued to go back and forth, suddenly we heard Principal Hessman's voice boom with frustration.

"Excuse me! Can we please get back to the subject of you being in a lot of trouble!" he said, as he threw-up his hands in disgust.

Realizing we had gotten carried away talking about ole-Chuck, we simmered down. Principal Hessman sat there shaking his head back and forth in disbelief.

"I don't understand it…; no, I just don't understand it."

"Sometimes we don't understand it either Principal Hessman. It's hard to explain, but when Katie and I get together, we just can't seem to pass-up a good adventure. It's just something inside of us."

He learned forward in his seat. "Well that something inside of you has gotten you into a lot of trouble!"

Seeing his frustration and disappointment in us, Katie spoke up with sincerity in her voice.

"Principal Hessman… I want you to know in all honesty, that Jess and I promise to never do anything like that again. We will never sneak off campus or do anything bad again—I promise."

He scanned the two of us back and forth with a penetrating stare. I could tell he was thinking very deeply about what Katie had said. He sat tapping his index finger on the table, as we anxiously waited in anticipation of what our fate would be. Finally, he exhaled a breath as he came to a conclusion.

"Well…, I would normally suspend the two of you, but this time I'm going to let you off with a warning. I don't want a suspension to be on your official records as I hope that someday you will both eventually go to college. However…, I am still sending a note to your parents which they will have to sign and return to me. The letter will be advising them that you are being given an official warning for this misconduct and the next time, you will be suspended for sure."

"Okay Principal Hessman," Katie said. "Thank you for only a warning."

After a few silent moments of us just sitting there, I asked if we could be excused.

"Yes Jesse, you are dismissed to go to your next class. And I mean *directly to class*!"

"Yes sir," we both said.

As Katie and I started to get up, he turned to us with an inquisitive look on his face.

"So tell me... You two actually found that secret room on the third floor?"

We turned to each other and smiled.

"Yes we did. Katie and I really found it."

"You know a few years ago my son and few of his friends tried to find that alleged secret room, but they never found anything. So what was it like in that secret room?"

We looked to each other once more before she answered.

"It was beautiful Principal Hessman. Like a miniature museum—it was pretty amazing."

He pressed out a half-smile. "Alright you two, back to class."

As we walked to our next class, I turned to Katie with an obvious question.

"So…, how long do you think your parents are going to ground you?"

"Oh, probably for the rest of my life."

"Yeah me too; but I still think our little adventure was pretty fun, don't you?"

"It was. But looking back, we never should have done some of the things we did. A little voice inside me knew it was wrong; especially the part about lying. And come to think about it, a few nights before the trip I was reading the Bible when I came across that scripture which says, 'Be sure your sin will find you out.' I should have listened to that voice inside of me."

"I wouldn't be so hard on yourself; I don't think God expects you to be perfect or anything. I mean you're only 13 years old; you're going to make mistakes."

As she sadly walked away, I could tell she felt really bad about it; like she had let herself down. As I headed to my class, I felt bad also, that as her friend I had let her down too.

When I got home that day, I had to face the music with my mom and dad about the whole museum incident. I informed them I was going to receive a warning letter for my actions. My parents were very upset and had a long talk with me about responsibility and lying to people. They grounded me for two weeks, which included not being able to see or talk to Katie. It's funny; I thought I had gotten off easy with only being given two weeks restriction with no extra chores, and I still got my allowance. But I guess they knew what they were doing, because those two weeks not being able to talk to Katie… was sheer torture!

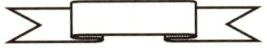

CHAPTER FIVE – HOLIDAY VACATION

The following week in drama class, we began to rehearse for next month's Christmas play. It was going to be the traditional story of the wise men, the shepherds, and the baby Jesus in the manger. Becky was going to play Elizabeth in the scene where Elizabeth says to Mary that she is "Blessed among women." Melissa was going to be the Inn Keeper's wife; and Marc, the guy who likes Katie, got the part of Joseph. I'm sure he was thrilled to get that part because you guessed it...Katie was going to be Mary. Miss Simms, our drama teacher wanted me to be the narrator. She says I have a way with words, and felt I could emphasize certain parts of the story when needed. As we were getting ready to rehearse, Becky came up to us with a camera in hand.

"Hey you two; smile for the camera," she said, bringing the camera to eyelevel.

We leaned close to one another, check-to-cheek, as she took our picture.

"Why are you taking our picture?" Katie asked.

"I'm taking some pictures for the yearbook."

"Oh that's right; I forgot you're in the yearbook club."

"Yes, we need a few photos of the Christmas play so we can place them on the events page."

As we were discussing the yearbook with Becky, Melissa motioned to me from across the room. Katie saw her hand gesture.

"Looks like someone wants you, Jess."

"Yeah, I think I better go over there, I'm already in the doghouse with her."

I walked over to where Melissa was standing near one of the props for the play. I could tell by the tone of her voice she wasn't too happy with me.

"Jess... I need to ask you something. I know we are not buddy-buddies like you are with your little friend over there; but why do you do things with me? Like going to the movies and meeting each other at the mall? I mean do you like me or not?"

"Of course I like you; that's a dumb question."

"I don't think it's dumb when you consider that I was the one who had to make the first move after the movies. Then there are times when you just don't seem interested. Not to mention of course how you ditched me at the museum and took off with Katie. I want to know if you like me as a girlfriend."

I thought about it really quickly. *On one hand, I do think she's a very pretty girl. And I now have this popularity because people think we're a couple. On the other hand, I'm really not sure I like enough to be my girlfriend.*

"Well Melissa, let me put it this way. When I am able to answer that question, you'll be the first to know. Well..., maybe the second to know, because I would be the first to know, wouldn't I?"

She rolled her eyes. "Jesse, you talk in circles sometimes. Either that, or you're trying to avoid the question. Anyway, on another subject...I heard that you and Katie were called into the Principal's Office. What was that about?"

By the inflection in her voice, it made me think she already knew what we were called in for. It was the same kind of inflection my dad has when he asks me something, yet I know he has already talked to my mother about it. This made me wonder if Melissa was the one who told on us. I answered vaguely.

"Principal Hessman just wanted to talk to us about our academic future."

She answered with skepticism. "Your academic future? Oh really."

"Yeah, you know, taking the right classes and stuff like that."

I know that wasn't exactly the truth. But in a way it did have to do with our academic future. After all, we almost got "academically" suspended.

*****

The week of Thanksgiving, I approached Katie in drama class about the upcoming holiday. We were going to have a full week off from school, as we got the Monday through Wednesday off before Thanksgiving Day.

"Hey…I wanted to ask you if you wanted to go with us on vacation during the week of Thanksgiving. I know you probably can't go considering you're still grounded, but I just thought I would ask."

She perked up with interest. "Really? Where are you going?"

"My father knows this guy from work who has this cabin up in the Sierra Nevada Mountains. He offered the cabin to my dad, so we're planning on going there for the Thanksgiving holiday. There should be lots of snow, and my mom is going to make a roasted turkey while we're there. Brian is going too, and I heard there's a couple of caves and all kinds of interesting trails we can explore."

"It sounds like fun. I might be able to go because my restriction is almost over. And thinking about it, this may be the perfect year to ask my parents. You see, my grandmother on my mom's side is coming to visit us, and she can be very controlling. When she comes to visit, she takes over the house and treats my mom like she's still a little girl. With our house being packed with aunts, uncles and other relatives, my mom will be so stressed out, that I don't think she'll mind me not being there. I'll ask them tonight about going."

"Alright, sounds good."

*****

The very next day I met up with Katie first thing before school started, as we made our way to the lockers.

"Jess, guess what? I can go!"

"Really?"

"Yeah, my parents said they like you and trust your parents, so it would be fine."

"That's great! I know we're going to have a great time up there. I'll tell Brian and let him know you're going. This is going to be so neat, the three of us camping together."

She smiled, as I could see the wheels turning in her head about the upcoming trip. However, her expression suddenly changed, as her thoughts veered in another direction.

"Jess, I was just thinking… is this going to be alright with Melissa? I mean her being your girlfriend, or sort of your girlfriend and all. Won't that cause a problem if she finds out we went camping together? I heard from a few people that she isn't very happy with me right now."

"No, it'll be alright. I talked to Melissa the other day and I explained to her where our relationship stands."

"Which is…?"

"Which is right now, we're just friends."

"Okay, I just don't want her to get mad at me or cause any problems between you two."

"No it's fine, besides, the two of us have been friends a lot longer than me and her. Don't worry about it; it'll be fine."

*****

The week before Thanksgiving, we began to get ready for our trip. My dad rented a four-wheel drive Jeep since we were going to be traveling off the main road. My sister Tami didn't want to go with us, and she made her displeasure known in that typical sarcastic way of hers. And as she put it, "why would I want to go to some rusty ole' cabin and get totally bored out of my mind!" My parents, not wanting to deal with her attitude, let her stay with my aunt and uncle—thank God.

On the day of the trip, we all packed our equipment in the Jeep rental and drove to pick up Brian. After loading his gear, we headed over to Katie's and packed up her things as well. When we were about halfway to the cabin, I tapped my dad on the shoulder from the back seat to get his attention.

"Dad…when we get to where the ski resort cut-off is at, can we go exploring a little? Katie and I found out there's this cave near that area, and we want to go exploring in it."

He glanced in the rearview mirror. "I guess that will be alright. Your mother and I will continue up to the cabin and start to set things up. I don't want you to be too long though. Part of camping is pulling your weight and doing some chores. There will be firewood to gather and other chores to do."

"Okay, we won't be too long—just for about an hour or so."

As we continued on our way, Brian and my dad really seemed to be hitting it off. My dad knows a lot about camping and fishing; so he began to explain a lot of things to Brian, who surprisingly seemed very interested. I guess Brian liked talking about that stuff because he has never really gone camping before. His father really doesn't like to go camping, as he is more into fixing up cars and things like that. Then last year when he was finally going to go camping up in Oregon somewhere, those plans got cancelled. As he and my dad continued their conversation, he suddenly turned to ask me a question.

"Jess, I think I want to go with your dad and help him set up at the cabin. Is that cool?"

When Brain said that, it kind of took me off guard. I guess when you look at your own family; you can't see them as other people do. The way Brian was acting around my dad was almost as if he admired him or something.

"Are you sure Brian? You don't want to go exploring with me and Katie?"

"I'll go exploring with you guys tomorrow, but I'd like to help your dad with setting up."

My dad spoke up from the front seat. "I'd love to have you help me, Brian. I can show you about gathering and chopping the proper wood and starting a fire."

Just then we arrived at the Ski Resort area which is the final stop before you head up towards the higher elevations, which has a few scattered cabins. My dad pulled up to this country market and had a few instructions for us.

"Okay everyone…we are going into this little market to pick up a few last minute supplies. Get everything you need, because once we're up there, we're up there. The weather report says we could get up to a foot of snow, so we need to be prepared."

I think my dad said that for Brian's sake. You know; kind of making it out to be a real adventure, like an "us against the elements" kind of thing.

As we went into the little market, Katie and I grabbed a few snacks to put in our backpacks for our hike. I noticed her scanning the isle, as if looking for something in particular before going to the counter to pay for our snacks. When we got outside, I questioned her about it.

"What were you looking for in the store?"

"Jess, that market was a dud!"

"Why do you say that?"

She pouted her lip. "Because they didn't have any Starburst, and I forgot to bring some with me from home."

I playfully squished her checks. "Oh poor baby, Katie doesn't have any Starburst…"

She smiled at my teasing, and then slugged me on the shoulder. "Come on Jess, let's hit the trails!"

We started up the trail, when I happened to notice her shoes. "Are you sure you're going to be alright in just your tennis shoes? Where are your hiking boots?"

"They're in my suitcase that your parents are taking up to the cabin. It's okay, looking at this map, it doesn't look like the trails are too steep or anything—I'll be fine."

"Okay, but I'm wearing my hiking boots just in case we encounter some *big huge snakes*!"

"Jess, don't try to scare me about snakes. Snakes generally don't live in the mountains. What you really need to worry about, are *the big black bears*!" she said, raising her hands in clawed fashion.

"I'll give you a big black bear!" I said, and began chasing her while snarling and growling.

She screamed and started running away from me, but it was uphill, so we slowed back down to a walk. The wind suddenly kicked-up, so we pulled out our jackets from our backpacks. She wrapped her arms around herself in a shiver.

"Wow…all of sudden it's gotten really cold, hasn't it?"

"Yeah, and now there are a lot more clouds starting to come in."

We continued up the trail, when we saw a couple of other people coming down the same trail. They stopped to talk to us.

"Are you two going up to the Iron Rock Caves?"

"Yes," we answered.

"Then I'd hurry up if I were you; we heard there's a big storm coming. You never know up here in the Sierras what a storm is going to do."

"Okay thanks," we told them. "We're not going to be that long exploring."

We continued up the trail for about a half mile more when we came to the Iron Rock Caves. There was a sign outside explaining all the facts about it, like who discovered it and the type of rock the cave was set in, which was iron ore. I guess that's why they called it the Iron Rock Caves. We went into the cave and explored a little bit, but it wasn't that exciting for us. Katie and I are used to exploring in caves and mine tunnels that no one had been in for a long time. This was like a tourist attraction and so it wasn't a big thrill for us. After we explored inside the cave she suggested we go for a little hike. We walked around the hillside and down this trail for a while, when the trail ended. We continued to hike off the beaten path when we came upon another cave. She moved ahead of me with caution and interest.

"Look, Jess! There's a cave right there; let's check it out."

As we began to look into the entrance of the cave, you could tell it was definitely not a tourist attraction. Part of it was covered with overgrown grass and a few cobwebs. However, it also looked like some animal might be using it. The entrance was matted down as if something had been going in and out of the cave.

A look of concern grew upon my face. "We need to be careful if we're going to explore in this one. There may be some kind of animal still using it."

"I was thinking the same thing. Let's just take a quick peek inside."

Cautiously we moved a few cobwebs from the top portion of the entrance and peered in. It was very dark, so I pulled out my flashlight from my backpack and moved it back and forth through the cave. You could see in about thirty feet, and as far as we could tell, there was nothing in the cave.

She motioned for me to follow. "Come on Jess, let's go in, it looks clear."

You know, to look at Katie who isn't that big and kind of skinny, you would never think she has as much guts as she does. I mean, *even I* was a little afraid of exploring in this cave.

As we cautiously moved forward, we were alerted by some kind of sound. I quickly grabbed her arm, as we stood silent and listened intently to try to identify what it was. A few moments later we could hear what sounded like the cries of some type of small animal.

"What is that, Katie?"

We stood quietly once more when we heard it again. Suddenly she burst-forth with excitement.

"Puppies…! It sounds like puppies!"

She rushed forward and found the tiny animals all huddled together. She picked one of them up and cuddled it to her face.

"Look Jess, aren't they so cute!"

"Katie, I would put that down if I were you. I don't think they are puppies, I think they are…"

Suddenly, there was an awful hair-raising growl! A rush of fear shot down the length of my back as I turned to see a large grey wolf slowly coming towards us—growling as it moved forward. Katie gently placed the baby wolf down, and slowly moved closer to me. I saw a stick on the ground and leaned down to pick it up, when the wolf growled even louder and more ferociously.

She placed her hand on my shoulder. "No Jess, she'll think you're trying to hurt her or the pups."

"You're right; I didn't think about that."

The wolf stood its ground with piercing eyes, and its fangs glistened from the reflection of the flashlight. As we stood there in a standoff, Katie glanced down at her backpack.

"Jess, I have some Twinkies in my backpack, should I try to give it to the momma wolf?"

"Yes, but do it slowly."

As she slowly reached for her backpack, the wolf growled and its mane raised up on its back in the attack position. Suddenly, the wolf lunged forward! I placed myself between the wolf and Katie and covered my face. Thankfully, the wolf only lunged so far and then backed off, but continued to hold its ground. Katie took the Twinkies out of the wrapper and threw them to the far side of the cave. Immediately the wolf went over to where they were. As she began to eat them, we slowly walked backwards, making our way out of the cave. I was taught to walk backwards when dealing with an animal that might want to attack. With each cautious step, the wolf continued to growl while she ate, as we cautiously moved out of the cave. Once we cleared the cave entrance, I yelled, "Run!"

We ran as fast as we could back down the trail, looking back to see if the wolf was coming after us. When we finally made our way back down the trail, we stopped to catch our breath.

She turned with a look of relief etched across her face. "Oh my God, can you believe that?"

"Yeah, that was incredible! Looks like we're going to have some story to tell Brian and my parents when we get up to the cabin."

"Yeah, that's true. Well...so much for my Twinkies."

"Yeah, who would have thought that wolves like to eat Twinkies."

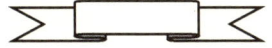

CHAPTER SIX - THE BLIZZARD!

As we approached the main road we began to hike towards the cabin which was a couple miles away. As we made our way, snow began to fall and the winds started to blow pretty hard. I put on my "hoody" that was attached to my winter jacket, while Katie placed a scarf around her neck and a little blue beanie cap on her head. I pulled out my camera from my backpack.

"Katie, stop and let me take your picture. I have got to take a picture of this. You look so cute with your little beanie on."

She abruptly held her hand in front of the camera.

"Jess, stop messing around, it's starting to get really cold out," she said, and wrapped her arm around herself in a shiver.

I lowered the camera. "Yeah you're right, we better get going. *It is* starting to get really chilly out."

I put my camera away and we started up towards the cabin. My dad had previously showed me on a map which way to take once we reached a fork in the road about a mile up. As we continued, the weather suddenly took a turn for the worse. The snow, which started out as light flurries was now coming down heavily in a blustering wind. The higher we traveled up the road, the deeper it got, as we trekked through the snow.

"Jess...where's that split in the road you said we had to go on?"

"I don't know...the snow is so deep, I can't even tell where the road is going anymore."

I stopped and looked around, but looking for a familiar landmark was useless, since I had never been in this area before in my life.

I tapped her shoulder and pointed in a certain direction. "See those trees over there? They seem to spread wider in that area. I figure the road must go in that direction."

She nodded her head in the affirmative. "Okay, let's try it."

As the snow continued to fall heavily, we traveled for about fifteen more minutes when I realized we were totally lost.

She pointed to an object in the distance. "Jess, I thought I saw what might be a cabin."

"Okay, let's head that way and see what it is."

As the snow continued to fall, the driving winds made it hard for us to walk in a straight line. Driven by what seemed like forty mile-per-hour winds, the frozen snowflakes stung across our faces, as we were being pounded by the elements. I shouted to be heard over the howling winds.

"I think we're in a blizzard! We need to try to get out of this and find some shelter!"

Pushing forward, we saw something that might have been the cabin Katie had mentioned. As we headed in that direction, suddenly we stumbled into a small river bed which we didn't realize was there because of the depth of the snow. This river bed had about a half a foot of water in it, and we almost lost our balance and fell in. Thankfully, we managed to hold each other up, and were able to make it up the other side of the embankment. Both of our feet got wet, but I had on my waterproof hiking boots to protect my feet. Unfortunately, Katie only had on her tennis-shoes which were now soaking wet.

As we traveled a little further, we finally got to a point where we could see what we thought was a cabin. However, disappointment draped across our faces, as our hope of finding shelter soon left us—the cabin was completely burnt down. All that remained was the burned out timbers and basically the fireplace. Disappointed, we continued on our way struggling through the freezing snow for about ten minutes more, when I could tell she was really hurting.

"Jess…!" she said, and placed her hand on my shoulder. "I can't go anymore! I can't feel my feet and my legs feel like they're on fire!"

"Katie, we can't stay out here in the open like this or we'll freeze to death! We need to continue and find shelter!"

We struggled for about five minutes more, when she buckled to the ground in pain.

"Jess, I can't! I can't go anymore!" she cried out, as the tears began to trickle down her cheeks.

I sat down next to her, and we huddled together in the freezing blizzard. Then she turned to me with a sorrowed, yet caring look upon her face.

"Jess… go find help; I'm just slowing you down. I'll stay right here—you try to make it."

I could tell by the way she said, 'you try to make it,' that what she really meant was, 'I know I'm not going to make it, so try to save yourself.' The thought of those surrendering words cut me to the core. Then something stirred inside of me and I became angry and stood to my feet.

"No Katie! I can't believe that God would have saved us from all those other situations in our lives, only to have us to die out here in this blizzard!"

I tried to help her up, but she could barely keep her balance. I tried to pick her up, but trying to carry her in the midst of a freezing blizzard was too hard, and we tumbled to the ground. As I picked up my head from falling in the snow, I was startled by a ferocious wolf staring me in the face. But then I realized, it was not just an ordinary wolf, but the same grey wolf we had encountered earlier in the cave. As the wolf stared us down, it growled and then started to pace back and forth.

"Katie, just sit still. Maybe it will go away."

I told her that out loud to try to calm her fears. But what I was really thinking, was this wolf had sensed we were in trouble and now we were its easy prey!

The wolf edged closer and closer, and was now within a couple of feet of me.

"Yah...!" I yelled out, with an angry inflection in my voice.

The wolf jumped back, but held its aggressive posture and continued to growl with its fur risen on the back of its neck. As this stand-off continued, my heart was pounding and every inch of my being was on full alert; trying to anticipate its next move. Katie was huddled close behind me when she took a peek at the wolf from around my shoulder. The wolf then focused-in on her for a moment, then back to me. The wolf began to back away and the hair on her neck lowered, as it seemed to relax. The wolf walked away about twenty-feet, and then gave this half-bark/ half-howling kind thing, and then just stared at us.

Now... I don't know why I would even think this, but a strange thought entered my mind that this wolf wanted us to follow it. I rose to my feet and extended my hand.

"Come on, Katie; I want to follow this wolf."

"No Jess, I can't."

"Please, you have to try!"

She looked at me with sorrowed eyes. "I can't—I have no strength left."

She had previously given me a Bible sometime back as a gift. And for some reason a particular part of what I read came to mind.

"Katie, doesn't it say in the Bible somewhere, that you can do all things through Christ because he gives you strength?"

She looked at me with surprise. "How did you know that is my favorite scripture verse—Philippians 4:13."

"I didn't. I just happened to read that verse one time, and for some reason it popped into my head right now."

Upon hearing that scripture verse, I could tell it seemed to give her strength. And her eyes which earlier were starting to look glossy, cleared up, and she seemed more alert.

She extended her hand out to me. "Help me up, Jess. Maybe I can try to walk, if you help me."

I helped her to her feet as she placed her arm around my neck and we began to follow the wolf. The wolf continued to walk ahead of us, periodically looking back as we struggled together through the snow. The strange thing was… that every time we stopped to rest, the wolf seemed to also stop. We continued for about fifteen minutes more, when I could see a cabin in the distance.

"Look, Katie; there's a cabin up there! It shouldn't be much longer."

As we approached the cabin, the wolf looked back at us one more time and then disappeared around the side of the cabin. We struggled up the front stairs and I placed her on a bench on the front porch.

"Wait here while I find a way in."

I began to try all the windows to see if any might be open. Fortunately, I found one where the latch was only partially closed, and with a little effort it slid open and I was able to crawl through the window. I went to the front door, unlocked it, and helped her to her feet.

"Come on; let's get you onto this couch in here."

She placed her arm around my neck and we made our way into the cabin. I sat her down on the couch in the living area, and we took off our backpacks. I found a couple of blankets in one of the rooms and brought them over to her.

"Here Katie, place these around yourself—you need to get warm."

"Jess, my clothes are soaking wet and cold; I need to get out of them. I have a long sweatshirt that is dry in my backpack; I can put that on."

"Okay, while you're changing your clothes, I'll go outside and find some firewood."

I had previously seen a pile of wood on the side of the cabin, so I gathered a few pieces and knocked on the door.

"Is it safe to come in? Are you dressed?"

"Yes, come-on in."

Holiday Blizzard: The Moment of Truth!

I began to stack the wood near the fireplace, when she called me over with worry in her voice.

"Jess, come over here and look at my feet. They are all red and discolored."

I went to her side and examined her feet. When I saw them, a measure of shock and fear ran through me. One of the things we learned in Boy Scouts to earn our first-aid badge was frostbite. They showed us a few pictures of frostbitten hands and feet. By the look of Katie's feet; I believed she had a pretty bad case of it—and that worried me. With fear and anxiety building within me, I tried not to over react.

"I think you just have a little frost-bite Katie—you'll be alright. We just need to get your feet warm."

On the outside I tried to act calm, but on the inside I was frantic! I tried to remember all the stuff I was taught about treating frostbite. *Soak her feet in cold water..., no, hot water..., no...., cold water first, then warm water...*

As the frustration of not remembering pressed on my mind, I knew I had to do something fast. If frostbite wasn't treated quickly a person could lose some toes, or maybe even worse. I looked at the stove in the kitchen, but it was an electric stove, which wouldn't do us any good considering the electricity was turned off. I hurried to the fireplace and gathered some wood to start a fire. There was no running water in the cabin, but fortunately there was a five-gallon water tank in the kitchen. There was also a big black cast-iron pot near the fireplace where I could heat up the water. I started a fire with matches I found in the kitchen, and got the fire going really good. Then I put water in the pot and set it on a hook above the fireplace. After about ten minutes I checked the water, but it still needed a little more time to heat up. Fortunately, I was now starting to remember the remedy. Use warm water, but not hot water, to treat frostbite. I also remembered that after soaking her feet, they needed to be kept warm after that. I went to her side once more.

"Katie, do you have any other clothes? Like an extra pair of socks in your backpack?"

"No, just this extra sweat-shirt I have on."

I needed to dry out her clothes, so I found a rope in a drawer in the kitchen and made a clothesline and placed it above the fireplace. Then I gathered up her pants, sweater and socks and placed them on the line above the fire to dry. I tested the pot of water and it seemed to be about the right temperature to thaw out her feet. I found a large broiler pan in the stove and poured the water in it. Then I brought it over to her side.

"Katie, try to sit up and put your feet in this water; it will help with the frostbite."

She swung her legs over the edge of the couch and pulled up the blanket that was covering her legs.

"Jess, don't look at my skinny legs," she said, as her cheeks slightly blushed.

At that point I was more worried about the color of her toes, than her skinny legs. I pushed the pan of water closer to the couch.

"Here, slowly put your feet in here."

She began to lower her feet as I gently guided them into the pan of water.

"Do you feel anything," I asked, with hope reflecting in my voice.

"No, I don't feel anything. I still can't feel my feet."

Now I was really worried. I knew that was a very bad sign when a person can't feel their feet. After about twenty minutes of letting her feet soak, I got the pot and poured more water into the pan to maintain the temperature. When I did that, she started to scream.

"Jess, it's hurting my feet! Is it supposed to do that?" she grimaced, with tears welling in her eyes.

Relief filled my smile. "That's good Katie; I'm glad that you're in pain."

She looked at me with hurt in her eyes. "What? How can you say you're glad that I'm in pain—that's so mean."

I laughed half-heartedly. "No, you don't understand. The fact that you're starting to feel pain is a good sign. It means that the frostbite hasn't killed the nerves in your feet and toes."

As she continued to fight the pain, I came and sat by her side. I began to gently run my hand down the length of her hair to comfort her. She looked to me with caring eyes.

"Jess… why are you so good to me?"

"Why am I so good to you? Gee Katie, that's a dumb question. If you weren't already in so much pain, I would slug you! Don't you know by now how much you mean to me?"

As my words lingered in air, I could sense we were starting to have a moment between us. Moments like that sometimes scare me, so I decided to lighten it up a bit.

"Wait right here, Katie; I'll be right back."

I walked over and searched my backpack for what I was looking for. I had previously brought this particular item to surprise her, so I felt this was a good time to give it to her. I held it behind my back as I brought it over to her.

"Here, I have a surprise for you. But you need to close your eyes and open up your hand."

She did as I asked, and I placed the item in the palm of her hand.

"Okay, you can open your eyes now."

When she focused on the item, her eyes lit-up with surprise. "A Starburst! Where did you get it from?"

"I bought a pack of them before our trip—I wanted to surprise you."

"Thank you; that was a nice surprise," she said, and popped it in her mouth.

"So, is that Starburst helping you? You're always telling me to have a Starburst and it will make me feel better."

"Actually, *I am* feeling better, but I don't think it's the Starburst. I think your soaking my feet is really helping me. I am feeling a lot less pain and can feel my feet now."

"That's good; let me have another look at them."

I examined her feet once more, and I could tell there was a big difference in the color—especially at the tips of her toes.

"They look good, Katie. I think you're going to be just fine. We'll let them soak for a while longer, then I'll find something to wrap them up to keep them warm."

By this time the firewood was starting to dwindle, so I grabbed my coat to get some more wood. I went outside and made several trips to stock up, as I knew we were probably going to be here all night long. After I brought in the last load of wood, I saw that her socks had dried so I brought them over to her. She dried off her feet with a towel, and put them on. The rest of our clothes were not dry yet, so I left them hanging above the fireplace. I found a couple more blankets and gave her one to keep her feet nice and warm. I took a blanket for myself, and sat on the loveseat. I could see through the window that it was now dark outside. The snow continued to fall, but the wind had stopped blowing so hard. As it got a little later in the evening, I placed a bunch of wood on the fire, as Katie fell asleep on the couch. It wasn't much longer before I fell asleep myself.

I remember starting to dream about the upcoming Christmas play and I saw myself narrating up on stage. As I was talking, I saw Katie in one of the scenes. I also remembered seeing Derek and Jason in my dream. This was kind of strange because those guys didn't go to our school anymore, so I wondered why they were in my dream. As I was narrating the play, I kept hearing a knock on a door. The knock kept getting louder and louder as I looked around the auditorium to see where it was coming from. Suddenly, I awoke from my dream. It was then that I realized the noise I was hearing was someone knocking on the door to the cabin. The cabin door then burst open as my mom and dad, Brian, and some forest ranger guys, had come to help us. My mom quickly rushed to my side

"Jesse...are you alright?"

I sat up and quickly covered myself with the blanket, as I only had a thermal shirt and my boxers on.

"Yeah, I'm alright, Mom."

Katie had woken up with all the noise, sat up, and covered her legs with the blanket. My mom turned to Katie and asked her if she was also alright.

"Yes, Mrs. Thompson. I'm alright; thanks to Jess."

There was a guy with the forest rangers that looked like a medic, so I got his attention.

"Mister...can you please look at Katie. I think she had frostbite on her feet."

Immediately the man went over and began to examine her feet. I rose from the loveseat and gathered our pants that were hung over the fireplace. I gave Katie hers, then placed mine on. About that time, one of the forest ranger came to my side to ask me a few questions.

"So Jesse...how did you find this cabin in that blizzard? Last we heard, you two had hiked up to Iron Rock Caves and that's where we started our search. How did you end up here, miles from those caves?"

"Well, when the blizzard started, we lost our way because you could no longer tell where the road was at. We must have gone way off course, when this big grey wolf led us to this cabin."

"What? Did you say a wolf led you to this cabin?"

"Yes, sir."

"Wolves don't do that, son. Wolves generally shy away from humans. Never have I heard of a wolf that would lead a human somewhere or let humans follow them."

"Well this one did. In fact, when Katie and I stopped to take breaks from walking through the snow, the wolf would actually wait for us."

As usual I could tell the forest ranger did not believe me about the wolf. At that point, I didn't want to tell him about the wolf's den and the wolf pups. I feared they might want to do something to them, so I just dropped the subject.

The medic guy turned to face me. "Are you the one who treated this girl for her frostbite?"

"Yes sir, I am."

He glanced over at the pan of water. "How did you know how to treat frostbite?"

"From when I was in the Boy Scouts. I took a survival training class as part of getting my first-aid badge."

"All I can say young man, is you probably saved this young girl a couple of toes."

Katie immediately sat up with a look of concern. "You mean it was that bad? I could have lost some of my toes?"

"Yes young lady. Had it not been for your friend knowing what to do by treating you right away, it could have been really bad."

Katie looked over to me and mouthed the words "Thank you" from afar. I smiled and mouthed the words, "You're welcome," in return.

About that time, Brian came over to talk to me.

"Hey man…for a while there we didn't think you guys were going to make it. The blizzard was so bad that we were stuck in the cabin and had to wait until this morning to try and find you. I'm serious dude, those ranger guys really didn't think we were going to find you two alive. I know they didn't want to say anything to your parents, but I could tell they were thinking it."

"Brian, it's a long story of how we were led to this cabin. But as it has been with me and Katie many times before…we had a mysterious unexplained rescuer."

CHAPTER SEVEN – BIG MAN ON CAMPUS

After we arrived home from our holiday blizzard, I rested for several days. I caught a bad cold with a sore throat, and had to miss a couple of days of school. Katie missed the first two days of school also, as she was still recovering from the frostbite on her feet. When I finally made it back to school, I could tell from the moment I stepped onto our middle-school campus, that something was different. As I began to work on a project in my first period class, this guy named Ronny approached me. He then motioned to some of his friends who came over to where we were standing.

"Hey guys...Jess *the man* is back in school."

When he said that, the rest of the guys looked at each other and smiled.

"So Jess," Ronny continued. "I heard you had a 'real nice time' with Katie over the Thanksgiving holiday."

His friends chuckled and nodded their heads at one another; like they had a secret.

"I don't know if being caught in a blizzard and almost dying is what you would call a 'real nice time' but I'm glad to be back in school," I replied.

The guys laughed and then a couple of them patted me on the back saying, "You're the man, Jess... Yep, you're the man..." and then they walked off.

With a perplexed look on my face I shrugged off their comments. I had no idea what they meant, but I guess I was "The Man" for the day or something.

My next class was English Literature where I sit next to Becky. Just prior to the class starting, I tapped her on the shoulder.

"Hi Becky, how's it going?"

She turned in her seat to face me. "How's it going? I don't know; why don't *you tell me?*" she said, with a bit of anger in her voice.

"What are you talking about? And why does it seem like you're mad at me?"

"You know very well what I'm talking about!" she snapped, and then abruptly turned around in her seat.

I thought. *Man..., what is her problem anyway?*

After class I tried to catch up to her to find out why she seemed so upset with me. However, she walked off in a rush like she didn't want to talk to me. As I was making my way to my next class, I saw Brian in the hall. He motioned me over with a sense of urgency.

"Hey man, I can't talk right now, but I need to talk to you about something really important. I'll meet you in the cafeteria at lunchtime."

"Okay, I'll see you then."

Curious about what he wanted to talk to me about, I made my way to my next class. As I did, I could tell a lot of people were looking at me in the halls.

Geez... I thought. *Do I have a booger in my nose or something? Why is everyone looking at me so strangely today?*

During all my morning classes, it seemed to be this same theme. People staring at me, and then whispering something to their friends. Not only was I feeling self-conscious by the time it was lunch hour, but I started to worry I had done something wrong but didn't know about it. Finally the bell rang, and so I headed out to the cafeteria. Katie and Becky entered to get their food, and then sat at a table a ways off. This was unusual because they usually sit close to our group of friends. Just then Brian came over in a rush and sat down at the table.

"Jess, I need to talk to you. Something is happening and I think it may be my fault. I don't want you to be mad at me, and I really didn't mean for this to happen."

Now I was worried. I had never seen Brian like this before. Brian is always cool-headed about things, and I could tell he was in a panic.

"Calm down Brian, just tell me what's going on."

"Well, this all started a couple of days ago when you and Katie were still recovering from the blizzard. At lunchtime, some of the guys were asking me about what had happened on our trip. I started to tell them the story how you guys got caught in the blizzard. I explained how you went on a hike, and how we found you the next morning in the cabin. In the process of telling the story, I kind of mentioned that you and Katie had spent the entire night together."

"So, what's wrong with that? *We did* have to spend the night together."

"I know Jess, but then I also kind of mentioned that when we found you in the morning, you were both in your underwear."

A look of shock ran across my face. "What!"

"Yeah, and it gets worse. You know how you play that game where you have like ten people in a line. Then the first person tells a story to the person next to them, and then that person tells the person next to them the story, and so on and so on?"

"Yeah, I know that game. So what's the point?"

"Well, within the last couple of days the story has changed a lot. Now what everyone is saying, is that you and Katie spent the night together in the same bed; you were in your underwear when we found you; and that you guys might have 'done something' together—if you know what I mean."

"Oh my God! You know that's not the truth!"

"I know, and I tried to fix it by telling those guys that I never said those things. But it has spread so much that I couldn't control it. Jess, you have to believe me…I never meant for this to happen. I was just telling the story and those jerks turned it into something else."

I was pretty mad at Brian, but given my experience with rumors I could see how it can happen. I could see by the downcast look on his face that he felt really bad about it and didn't want to look at me in the eye.

"I know you didn't mean it, Brian," I said, and placed my hand on his shoulder to show him I wasn't mad at him. "Right now I'm just concerned about Katie and what is being said to her."

"And what about Melissa?"

"Yeah, you're right, I didn't think about Melissa. I'll have to explain things to her too."

On my way to drama class my stomach was doing flip-flops, knowing all the people who were in that class. Thinking about Katie, Becky, Melissa, Marc and myself; all being in the same room, made me want to hurl my lunch. I thought about maybe going to nurse's office to try to be excused for the rest of the day. But after thinking about it, I decided I would have to face the music sometime. I heard that expression from a movie I saw once.

When I stepped into the classroom a world of eyes were upon me. First I looked at Marc, who basically gave me a dirty look—I kind of expected that from him. Melissa was over in a corner with some of her friends talking. When she saw me, she glanced at me with a blank stare, and then turned the other way. Katie looked over to me with hurt in her eyes, which made my heart stir with concern. Becky looked at me with distain, and quickly turned away. Talk about a tough crowd!

About that time, Miss Simms directed us to our places to rehearse some of our scenes for the upcoming Christmas play. She clapped her hands together to gain our attention.

"I need Joseph and Mary to take their places. Katie, Marc…come stand over here near the prop. I want you to rehearse the part where you try to get a room at the inn."

Katie and Marc walked over to the half-opened prop door to begin their scene. Melissa, who was the inn-keeper's wife, answered the knock of the door. That's when things started to get ugly.

"May I help you?" she said.

"Yes, we have been traveling a far ways and my wife, she is with child. Do you have any room for us?"

Melissa looked directly at Katie, and in a snooty tone replied, "There's no room at the Inn *for you, Mary*!"

"Cut!" Miss. Simms interjected. "Melissa, the line is; we're sorry, but there is no room here at the Inn. And Melissa, you just say it straight, not so mean."

"Yes Ma'am," she said, while giving Katie a dirty look.

Katie turned to me with hurt in her eyes once more. I shrugged my shoulders signifying that I didn't know why all this was happening. She turned away and they rehearsed it one more time.

Miss Simms then gathered my attention. "Jesse…I want you to practice your narration where Joseph and Mary already have the baby, and are in the stable with the wise men and shepherds."

"Yes Ma'am."

As I begun to narrate, my voice was weak and began to shake. Miss Simms interrupted me.

"Jesse…you need to be more confident than that. Speak up with a strong voice, please."

"I'm sorry Miss Simms, but my throat is still a little sore from when I was sick."

I said that because I really didn't feel like narrating with all that was going on with Katie and Melissa. Fortunately, Miss Simms moved on to another scene of the play.

When I arrived home from school that day, all I could think about was calling Katie to explain what Brian had told me. After doing a few household chores, I went to my room and dialed her number. Mr. McCullough answered the phone.

"Hello…"

"Oh, hi Mr. McCullough, this is Jess. Can I talk to Katie?"

"No Jesse, she can't talk right now." Then there was just silence.

"Do you know if I can call her later? I really need to talk to her about something."

"Not today, Jesse, maybe another time." Then more silence.

Feeling I shouldn't push the issue, I backed-off.

"Yes sir, maybe another time."

As I hung up the phone, I noted the firm tone and short answers he had given me. I figured he must know something about the stuff that is going around in school, and so he was upset with me. Feeling downcast at not being able to talk to her, I went into the living room to watch TV. My mom and dad were in there watching a program, so I plopped on the loveseat and quietly sat there watching the program.

"What's wrong, Jess?" my mom asked. "You seem very quiet tonight."

"Nothing…just some stuff going on in school."

"You know if you need someone to talk to, both your father and I are always here."

"Yeah I know; thanks."

I didn't feel like watching TV, so I went upstairs to play a few video games. Suddenly, there was a rapid knock on the door, as Tami came barging in.

"Hey squirt, I need to talk to you."

I shook my head in annoyance, as I wished she would stop calling me squirt.

"What do you want, Tami? I'm really not in the mood right now."

"Jess, there are some really bad rumors being spread in our high school about you and Katie. A lot of the ninth-graders still keep in contact with your class. For example… Jason still talks to Becky and some of the guys from your school talk to Derek. Now I know you and Katie did not 'do anything' up at that cabin, but a lot of people are saying all kinds of things."

"Tami, I never said any of those things. Brian was the one who was simply telling the story, and some friends of his twisted it all around."

"Well, I'm not trying to tell you how to live your life kid, you know me; live and let live. But you need to try to put a stop to these rumors before they get out of hand."

"Do you really think it's that bad? Don't you think this will all blow over pretty soon?"

"I don't know; I would hate to see you ruin your friendship with Katie."

"I won't, it'll be fine."

"I hope so, but if I were you I would somehow try to control this before it goes too far. By the way…a lot of us ninth-graders will be going to your Christmas play since you are having it at our high school. When is it again?"

"It's the 20th; that Friday afternoon before Christmas vacation."

"Alright, good luck kid."

"Yeah, thanks."

*****

For the next couple of days things got really crazy. Most of the guys in school thought I was "The Man," as they would come up and pat me on the back. On the other side of things, a lot of the girls were not happy with me and were giving me dirty looks. All of this was getting me upset because I was not the one who started this in the first place.

This is not my fault, so why should I be expected to do something to fix it. And as far as I'm concerned, people can believe what they want to believe; they're going to think what they want anyways.

With that train of thought, I went and sat by myself at lunchtime. As I began to eat my lunch, I felt a familiar hand touch my shoulder.

"Jess…, we really need to talk."

I looked up to see Katie standing by my side, with worry and disappointment draped across her face.

"I know, Katie. How about we talk about it after school when we walk home?"

"Okay, I'll see you then."

A couple of minutes later, Melissa walked over and took a seat beside me. As usual, sarcasm stemmed from her voice.

"I saw you talking with your little skank. What did she want?"

My face flushed with anger. "Don't you dare call her a skank! You have no idea what went on in that cabin. Only Katie and I know the truth, and everyone else should just mind their own stinkin' business!"

Infuriated, I got up to leave as she called out a few departing words.

"You know Jess, you need to make up your mind about what you want. Do you want someone who can actually be a girlfriend to you, or do you want your little friend over there?"

I walked up to her face to face. "Melissa, remember when you asked me if I liked you? And I said you'd be the first one to know? We'll since you just called Katie a skank, you'll be the first one to know. And the answer is… NO, I DON'T LIKE YOU!"

Later that afternoon, Katie and I began to walk home. At first there was just this uncomfortable silence. Finally, she turned to open the conversation.

"What's going on, Jess? I know you didn't start those rumors about us. So how did this get started?"

"It was Brian, but he didn't do it on purpose. He was just telling the story of what happened, and then some of the guys took it from there."

"People are talking about me and looking at me different. Do you know how that makes me feel?"

"I know it's bad, but what can I do; people are going to talk."

"Jess, I don't want people to think of me that way. I have tried hard to live a Christian life that is pleasing to God. I know they call me things like 'church girl' and 'goody-two-shoes,' and I can deal with that. But now they are saying such terrible things about me, and I am getting this other reputation—it hurts, Jess."

As she stood silent, tears began to form in her eyes. I placed my hand caringly on her shoulder.

"I don't know what to say, Katie. There's nothing I can do."

She burst into tears, and quickly walked away. I called out to her to get her to stop, but she just kept walking home.

*****

Throughout the following week the rumors kept circling around campus. The bad thing, is that they weren't going away. And although this was good for my reputation, as the guys thought I was "The Man," it was doing the opposite for Katie and her reputation. There were names being said about her that, let's just say, were not very nice.

When I arrived home from school that day, my mom came up to my room, and sat on the edge of my bed. By the expression on her face, I knew a lecture was coming.

"Jess, let's have a little talk, alright?"

"Okay."

"Your sister told me about some rumors that are apparently going around your school about you and Katie."

I shook my head. "Figures Tami would tell you; she has such a big mouth."

"I know you and your sister fight sometimes, but I don't think you realize just how much she loves you and looks out for you."

"Well she has a funny way of showing it."

"Getting back to the subject…I would like to tell you a story. When I was a little girl I had a very close friend of mine by the name of Sandy. Sandy and I did everything together, like true friends do.

One of the things we liked to do was go with her mom and dad to the Five & Dime. The Five & Dime was a small department store that had a pharmacy and sold a variety of items. Sandy and I liked to go there because we would always get to pick out a candy bar or some small item at the end of our time shopping there. One time while Sandy and I were looking over the selection of candy bars, her mother called her over to help with carrying a few items. Sandy placed the candy bar in her pocket and then went over to help her mother. When it was time to leave, her mother told us to pick out a piece of candy. Sandy had forgotten she had placed that candy bar in her pocket, so she choose another one. After her parents paid for their items and were about to leave the store manager stopped us. He told Sandy's parents that Sandy had stolen a candy bar and it was in her pocket. She pulled out the candy bar and tried to explain that she was not trying to steal the candy, but forgot it in her pocket. Her mother and father were very angry and started to yell at her. They apologized to the store manager; saying that Sandy would be disciplined for her actions. As Sandy's parents continued to yell at her in the car, I was afraid to say anything because I thought that I was going to get in trouble myself. As part of Sandy's punishment, they told her she could not play with me for a whole month. After that incident, Sandy's parents were always reminding her of what she did. And any time something turned up missing around the house she was always blamed for it. As the years went by and we were no longer friends, Sandy began to steal things in stores. I guess she figured since everyone else thought that she was so bad and had this bad reputation, that she might as well be that way. During my years in high school, she spent time in Juvenile Hall and eventually in youth prison." My mom then turned to me as regret stemmed from her voice. "Jesse… even after all these years that still haunts me and I feel so bad about it."

"Yeah, but Mom, that wasn't your fault. You didn't do anything wrong."

She rose to her feet, walked to the door and turned to face me. "Jesse...sometimes it's not what you did wrong that matters. Sometimes it's what *you should have done* that can make all the difference in someone's life."

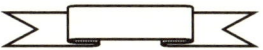

CHAPTER EIGHT – THE ANSWER

Later that evening my mind was filled with everything that was going on. I remember Katie telling me that when she needed a "word from God," she would pray and read her Bible. She said there were times a particular scripture verse would just jump out at her, and give her the answer she needed for her life. Right now I needed an answer to this whole situation, so I opened up my nightstand drawer and pulled out my Bible. I began to read several verses, but nothing seemed to jump out at me or even related to what I was going through. I tried to read another section, but once again, I got nothing. Then I thought, *Maybe it doesn't work unless you are "Saved" or "Born Again". Or maybe I just don't know the right way to read the Bible or something.*

*****

The next day was Saturday and I decided to give Brian a call.

"Hey Brian, what's up?"

"Not much. I was about to get something to eat and just hang out in my room. Do you want to come over?"

"Yeah, actually I do. I could use a bud right now."

"Yeah man, come on over."

"Alright, I'll be there in a few."

I took my bike out of the garage and headed towards Brian's house. I probably got about halfway there, when ka-blam!—my tire popped. It totally went down to the rim as I came to a bumpy stop.

"Oh man, not now!" I shouted in frustration.

I got off my bike and headed towards Brian's, thinking his house was closer than mine at that point. I also remembered that Brian's dad had all kinds of automotive equipment and he could probably fix my flat. As I continued to push my bike, a man in a pickup truck came by and pulled over to the side of the road. He proceeded to roll down his window.

"Hey there young man," he greeted. "You go to Fuller Creek Middle School, don't you?"

"Yes sir, I do."

"I thought I have seen you before. You're Jesse, right? I am John Burke; I believe you know my daughter, Patty Burke."

"Oh yeah I know Patty; we used to be lab partners last year."

"Yes, one time I was picking Patty up from school, and she pointed you out as being her lab partner. So, I see you got a flat tire. Can I give you a lift?"

Normally I wouldn't take a ride from someone I didn't know, but since it was Patty's father I thought that I would be alright.

"Sure Mr. Burke, I would appreciate a ride. Can you drop me off at my friend's house? He just lives over on 4th Street."

"Sure, just put your bike in the back of the pickup."

I placed my bike in the back of his truck, and hopped in the front seat.

"So Jess... do you and Patty have any classes together this year?"

"No, not this year."

As he was about to turn down Brian's street, I looked down and saw this little booklet with the title of "Your Daily Bread."

"Can I look at this Mr. Burke?" I said, pointing to the booklet.

"Sure, it's a booklet of daily scripture verses from the Bible."

I took a hold of the booklet, which was opened about half way, and read what was on that page. It read; *'A righteous man hates falsehood, but a wicked man acts disgustingly and shamefully'. Proverbs 13:5 (NAS)*

At first it didn't mean much to me. But then all of a sudden, all these thoughts just seemed to pop into my head all at once—it was really strange. One of the thoughts that came to mind was in the form of a question. "What was the falsehood in my life?" What came to mind, were all the rumors and false stories that were going around in school. The second question was, "Did I hate the falsehood or did I like it?" Did I really hate all that was going on? Or did I like the part about me being "The Man" and becoming popular. When I thought about it, I realized that by keeping silent about these rumors, I was trading Katie's reputation for a chance to be popular. As I thought on that I felt disgusted and ashamed for letting this go on for as long as I have without speaking out against it. This I related to the part of that scripture that said, "But a wicked man acts disgustingly and shameful."

Mr. Burke's voice suddenly broke my thoughts. "Is something the matter, Jess? You seemed to be in deep thought when you were reading that."

"Actually sir, I think it's an answer to something I have been dealing with in my life."

About that time we arrived at Brian's house, so I thanked Mr. Burke and pulled my bike out of the back of his truck. Brian came out of the house and looked over my bike.

"Dude, what happened?"

"I blew a tire on the way over here. Mr. Burke happened to be passing by and gave me a ride. Mr. Burke is Patty Burke's father."

"You were lucky he came along when he did, otherwise you would have had to walk your bike all the way over here."

"Yeah, I guess I was pretty lucky."

I agreed that I was lucky that he happened to pass by when he did. But I also felt like Mr. Burke coming along and having that booklet opened to that particular spot was meant to be.

"Brian, do you think your dad can fix this flat for me?"

"Sure I'll go get him; he fixes my tires all the time."

As his father began to work on my bike, we went into his room to hang out. He walked over to his stereo and began to scan through some of his cassettes.

"You want to listen to some tunes? I have Boston, the Eagles, Chicago, Aerosmith; all kinds of stuff."

"Yeah that's cool; maybe something that can keep my mind off of things. I want something a bit on the mellow side. How about the Eagles."

He placed the cassette in his stereo as we began to talk.

"Jess, I really feel bad about what has happened. I feel like I let you and Katie down."

"It's not your fault. Once the rumors got out at least you tried to stop it—which is more than I can say about myself."

"What do you mean by that?"

"Oh nothing, just something I have to figure out."

Just then the song Desperado came on.

"There you go Brian, that's me, a 'Desperado.' I'm desperate to come up with a solution to fix all of this."

"If I can help in any way, just let me know. Oh by the way… I heard that you and Melissa got into it and you guys broke up?"

"I wouldn't call it breaking up. I mean you can't break up with someone unless you're officially going out with that person in the first place."

"So what happened?"

"She called Katie a skank."

"What! No way, that's so messed up."

"Yep, and to me, that really showed what type of person she is. So that was it for me, I didn't want to be her friend anymore."

"Well, since me and Michelle don't hang around anymore either, I guess that kind of works out. Easy-come, easy-go, right Jess?"

"Yeah, I guess so."

"So…the big Christmas play is coming up at the high school for you and the rest of your drama class."

"Yeah, I hope it turns out alright, but with all that's going on, people are starting to take sides. Like Becky and her friends are trying to defend Katie, while Melissa and her friends are bad-mouthing her. I guess it will be interesting if nothing else. You're going, aren't you?"

"Oh course man, I got your back."

"Thanks man," I said, as we gave each other the particular handshake thing we do.

*****

The following day after school, which was the day before the Christmas play, I arrived home. I grabbed a snack to eat and went up to my room. I started to rehearse my lines for the play so it would come out nice and smooth. I was fortunate to have my lines right in front of me being the narrator. Not like the rest of the cast who had to learn their lines by heart. I read over some of the narration leading up to where Mary has this revelation of her being chosen by God to bring a savior into the world. As I was doing that, I began to think about Mary and how hard it must have been for her when she discovered that she was "with child." She wasn't married to Joseph yet, and I could only imagine what the people would have said about her—especially in those times. I then thought about Joseph and the position he was in and thought how hard it must have been for him also, to make the decision on whether to marry her or not.

That night as I feel asleep I had almost the exact same dream as I did when Katie and I were stuck in the mountain cabin. It was the dream where I was narrating the play and saw Katie kneeling over the baby Jesus in the manger. I also remembered seeing Derek and Jason and wondering once again why they were in my dream. When I awoke the next morning, I dismissed the thought that it had any significance. I passed it off as being nervous about the play, and that's why I had that particular dream again.

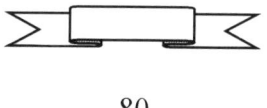

CHAPTER NINE - THE MOMENT OF TRUTH!

On the day of the Christmas play our drama class went over to the high school auditorium. We were allowed to be excused from our afternoon classes to go through a final dress rehearsal. We had a full dress rehearsal and went over some final details. For the most part it seemed to go smoothly.

After the rehearsal, we were allowed to go home to get something to eat before the evening performance. When I arrived at home, my family was getting ready for the big event. Surprisingly, even my father had taken off from work early to see my play. As I began to get ready, Tami stopped by my room.

"So squirt... are you ready for this play?"

"Yeah, I think so," I replied, and adjusted my tie.

"So how are things going with Katie and all the rumors flying around?"

"Not good. In fact it seems to be getting worse. It seems like half the school is taking sides in this whole mess."

"Jess, I know we haven't talked much in the past on a personal level, because to be honest, it was just kind of weird. But now that I'm in high school and you're a little older, I feel we can talk a little better. I just wanted to tell you that I think you're growing up to be a pretty good kid. I have seen a lot of changes in you, and I think some of those changes are because of your friendship with Katie. One thing I can say about her is that she's not a poser. Do you know what a poser is?"

"No, not really."

"A poser is someone who tries to act like someone they're not. In high school you see a lot of different people with a lot of different beliefs. But let me tell you, there are a lot of people who say they're Christians or religious, but they're really not. You'd be surprised at some of the things they do. These are the posers. But Katie, she's not a poser. I can tell there is something different about this girl. I don't know how to completely explain it, because I'm not into all that religious stuff myself. The only way I can put it, is that some people try to live by the teachings of their religion because that's what they are taught to do—like a set of rules. But with Katie, what she believes is who she is. It's her nature to be that way. All I'm saying, is I think your friendship with her is good for the both of you. Jess, don't lose her friendship over this mess."

A look of surprise rose upon my face, as I had never heard Tami talk like that before. It was kind of nice considering how we were always fighting and calling each other names. I guess my mom was right when she said that Tami cares about me more than I thought.

I turned to her with a smile of appreciation. "Thanks Tami for telling me that; it really means a lot to me. Really... you're a good sister."

"Now don't you go get all mushy with me, you're still a little twerp!" she said, and then gave me a playful shove.

I playfully shoved her back. "Yeah, and you're still a dorkface."

She headed for the doorway. "Alright, now go break-a-leg, as they say."

"Thanks."

When we arrived at the high school for the evening's performance, there were a lot more cars in the parking than I expected. I really didn't think that many people would be there; being a middle-school play. However, in thinking about it, I remember Mr. and Mrs. McAllister telling us that this town supports each other. Speaking of the McAllisters...I saw them come into the auditorium and I waved to them as they came in and took their seat.

As my family looked for a place to sit, I went backstage to start to get ready. Everyone was getting dressed in their costumes, and the lighting crew was making last minute adjustments to their equipment. With a quick signal of her hand, Miss Simms motioned me over.

"Jesse…I wanted to go over a few things with you before we begin. Make sure you speak clearly and don't rush through it. I chose you to narrate because I like the way you emphasize key parts when you're reading. I remember when you read your poems and other writing assignments when you were in my English class. Use those same skills with your narration."

"Yes Ma'am, I will. I have gone over it several times at home so I would know my readings much better."

As Miss Simms went to talk to some other cast members, I saw Katie walk out from the dressing area in her "Mary" outfit. I walked across the stage area to talk to her.

I scanned her up and down. "You look good—like a girl from the Bible days. So, are you ready for this?"

She took a blue scarf and wrapped it around her head. "I think I'm ready. But now that I see so many people here, I have butterflies in my stomach."

"You'll do great. Don't worry about it. Hey…are your parents here yet?"

"Yes, they just came in. They're sitting right over there next to your parents."

"Katie, I've been meaning to ask you… is your father mad at me? Last week when I called, your dad acted kind of cold with me."

"I think he was a little upset at first. I think he felt you could have done something to stop those rumors. I think he thinks that all boys are the same, and you might have been going along with those stories to make yourself look good. I had a talk with him and I told him that you had nothing to do with starting those rumors; so I think he's okay now."

"I hope so; I don't want him to be upset with me."

"He'll be fine. But I better go now; I have to get ready for my first scene."

"Okay, good luck."

"Thanks, you too."

As the people filtered into the auditorium, it seemed like the whole town was there. I know that wasn't the case, as the auditorium only holds about twelve hundred seats; but it sure felt like that way. When it was time to start, Miss Simms made her way and stood in front of the stage curtain. She then began to address the audience.

"Ladies and Gentlemen would you please take your seats, as we are about to commence with the performance."

As the people settled into their seats the lights dimmed over the audience, and the full spotlight shown on the center of the stage. Miss Simms began the introduction.

"Ladies and Gentlemen, children of all ages. I would like to present Fuller Creek Middle School's rendition of: A Savior is born unto the World."

The audience applauded as the curtain came down to start the first scene of the play.

Katie (Mary) and Becky (Elizabeth) were on stage as Mary came to the door of Elizabeth's house. I then began to the read the narration that leads into the first scene.

"Mary got ready and hurried to a town in the hill country of Judea where she entered Zechariah's home and greeted Elizabeth. When Elizabeth heard Mary's greeting, the baby leaped in her womb, and Elizabeth was filled with the Holy Spirit."

(Mary): "Elizabeth, it's me, Mary. I am here on a visit."

(Elizabeth): "Come in Mary! Blessed are you among women, and blessed is the child you will bear!"

(Mary): "But why am I so favored that the mother of my Lord should come to me?"

(Elizabeth): "As soon as the sound of your greeting reached my ears, the baby in my womb leaped for joy. Blessed is she who has believed that what the Lord has said to her will be accomplished!"

With the end of that dialog, the eighth-grade band began to play softly in the background as Katie knelt to her knees and looked towards the heavens.

(Mary): "My soul glorifies the Lord and my spirit rejoices in God my Savior, for he has been mindful of the humble state of his servant. From now on all generations will call me blessed, for the Mighty One has done great things for me, holy is his name."

As Katie continued to recite the whole passage, I took a deep breath as I was still a little nervous. I looked towards Miss Simms who signaled me to stand up straight and project my voice. When the scene and song ended the curtain closed to a round of applause, as that concluded the first scene.

The next scene was where Joseph (Marc) is sleeping, and an angel of the Lord comes to him in a dream. As everyone took their places, the curtain rose as Joseph was lying asleep and the Angel enters his room. I opened the scene with a brief narration.

"But while Joseph thought on these things, behold, the angel of the LORD appeared unto him in a dream."

(Joseph): "Who art thou that thou hast come to me?" he said, and covered his eyes from the Angel who was illuminated by the spotlight.

The Angel said, "Joseph, thou son of David, fear not to take unto thee Mary thy wife. For that which is conceived in her is of the Holy Ghost."

Just then a voice from the audience yelled out… "If I were you Joseph, *I would fear* taking Mary as thy wife!" Then you heard a few guys laughing.

It wasn't that loud, but some of the people in that area turned around and said to be quiet. I thought perhaps it was Melissa's friends or maybe some of Marc's friends just messing around, but I wasn't sure. As the scene ended and the curtain closed, I saw Melissa look towards some of her friends who were smiling and snickering.

There was a short break between scenes where the band was playing and the choir sang a couple of songs. After they finished, we went through two more scenes where the wise men see the star in the sky, and the shepherds are with their flocks by night. Now it was time for the scene where Joseph and Mary try to get a "room at the Inn." The scene had a prop door that opened about half way as Mary and Joseph walked up and knocked on the door.

(Knock, Knock)

(Joseph): "We have been traveling a far ways and my wife is with child. Do you have any room for us here at the inn?"

Innkeeper's wife (Melissa): "I'm sorry but there's no room at this inn *for you Mary*!" she said, in a snotty tone.

I looked at Miss Simms and saw she was furious. Melissa had once again said her line in that same snotty tone like she did in practice. I looked at Katie and Marc who were both upset at the way Melissa said her line. Marc shook it off and continued with his lines.

(Joseph): "Thank you for your time; we will seek shelter someplace else."

Melissa then slammed the door and commented. "You're not welcome at the inn, or at our school, Mary!"

With that, the scene ended and the curtain came down. By this time I was so upset that when the spotlight was off of me, I tried to sneak backstage and give Melissa a piece of my mind. However as I took a few steps in that direction, Miss Simms motioned for me to stay at the podium. Then she pointed at herself like saying, "I'll take care of this." I peeked behind the curtain and I could see Miss Simms really laying into Melissa. Then she motioned for Melissa to leave the stage area.

Now we were at the final scene at the manger with Joseph and Mary, the wise men, and the shepherds. The scene opened with the band and choir singing Away in a Manger. After they finished, I began my narration summarizing the scene.

"As Joseph and Mary beheld their newborn son in a humble manger, wise men from the east came to worship the child bringing gifts."

Just then another voice from the audience yelled, "Hey Joseph... are you sure that's your kid? I think we all know whose kid that is!"

This time, a lot of people in the audience heard what was said, including my and Katie's parents. The people in that area turned around, as you once again heard them say to be quiet. I looked at Katie's dad and I could tell he was furious. Then I looked to Katie and I could tell all of this was starting to get to her. Tears began to form in her eyes, as Marc leaned over and said something to her, then he shook his head in disgust. My mom and dad had a look of shock draped across their faces as to what was going on. I looked over at Miss Simms and she motioned for me to continue. I was so upset I almost couldn't think straight. I cleared my throat to gather myself, and continued my narration.

"And the wise men brought their gifts unto the child and laid them before him. And they called the child Jesus—Emmanuel, meaning 'God with us.'"

Then once again someone shouted from the audience. "Shouldn't that baby be called Jesse Thompson Jr.!" Then you heard a bunch of kids laughing.

This time, both my dad and Mr. McCullough stood up with anger raging on their faces. By Mr. McCullough's expression, it looked like he wanted to go beat someone up. Most of crowd didn't know what was going on and thought that these kids were just being stupid. But those of us closest to the situation knew very well what they meant. And although those awful comments were hurtful to all of us, for Katie... they were unbearable.

Katie was supposed to begin reciting a dialog about being blessed and calling the child Jesus. As I looked at her on stage, she had her head bowed, and I could tell she was crying. To his credit, Marc tried to console her, as he leaned in saying something to her. She responded by shaking her head back and forth in the negative. I knew she was telling him she could not continue, as she was filled with tears. The spotlight then re-focused on me, as Miss Simms knew that Katie could not continue with her lines. Miss Simms then motioned for me to continue and move on to the final part where I recite that famous passage in Luke Chapter 2 of the Bible. You know, the one that you hear Linus recite on a 'Charlie Brown Christmas.'

As I stood there in disbelief of what was happening, I remembered the story my mom had told me about speaking up when the truth needs to be told. I also remembered that scripture verse from my ride with Mr. Burke, and the thoughts that entered my mind after reading it. All those things came to me perhaps in preparation for this very moment—the moment of truth!

I looked towards heaven as if to say, "God give me the right words." I placed my script on the podium and looked out into the audience and began to speak.

"We have come here tonight to celebrate Christmas by the performance of this play. We have all heard this Christmas story many times before about Jesus in a manger, and we think it's such a nice little story. But tonight I want to tell you, it is much more than just a story. This story is about real people and the events going on in their lives. What I feel gets lost in the Christmas story, is the decisions that both Joseph and Mary had to deal with knowing that Mary was pregnant with a child. Imagine you are a very young girl like Mary was, barely into her teen years. You have just been told that you are going to have a baby. Mary knew she had never been with a man before; so how could it be that she was pregnant? She must have gone through a lot of emotions wondering what she was going to tell Joseph.

What were the people in her community going to say about her? Mary had a reputation in the community as a 'good girl' a godly young woman; so what was she going to do. At that point Mary could have backed-off from what she believed and could have run away from this responsibility. But Mary knew the truth, and knew she was a pure young lady and kept to her beliefs. Now think about Joseph. Here was a young man who cared deeply for Mary and had just found out that the girl he was going to marry was pregnant. He probably thought about all the ridicule and the gossip that would spread about her if all of this was to be found out. And although he was told by an angel it was okay to marry her as illustrated tonight in the play, I am sure he had many decisions to make. Joseph could have let his pride and fear get in the way and just left Mary to fend for herself. This was real… real life, real emotions, real decisions that he and all of us have to make at one time or another in our lives. But Joseph knew Mary. He knew her character and trusted in her integrity and devotion to God. He knew this girl better than anyone else…" I said, raising my voice. "Better than those who would make up false stories about her…! Better than those who would want to call her names and tarnish her reputation…! And better than those who didn't know the real story of what was going on in her life! If I were Joseph I would stand before you tonight as a testimony to my knowledge of the purity of this young woman. And it's because of this knowledge that I can confidently and proudly declare to the world, that she is in fact a pure virgin girl, never knowing any man and chosen by God for great things!"

As the last of my words echoed throughout the auditorium, the audience fell completely silent. I saw my mom and dad staring at me in amazement. I looked at Katie's mom who had tears welling in her eyes. I then looked to Katie, who had a glow about her—like a tremendous weight was lifted off her. As the auditorium stayed silent, suddenly I heard a single person start to clap from the back row. That person then stood up and continued to clap as the lights started to come on over the audience. As the lights filled the auditorium, I focused on the person who was clapping, and to my amazement... it was Derek. Yes Derek...The same guy who started those rumors about me last year. The same guy who I had been calling a jerk for the past year. And the same Derek that I thought would never apologize to me unless "Pigs learned to fly." Then Derek's friend Jason stood up and he began to clap also. Then all of Derek's friends stood to their feet clapping along with them. Moments later, my mom and dad, Tami, and Katie's parents, joined in clapping as well. Before I knew it, the entire audience rose to its feet and gave a standing ovation. I looked over at Miss Simms who nodded her head in approval, and motioned for me to finish the last part of the narration to the Christmas story. As the audience settled back in their seats, I cleared my throat and began to narrate the final passage of the play.

"And it came to pass in those days, that there went out a decree from Caesar Augustus that all the world should be taxed. And all went to be taxed, every one into his own city. And Joseph also went up from Galilee, out of the city of Nazareth, into Judaea, unto the city of David, which is called Bethlehem; (because he was of the house and lineage of David) To be taxed with Mary his espoused wife, being great with child. And so it was that while they were there, the days were accomplished that she should be delivered. And she brought forth her firstborn son, and wrapped him in swaddling clothes, and laid him in a manger; because there was no room for them in the inn.
And there were in the same country shepherds abiding in the field, keeping watch over their flock by night. And, lo, the angel of the Lord came upon them, and the glory of the Lord shone round about them: and they were sore afraid. And the angel said unto them, Fear not: for, behold, I bring you good tidings of great joy, which shall be to all people. For unto you is born this day in the city of David, a Savior, which is Christ the Lord. And this shall be a sign unto you; ye shall

Holiday Blizzard: The Moment of Truth!

find the babe wrapped in swaddling clothes, lying in a manger. And suddenly there was with the angel a multitude of the heavenly host praising God, and saying, Glory to God in the highest, and on earth peace, good will toward men." Luke 2: 1-14

As the curtain came down and the lights came on signaling the end of the play, the entire audience stood to its feet and gave another standing ovation. All of us in the cast gathered behind the curtain, and when it rose we all took a bow. One of the students came and gave Miss Simms a bouquet of flowers as she took a bow with a smile of appreciation. After it ended, the families of the cast members came up to give their congratulations. I walked over to Miss Simms, who reached out to me with a big hug.

"Jesse, I knew I picked the right person to narrate. What you did up there was simply inspiring!"

"I'm sorry Miss Simms about not sticking to the script at the end. But with all of that going on, I just had to do something."

"Jesse, I would normally not approve of a cast member deviating from the script. But what you did up there was not only necessary, but appropriate given the circumstances. Did you already have something prepared just in case something like this was going to happen?"

"No, it just came to me on the spot."

"That's amazing; and the way you intergraded it with the Christmas story was wonderful. You have talent, Jesse. I hope you continue with those writing skills in the future."

"Thank you, Miss Simms."

Just then Brian came up and tapped me on the shoulder. "Hey man, congratulations—you did a great job."

"Oh, hey Brian, I see you made it after all?"

"Oh course man, I told you I would have your back. Although, I don't think you needed me tonight; you really took care of this whole thing with that speech."

About that time my mom and dad came to give their congratulations. My father patted me on the back.

"I wasn't sure I was watching my own son up there. I'm very proud of you."

"Thanks, Dad." I turned to face my mother. "And *thank you*, Mom. That story you told me the other day was part of what gave me the courage to do something like that."

She smiled, and ran her hand caringly down the back of my head. "You're welcome, son."

Just then I saw Derek making his way over to talk to Katie. As he stood waiting until she was finished talking with another cast member, I saw my chance to talk to him.

"Hey, Derek," I greeted, and extended my hand to him.

"Hey, Jess," he replied, with a firm handshake.

"I wanted to thank you for what you did tonight. That was really cool standing up for us like that."

"Let's just say it was my way of apologizing for what I did to you last year and the whole rumors stuff. I meant to apologize before this, but then the whole Boomy thing came up and you know how it is, I just never got around to it."

"That's cool, I think you more than made up for it tonight."

"You know Jess, Katie is a very special girl as you probably know better than anyone else. When I heard those stories about you guys getting stuck in that cabin, I said no way, Katie would never do anything like that. Like you said up there tonight, she is a good girl and you're lucky to have a friend like her. And by what I saw up on stage tonight, I think she's pretty lucky to have a friend like you too."

"Thanks, that means a lot to hear you say that."

"Well I'm going to talk to Katie for a minute and then split. But maybe we can get together and do something next year when you get to high school with us?"

"Sure, that would be cool."

Derek went over to Katie, congratulated her and then said something to her that made her turn and look at me. Katie then walked over as we gave each other a warm hug.

"Congratulations, Katie. You were great up there tonight."

"Thanks. But that was nothing compared to what you did. It looks like the Knight in Shining Armor has saved the Damsel in Distress once again. It seems like every time I'm in trouble you are there to rescue me."

"Oh, I don't know about that, you have done a lot for me too. And besides, I am definitely not a Knight in Shining Armor."

"I don't know, Jess; you should have seen yourself up there tonight. It was like you were shining up on stage and you had a glow about you—like you were anointed."

"Anointed? What's that?"

"Anointed is a term that Christians use when someone is either speaking, preaching, or singing, and it seems like God's Spirit is upon them."

"Well I don't know if that's what it was, but I'm not sure where some of those words came from."

She looked past me to where Derek was talking with some friends. "So… I saw you talking with Derek. What did you guys talk about?"

"Actually I was thanking him for standing up for us. He then apologized for spreading those rumors about me last year. Which means I'm going to have to start to look for flying pigs."

An inquisitive look rose upon her face. "Flying pigs? What do you mean by that?"

I half-laughed. "Oh nothing, just a little joke I had with myself about Derek. I guess it just goes to show, that you never know what's inside a person's heart."

"That is very true. Oh by the way… my family is taking me out for a celebration dinner. I invited Becky to come with us. Do you want to come too?"

"Thanks, but I think I'll just go home. This whole thing was exhausting and I just want to go home and rest."

"Okay, but you're still coming over on Christmas Eve, aren't you?"

"Oh yeah, I'll be there Christmas Eve. How about five o'clock?"

"Yes, that will be good."

"Okay, I'll see you then."

On their way home from their celebration dinner, Katie and her father began to discuss the evening's events.

"Katie..."

"Yes, Dad?"

"I didn't bring this up because Becky was with us; but are you okay, pumpkin? It must have been horrible for you up on stage with all that was going on."

"You know, Dad, there are times in school when I'm called 'church girl' or 'goodie-two-shoes' because I'm a Christian and talk about God sometimes. Most of the time, I ignore those comments and just smile. Sometimes I take it as a compliment that I must be doing something right, that at least people know I'm a Christian. But when all of those rumors were being spread about me and Jess, it really affected me. Instead of being called a good girl, I was being called the names of someone who was a bad girl. There is so much going on in my life right now with school, my friends, boys, and growing up as a teen. At the same time, I'm trying to be a good Christian and stick to what I believe. When all of that was going on, I had a lapse in my faith and wondered if it was all worth it. Like maybe I should just give up trying to be good, and be like other girls who don't care about their reputations."

"Oh honey," Mrs. McCullough added. "We all go through periods where our faith might be weak. Both your father and I go through that even at our age."

"I know, Mom, but it was still very hard for me. Besides the two of you, Jess knows me better than anyone else. But tonight when he stood up and gave that speech, it said to me that he thinks my reputation as a good girl was worth preserving. When he did that, it confirmed to me that *I am* doing the right thing by living this way."

Mrs. McCullough turned to Katie and directed a smile. "*He is* a very special young man."

Mr. McCullough quickly countered. "He's a special *young boy;* he's not a man," he said firmly.

"Dad, you don't have to worry about me and Jess—we're just friends."

"Okay pumpkin, but I wouldn't be a good father if I didn't point things out like that. It's a father's job to watch out for his little girl."

Katie rolled her eyes. "Okay, Dad."

Mr. McCullough glanced in the rearview mirror. "I do have another question for you about him. Your mother told me you have talked to Jess about the Lord at times. But has he made any kind of commitment? Has he accepted the Lord as his Savior?"

"No, not yet. He believes *there is a God* and he has seen God's hand work in our lives, but he hasn't accepted the Lord yet."

"Honey..." Mrs. McCullough added. "Maybe you should invite him to your youth Bible study. You know they are starting that back up in the spring at the youth pastor's house."

"I plan to, but I don't want to rush him. We kind of had a conversation about this and he said he likes that I don't shove Christianity down his throat. I want him to come to the Lord on his own terms. Oh, speaking of Jess… you do remember that I invited him to come over for Christmas Eve dinner, right?"

"Oh sure honey, we would be more than glad to have him over."

When I arrived home that evening I went up to my room, laid down on my bed and turned on the radio to listen to some music. Just then there was a knock on the door.

"Jess…"

"Come on in, Dad," He walked in and began looking at some of the sport posters on my walls.

"How are you doing, son? Everything alright?"

"I'm fine; just came up to my room to think a bit."

"You know, other than the day you were born, I don't think I have ever been prouder than I was seeing you up there like that."

My dad is not the type of man to come out and say things like that, so I was kind of surprised to hear him say that.

"Thanks. I tell you, it was one crazy night."

He picked up one of my car models and looked it over. "She's very special to you, isn't she son?"

"Oh Katie? Yeah, she's pretty cool."

He half-laughed. "Pretty cool, huh?"

He walked over and gave me this "manly" pat on the leg, and then turned to me before leaving the room.

"Jess…"

"Yeah, Dad?"

"I know Katie is a church girl, so even though our family isn't into church, anytime you want to go with her that's fine with me."

"Okay, thanks. She invited me to go with her several times, so I may just take her up on that invitation sometime."

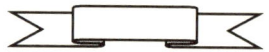

CHAPTER TEN – THE CHRISTMAS DINNER

On Christmas Eve my mom was doing some last minute shopping at the mall, so I went with her to get Katie a Christmas card. Since our parents had paid our way to the museum, we decided not to ask them for any money for gifts. We agreed that we would only give each other Christmas cards this year. When we arrived at the mall, we went into a gift shop and began to look around. I went to the greeting cards isle and began my search. I must have gone through tons of them, but none of them seemed right. They were either too mushy, too stupid, too lame, or just too whatever. None of them said the things I wanted to say; it being our second Christmas together as friends.

"Have you found a card for Katie?" my mom asked.

"No, I just can't seem to find the right one."

"You know that poem you wrote for Boomy was very nice. And what you said at the Christmas play shows you have writing talent. Maybe you could write your own Christmas card to give to Katie."

"Yeah, maybe. But won't that be lame just writing it on a plain piece of paper?"

"I'll tell you what… You write out the poem and I'll make the card out of construction paper. When I was younger I was pretty good at doing things like that. I used to always get good grades in art."

"Okay, let's do that. It'll also save us a few bucks on buying a store bought card."

Later that afternoon my mom got started on making the card. I went up to my room and decided I would write Katie a poem. At first I had trouble getting stared—writer's block I guess. I took in a deep breath to clear my mind and began to write. Once I got going the words seemed to flow, and it said all the things I wanted the card to say. My mom did a really good job on the card, with a picture on the front and everything. I was kind of surprised it came out as good as it did. I pasted my poem on the inside, and my mother gave me an envelope to place it in. She glanced up at the clock.

"What time are you going over to Katie's?"

"In about an hour. I'm supposed to be there at 5:00 O'clock."

She gathered up the scraps of construction paper and threw them in the trash. "Then I guess I better get ready if I'm going to drive you there."

"Okay, I guess I better get ready too."

When we arrived at her house, Mrs. McCullough invited us in and asked my mom to sit and visit for a while. Katie and I went into the den and sat down by the fireplace. Her father soon entered the room a few minutes later, and sat on a recliner chair a few feet from where we were sitting.

"Hi Mr. McCullough," I greeted.

"Hi Jess, Merry Christmas."

"Merry Christmas to you too."

He then looked at me with a questioning stare. "Do you happen to like baked ham and roasted potatoes, Jess?"

I nodded my head. "Oh yeah, I like that."

"Well too bad!" he abruptly countered. "We're having Pot Roast!" Then he laughed so I knew he was joking.

Katie then directed to him a telling look. "Dad... Jess and I are trying to exchange cards—if you don't mind."

"Oh, okay. You go right ahead," he said, and then leaned back in the recliner.

Katie cleared her throat and sent him a piercing stare. "Dad...!"

"What, pumpkin?"

"We would like a little privacy, please."

"Oh sorry, I got you," he said with a wink of his eye, and then left the room.

Once he left I turned to face her. "Boy, your dad seems to be in a really good mood."

"He gets like this around Christmastime, but he seems a lot happier since the Christmas play. I think he knows I feel much better now, so I guess he's happy for me."

"That's pretty cool that he cares about you like that."

She glanced to the side and a smile creased her lips. "Yeah, I guess it is. Speaking of the Christmas play... I wanted to thank you again for standing up for me. You really made me feel special by putting a stop to those rumors in front of hundreds of people."

"Well thank you for saying that. But had I said something sooner it might not have gotten to the point that it did—and I'm sorry for that."

"That's okay; it wasn't like you were the one who started all of that in the first place."

"I know, but someone told me recently that sometimes it's what *you don't say* that can make all the difference in someone's life."

"Well you certainly made a difference in mine."

I could tell we were starting to have a moment between us, so I suggested we exchange our cards. She pulled out a card that was nestled amongst some of the gifts under the Christmas tree.

"Read mine first," she suggested.

I took the card, opened the envelope, and began to read it to myself.

Christmas is the time, to think about the year.
The moments shared together, filled with fun and cheer.
The laughs and smiles of treasured times, and all the things we've done, that make the friendship that we share a very special one!
Have a very Merry Christmas, your best friend.
Katie...

"Do you like it?" she asked. "It took me a long time to find the right one."

I smiled and nodded my head. "It's perfect, thank you."

I then handed her the homemade card I made for her. She looked it over with a questioning stare.

"Jess, did you made this?"

"Yeah, with a little help from my mom."

"I was hoping that you would write me something."

She opened the card and started to read my poem silently to herself.

On this Christmas Day, there are many things to say; the adventures we've been through, give thoughts of me and you.
I think about the day, the "rat" helped find our way; and I think about the time, of our "golden" find.
And then there was the dance, the "dress"; I took a chance; and saw you standing there, a "bun" within your hair.
The river was a ride, but "someone" saved our hide. The "museum" was a rush, but we made it to the bus.
A blizzard made us stray, but "wolfy" found the way. When rumors were abound, the "answer" came around.
So now I say to you, on Christmas number two; a "treasure" I have found, as long as you're around...
Merry Christmas
Jess

After she finished reading, her eyes watered and she swallowed her emotions.

"Jess, I don't know whether to laugh or cry—that was beautiful. It means so much to me that you wrote about our adventures together. Thank you."

After a few awkward moments of silence, she finally said. "Merry Christmas, Jess," then she leaned forward to give me a hug, and I met her half-way.

"Merry Christmas, Katie."

Just then Mr. McCullough entered the den so we quickly separated.

"You two might want to think about getting washed up. As soon as a few of our other guests get here, we'll be eating dinner. And Jess..., your mother is going to stay with us for dinner and I think your father and sister are on the way over here too. We invited them also."

Just then the doorbell rang. He opened the door and Becky stood in the doorway with a gift in hand.

"Hi Mr. McCullough, is Katie here? I just came by to drop off her gift."

Katie and Becky began talking in the den and started laughing about something—like most girls do. Mr. McCullough invited Becky's parents in, but they couldn't stay. They did say however, that Becky could stay and have dinner with us. About that time, my dad and Tami approached up the walkway to the house. Mr. McCullough greeted them in.

"Come on in John, Tami. It's good to see you again."

Tami entered the den and playfully rustled my hair. "Hey squirt! Looks like Christmas Eve dinner is over here this year."

She made her way over to Katie and Becky, then joined in their conversation. About that time the preacher man from Katie's church arrived, and he escorted this older lady up the walkway. I found out later that her husband had recently passed away, and I thought that was really nice of Katie's parents to invite her to share this Christmas dinner. Seeing all these people enter the house, I thought, *Geez... I hope they made enough Pot Roast!*

It was now time for our Christmas dinner. Mrs. McCullough entered from the kitchen and wiped her apron with an announcement that it was time to say grace. She scanned around the table when her eyes fell upon me.

"Jesse... I don't want to put you on the spot or anything, but would you like to say grace?"

Shock and fear ran across my face. *Oh my God! Why me? I think there are much more qualified people at this table to say grace. Besides, the only prayer I know is, God's neat, let's eat!*

As I sat there trying to make up my mind, a world of eyes were upon me. First I saw Katie, who was looking at her mother like, "Oh Mom, why did you do that to poor Jess." Then I looked at my dad who had his eyebrows raised, like saying, "You wanted to come over here son." Mr. McCullough gave me a look like, "Hmmm... I wonder what this boy is going to do." Becky was looking at Katie like, "Wow, your mom really put Jess on the spot!" Tami had her usual brooding stare like, "Ah, what a burn, the squirt's got to pray!" My mom directed to me a smile like, "Go ahead Jess, be polite and say a prayer." And finally... the little old lady looked at me like, "Make up your mind kiddy; I'm hungry!"

At that point I felt like I had no choice but to do it, so I told everyone to bow their heads. I quickly tried to think of something to say, so when all else fails, I usually rely on movies or TV shows to come up with something. Just then, I thought entered my mind of how they say prayers on *Little House on the Prairie*. I tried to remember how they say their prayers from the show.

"Dear Lord, we are thankful for the wondrous blessings you have bestowed upon us. And we thank you for this bountiful harvest you have provided."

As the words left my lips, visions of Pilgrims surrounding a turkey dinner and a cornucopia centerpiece, swirled in my mind. I suddenly became self-aware.

Oh my God! What am I saying? Bestowed? Bountiful harvest? That sounded totally dumb!

Feeling the heat flush to my cheeks, I quickly remembered another prayer, so I tried that one.

"And Lord, we are thankful for the hands that were washed before preparing this food."

When I said that, sudden my dad pressed his lips together and his body was shaken—trying to hold his laughter. I guess that's when it hit me that I had said it wrong. I was supposed to say, "Bless the hands that prepared the food". Not that the hands *were washed* before preparing the food."

I glanced at my sister who gave me a look like, "What the heck are you saying?"

As panic set in, I quickly tried to cover my blunder with something to finish this disastrous attempt of a prayer. I remembered that sometimes you go around the table and mention each person by name, and why you are thankful for them. However, when I'm nervous, sometimes what I say comes out as jokes.

"And Lord, I thank you for the people at this table. I'm thankful for my mom and dad. I guess their pretty cool—when they're not punishing me. And for my sister Tami who can be a royal pain in the, *you know what*, but I love her anyways. And for my best friend Katie, who I'm sure you know very well, and who I wish was praying instead of me right now. And I'm glad that Becky is here, and the other lady from Katie's church. Also, for Mrs. McCullough who made the pot roast, which smells pretty good. Oh, and most of all… I'm thankful that Katie's dad didn't beat up those guys up at the Christmas play—Amen."

With a sigh of relief, everyone said, "Amen" that it was finally over. My dad, who was still trying to hold his laughter, excused himself to go to the bathroom.

Mr. McCullough then turned to me with a pressed smile. "Very interesting prayer there, Jess." Mrs. McCullough then kicked him from underneath the table.

Katie then came to *my rescue* at that awkward moment.

"Well I thought it was a very cute prayer for his first time." She said it in a firm tone like, "And nobody better not say another word about it!"

About that time, my dad returned to the table after composing himself and started us on another subject.

"Elizabeth (Mrs. McCullough), the food looks delicious. Everyone then chimed-in that it all looked very good.

"Well thank you, John. Now let's all enjoy a nice Christmas dinner."

As we enjoyed a wonderful dinner together, there was a lot of good and friendly conversation. During that time we brought up all kinds of subjects and really enjoyed ourselves. After we finished, we all went into the den as the grownups had coffee and began talking. Katie, Becky and my sister, hung out together for the rest of the evening, while my dad and I watched some college football on TV. Every now and then the grown-ups would bust-up laughing, commenting about something that Katie and I had done. Saying things like, "I don't know about the two of them; the things they get into."

Looking back at everyone laughing and having a good time made me wish I could have bottled-up and saved some of that laughter for another time. To a time in the near future when our parents would not be laughing. A time when Katie and I would be standing before a judge, and the judge would be pounding his gavel saying, that we were about to be in "Contempt of Court!"

THE CONCLUSION

A week later lying on my bed on New Year's Eve, I thought about this past year and all that had happened. Meeting new people like Melissa and seeing others leave, like Derek, was all part of realizing that you can never judge a book by its cover. I learned that some people may seem good at first on the outside, but then turn out to be bad on the inside. And those that seem bad at first, turn out good in the end. I learned that we shouldn't be so quick to judge, and to forgive those who truly ask for forgiveness.

Katie and I had another little adventure at the museum, but we also learned that you should never break any laws or lie to people in the process. Somehow life always seems to show you that there are always repercussions for your actions. Like being called into the principal's office and receiving a written warning. Getting grounded from our parents, and adding fuel to the fire of Melissa's anger towards me and Katie. I guess it's just like that one scripture Katie told me about; "be sure your sin will find you out." I know ours did.

As Katie and I went on another vacation together, once again we saw a watchful hand upon our lives. This only confirmed to me that there must be someone watching over us in our time of need. That watchful hand came in many forms this past year. Like a mysterious wolf coming to our rescue in a freezing blizzard… a Bible verse that helped guide me in making the right decision… and a heartfelt story from a caring mom about speaking up and telling the truth.

I was fortunate to see those signs so when that moment of opportunity arose, I was prepared to meet it. Throughout our lives we are given opportunities to say something or not to say something… to do something or not to do something. We must always take these opportunities because we never know when a person might be teetering on a decision that could affect them for rest of their lives. So keep your heart and mind open to the lessons that are being taught to you in preparation of a moment to come… the moment of truth!

                        To be continued in next episode of the series…

The Search for Rosemary Pullman
(Episode Four)

TABLE OF CONTENTS

INTRODUCTION

CHAPTER ONE – SUMMER AT LAST!

CHAPTER TWO – SETTING UP A PLAN

CHAPTER THREE – WORKING ON "CLUES"

CHAPTER FOUR – "OPERATION DGC"

CHAPTER FIVE – JUST A FAN

CHAPTER SIX – MORE MCALLISTER SECRETS

CHAPTER SEVEN – THE GREAT AMERICA ADVENTURE

CHAPTER EIGHT – THE UNEXPECTED "ROADIE" AHEAD

CHAPTER NINE – THE PURSUIT OF JUSTICE

CHAPTER TEN – A GATHERING OF EVIDENCE

CHAPTER ELEVEN – THE TRIAL BEGINS

CHAPTER TWELVE – PLAYING WITH THE "BIG BOYS"

CHAPTER THIRTEEN – DAVID AND GOLIATH

THE CONCLUSION

INTRODUCTION:

As I awoke that day and saw the morning sun filtering through my curtains I thought about having to get ready for school. Then suddenly it hit me. *Wait..., its summer vacation; I don't have to go to school!* I had completely forgotten that the school year was over. Now I had the whole summer to enjoy, relax, and just have fun.

My eighth-grade year was good in some ways, but very bad in other ways. Once again Katie and I had been attacked by some very bad rumors. Stories that could have tarnished her reputation, but fortunately it all turned out fine. I never expected stories like that could have gone around our school, especially considering we were barely in the eighth-grade. But I guess that's how the world is with kids maturing faster and thinking about sex and things at younger ages. I also learned many lessons that year, about speaking up and telling truth as you never know how it is going to affect someone's life. And although Katie and I had a fun adventure at the museum, we also learned there are always repercussions for your actions.

Within the past couple of years Katie and I have encountered quite a few adventures as most kids do during this time of growing up. Some of those adventures have been fun and exciting, while others have been filled with suspense and danger. I really enjoyed that aspect of our friendship, as that spirit of adventure has drawn us closer together.

As I looked ahead to a fun-filled summer, I thought that maybe this was our last summer to act like kids before starting high school. However, little did we know, we would once again find ourselves smack-dab in the middle of another investigation. An investigation where we would suddenly be thrown into a grown-up world!

CHAPTER ONE – SUMMER AT LAST!

That bright summer morning I brushed my teeth and headed downstairs to get something to eat for breakfast. The kitchen windows were open and you could hear the birds singing in the trees. My mom always says that if the birds are singing in the morning, it signifies that the hot days of summer are upon us. When I walked in the kitchen, Tami was already eating some kind of health bar and orange juice. I grabbed a box of cereal out of the cupboard, took a seat at the table and poured my milk.

"So Tami… what's with all that healthy stuff? You usually eat all those sugar-coated cereals."

"What's it to you, dweeb? I need to watch my weight and stuff."

"What for?"

"You'll soon learn that appearances in high school are very important. But since you're still a kid, you wouldn't understand."

I guess relationships go through their ups and downs. Last year it seemed like Tami and I had started to get along better. But hearing her sarcasm made me realize that she was back to mean ol' Tami.

I glanced around the room. "Tami, where's Mom?"

"At the store. She needed to pick up a few things. Oh by the way… tell Mom I went out with Cheryl."

"Where are you going?"

"Not that it's any of your business, but Cheryl and I are going to practice some routines to make the Pep Squad this year."

I raised my brow with surprise. "You, a cheerleader?"

She rose from the table irritated, and took her glass to the sink. "What's wrong with that? Besides, cheerleaders get all the cute guys."

"Yeah, but you're a total klutz. I've seen you play sports and stuff. Doesn't cheerleading require someone who is coordinated?"

She placed her hands on her hips. "I'm coordinated, you dipstick! Why am I even talking to you about this? Just tell Mom that I left with Cheryl, okay?"

"I'm not your messenger service, just leave her a note."

"Fine, whatever!" she said, then wrote a quick note and left out the door in a huff.

A few minutes later I heard a honk in the driveway. I looked out the window as my mom signaled that she needed help with the groceries.

"Thanks Jess," as she handed me one of the bags. "Where's Tami?"

"She left already to go with Cheryl somewhere."

"I wish that girl would at least let me know in advance when she's planning to go somewhere."

We walked into the kitchen and set the groceries on the kitchen table.

"Oh by the way… guess who I ran into at the grocery store?"

"I don't know, who?"

"Mrs. McAllister."

"Oh really. How is she doing?"

"Actually, she wanted me to give you a message. She asked if you and Katie could go over to their house sometime this week. She said she wants to make breakfast for the two of you. She said she was going to be making homemade blueberry pancakes."

I grabbed a jar of peanut butter and placed it in the cupboard. "Okay, I'll call Katie to let her know."

"Jess, I'm curious… why do the McAllister's seem to like you and Katie so much? And why do the two of you visit with them so much?"

I thought quick to remember our fabricated answer that Katie and I had come up with whenever someone asked us about them.

"Well, do you remember when Katie and I were doing that report on the Fuller Mine? After talking to the McAllister's; we realized we really did not have much of a story. They were the ones who recommended us to go to the Winchester Mystery House. They had a great story to tell about it, which we put in our report. After that, we just seemed to get along with them really well. After grandma and grandpa Thompson died; now we only have Nana Morgan who lives far away. The McAllister's are kind of like our step-grandparents."

She took a bag of carrots and placed them in the crisper. "I think that's really nice of you and Katie to be close to them. They are really nice people."

As I finished helping her unpack the groceries, I kind of felt bad about not telling the total truth. However, under the circumstances I felt liked a "little white lie" was okay. If they only knew the secret we kept for the McAllister's, they would probably do the same.

*****

The next day I gave Katie a call to talk to her about visiting the McAllister's.

"Hello…"

"Hi Katie."

"Oh, hi Jess. What's going on?"

"Nothing much. I wanted to give you a call to tell you that Mrs. McAllister invited us over for breakfast sometime this week."

"Oh, really? Did you talk to her or something?"

"No, my mom saw her at the grocery store and she said that Mrs. McAllister asked if we could go see them."

"What day do you want to go, so I can make plans for that?"

"I don't know, how about Wednesday?"

"Wednesday is fine with me. How do you want to get there?"

"I'll ask my mom to drop us off with our bikes. My dad can't take us because he'll be working. I'll just ask my dad to switch with my mom so we can put our bikes in the pickup."

"Okay, sounds good. I'll ask my parents after we get off the phone."

"So…, anything going on special with you?"

"Actually, I wanted to talk to you about possibly going with me to youth group on Thursday night. It's at our youth pastor's house, and I was hoping you would come with me."

"What's it about, and what do you guys do there?"

"Well it's a lot more casual than being in regular church. We sit on sofas or on the floor and sing a few songs and then talk about different subjects. Then the youth pastor usually has a short teaching of some kind. Then afterwards, we eat pizza or even barbeque sometimes—it's a lot of fun."

"Okay, I guess that will be alright. Do we have to bring a Bible or something?"

"You can if you want to. But usually they have a lot of spare ones there, or you can sit next to me and we can share mine."

"Okay, is your mom or dad going to take us there?"

"Yes, they drive me there and pick me up afterwards. We'll pick you up around six o'clock on Thursday, as it starts at six-thirty. Jess, my mother is signaling me that she needs to use the phone, so I better get off."

"Okay, remember about Wednesday morning at the McAllister's. We'll pick you up around 7:30 am."

"Okay, I'll be ready."

*****

On Wednesday morning I got dressed to go over the McAllister's house for breakfast. My mom drove over to Katie's to pick her up, and loaded her bike in the back of our pick-up truck. We drove over to the McAllister's and began to unload our bikes.

"Thanks, Mom. I'll see you later."

"Okay, you two have fun; and say hello to the McAllister's for me."

We entered the gate through the white-picket fence, and walked up the stairs and knocked on the door. Mr. McAllister answered with a friendly greeting.

"Well if it isn't the Bobbsey Twins!"

"Hi Mr. McAllister," we said at the same time.

"Who are the Bobbsey Twins?" I asked.

"You never heard of the Bobbsey Twins?"

"Nope."

"Well maybe they were a little before your time. It was a book series about two sets of twins; in which the older set of twins, a boy and a girl, went on adventures. I really didn't read those books myself, but that's just an old expression you use when you see a boy and a girl hanging around together all the time."

Katie turned to me with an acknowledging smile. "Well, then I guess were the Bobbsey Twins, because Jess and I do hang around together a lot."

"Come on in you two, Mrs. McAllister is just about done fixin' breakfast."

As we walked into the living room, Katie saw Mrs. McAllister working in the kitchen so she went in to see if she could help.

"Hi Mrs. McAllister."

"Oh Katie, come over here and give me a big hug—I just love your hugs," she said and squeezed her tight.

Katie looked around the kitchen. "Can I help with anything?"

"Sure sweetie. Can you get the china plates off the shelf and place them on the dining table?"

"Okay, no problem."

She went to the cupboard and brought down the plates and started to place them on the table. Mrs. McAllister came behind her with the forks, knives and napkins. Mrs. McAllister took note of how Katie was arranging them.

"Sweetie... I like for all the patterns on the china to be facing the same way. Can you please arrange them that way?"

Katie turned to me with a telling smile, as if to say. "See... I told you she's a neat-freak."

I nodded my head and smiled that I now understood what Katie meant. Mrs. McAllister then proceeded to arrange the forks and knives in their proper positions on each napkin. About that time, Mr. McAllister and I got up to sit at the table, as Mrs. McAllister instructed us where to sit.

"I made these blueberry pancakes especially for the two of you. We have a garden out back and these are fresh blueberries."

"It looks very good Mrs. McAllister," I said. "We appreciate you having us over."

Mrs. McAllister turned and smiled warmly at Katie. "Katie... would you like to say grace?"

"Sure."

We all bowed our heads and Katie prayed over the meal. Which I have to say was about a hundred times better than the prayer I said at last year's Christmas Eve dinner. As we continued to talk about different subjects, I could tell there was something else on their minds. Mrs. McAllister then spoke up to confirm what I was sensing.

"We wanted to invite you over because we just love having you visit with us. You are like the grandchildren we never had."

"Thank you," we said. "We feel the same way."

"However, there is another reason I wanted to have you over, as I have a very big favor to ask of you."

"Sure, what's the favor?" I asked.

"I need your help in finding someone."

"Find someone?" Katie asked, with an inquisitive stare.

"Yes. I have a very old and dear friend of mine who used to live in the Cedarwood Condominiums. I would like for the two of you to do some investigative work for us."

We looked at each other with curiosity and excitement.

"You need us to investigate something!" I asked.

Mr. McAllister got into the conversation. "Well considering how the two of you figured out those clues in finding that gold, we figured you are the perfect ones to do this for us."

The thought of conducting another investigation peaked our imaginations. Then Mrs. McAllister continued with what she was saying.

"You see… I have this dear friend by the name of Rose Pullman. Her full name is Rosemary, but I call her Rose and have known her for many years. From time to time I would go to her condo to visit her. About two months ago I went to visit and she seemed very quiet and almost scared about something. I tried to ask her if she was alright, but she would just say that she was fine. When I left there that day, I couldn't help but think there was something very wrong. About two weeks later I tried to call her, but the telephone was disconnected. We waited for a couple of weeks thinking that maybe the line was down or she had forgotten to pay her bill. Sometimes she can be a little forgetful. A few days later we tried calling again, but the phone was still disconnected. About a week later, Harold and I drove over to her place and knocked on the door for several minutes but no one answered. We went downstairs to the front desk and asked about her. There was a man at the front desk who told us she had moved out. We tried to ask the man more questions, but he was very rude and told us that tenant information is confidential, and he could not answer any questions regarding her. Harold and I left there feeling something was very different at her building. It seemed like none of the previous staff was there, and we did not see very many tenants walking around the building. This was a very nice complex for senior citizens over the age of fifty-five, and that's why Rose loved living there so much. It just doesn't make any sense to us that she would leave."

Mrs. McAllister then started to get emotional telling us about her friend. Katie went to her side and placed her arm caringly around her shoulder to comfort her.

"Don't worry Mrs. McAllister, Jess and I will find your friend for you."

As Katie continued to talk to Mrs. McAllister on a few other details, Mr. McAllister pulled me to the side.

"Jess… this situation with Rosemary might be nothing at all, but then again, we're not sure. As soon as you find something out, come and let me know. Emma and I are too old to be running around doing any investigating. This means a lot to her, so can we count on you?"

I answered strong and firm. "Yes sir, you can count on us."

"Good boy, or should I say, young man."

He reached into his pocket and pulled out forty dollars. "Here Jess, you and Katie may need this for bus fare or whatever you may need."

"Okay, thank you. Now you said she used to live at the Cedarwood Condos?"

"Yes, over by the new mall on the west side of town."

"Okay, I know which ones they are."

After we finished visiting with them, Katie and I got on our bikes and started to ride off when a strange thought occurred to me.

"Katie, you don't think they are just messing with us, do you?"

"What do you mean?"

"You don't think they are having us investigate this woman just to give us like an adventure or something. You know, kind of like how his father used to do with the two of them?"

"I hadn't thought about it, but I don't think so. Those tears of Mrs. McAllister were real. I don't think you can fake something like that."

"Okay, well I guess we have another investigation to look into."

"I'll tell you what, Jess… why don't you come over my house tomorrow about four o'clock and we can work out a plan of action on how to go about doing this. Then at six, we can leave to go to youth group. You did say you would go with me, didn't you?"

"Yeah I'll go with you. I'll have to ask my mom about going over early to your house, but I'm sure she'll say that it's okay."

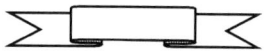

CHAPTER TWO – SETTING UP A PLAN

On Thursday afternoon I got ready to go to Katie's house. We were going to work on a plan of action on how to go about looking for this Rosemary Pullman. As I arrived at Katie's house, she let me in the door and we went into the den.

"So…, are you ready to get started?" she asked.

"Yeah, I'm ready. But where's your mom? I didn't see her car out front?"

"She had to run really quick to the Post Office."

"Okay, since you're the brains of this outfit. How do we set up a plan on how to go about finding this woman?"

"I'm not the brains of this outfit; we are both equal investigating partners."

"I like that, investigating partners; it has a good ring to it."

She smiled and took a hold of her pencil. "Okay, let me write down a few ideas on how to go about our search for Rosemary Pullman. Now Mrs. McAllister said the people at the Condos would not give them any information about the tenants there. This means we are going to have to figure out another way of getting information."

Katie began to write out her investigation notes.

Plan of Action - Notes
(The search for Rosemary Pullman)

1. *Need to find more information on Rose.*

"Katie, if those people at Cedarwood won't give us any information, then that means we're going to have to get it from them without them knowing it, right?"

"Yes, but how do we plan on doing that?"

"I guess like we always do. Find a way in, see what we can find, and sneak a little information."

"I guess that's the only way, but nothing illegal this time. I also don't want to write down 'sneak a little information' on our Plan of Action notes just in case someone sees them. We need to call it something else."

"I know, it needs a code name!"

With me saying that, the excitement ran through our bodies as this was starting to get fun with code names and everything.

"I know Katie, how about 'Mission Possible'. You know like Mission Impossible except that we hope our 'mission is possible'."

We thought about it for a moment, and then turned to each other and said in unison, "Naa."

"I know, now that I said it out loud, it sounded lame."

We sat there thinking for a moment, when her eyes grew large. "I know Jess, how about Operation DGC."

"Operation DGC? What does that mean?"

"It stands for 'Operation—Don't Get Caught'!"

My mind quickly flashed back to our last investigation at the museum, and I thought the name was pretty appropriate considering that we *did get caught*.

"I like it, Katie. Operation DGC it is."

"Jess, we also need to write down what we might need to bring with us on our investigation."

I glanced to the side thinking about it. "I know… how about a camera? Don't we need a camera just in case we see some records or a file on Rosemary Pullman? I'm pretty sure they have past records on all the tenants that lived there. Maybe those records might tell us where she moved to."

"That's a good idea! I just thought of something too. We need to have a cover story. You know, like you see in the movies."

"A cover story?"

"Yeah, you know, just in case *we do* get caught. We need to have a reason why we are there. And you know something, I have just the thing."

"What's that?"

"Becky's Journalism Badge. Becky is part of the Newsletter and Yearbook Club, remember? She has an I.D. Badge with her name on it, but it doesn't have her picture on it."

"That's a great idea!"

"You know, our cover story will fit perfectly with what's going on in that area of town. That west side of town is growing really fast. In fact my dad, who works for the Building Department, said they have been issuing a lot of building permits in that area. We can just say we are writing a story on all the new growth in our community."

"I didn't know your dad works for the Building Department." I glanced out the corner of my eye with a sneaky smile. "Hmm… that may come in handy someday."

"Oh no you don't, mister! Don't get any ideas of having my dad look up records illegally for us—it's not going to happen."

"Okay, but I still think your dad working for them might come in handy one day."

Katie wrote down all the information on our Plan of Action notes and showed them to me.

<u>Plan of Action - Notes</u>
(The search for Rosemary Pullman)

1. Need to find records for information on Rose.
2. Need camera
3. Code name: Operation DGC
4. Borrow Becky's badge
5. Cover: doing story on growth of town
6.

"I think we have some good idea so far. I can't think of anything else at the moment."

"So Jess…what day should we…?"

Suddenly the slam of the kitchen door halted her sentence, as Mrs. McCullough had returned from the Post Office. Her mother's irritated voice rang loud and clear throughout the whole house.

"Katherine Marie McCullough… you get over here this instant!"

"Uh-oh, sounds like your mom is really mad. You better go see what she wants, *Marie*."

"Shut-up Jess, I hate my middle name."

With worry draped across her face, Katie walked into the kitchen. Mrs. McCullough stood there with hands on her hips, and a miffed expression.

"Katie, I thought I told you I wanted those dishes washed before I got back from the Post Office."

"Sorry, Mom; I guess I forgot with Jess coming over and everything."

"I told you to get those dished done *before* he came over. I know you're working on some project, but I want those dishes done right now. Jesse will have to go home."

"But Mom…"

"No buts Katie, now!"

I heard what was going on, so I entered the kitchen to see if I could help.

"Hi Mrs. McCullough… I can help Katie with the dishes, and that way we can get them done twice as fast."

She glanced to the side, deep in thought. "I don't know; I'm not sure that's such a good idea."

"Come on, Mom. Jess was supposed to stay for the rest of the afternoon until it's time to go to youth group tonight."

"Okay, but make sure you do a good job and concentrate on what you're doing. I also want the floor to be swept and the trash taken out."

"Okay, Mom; we will."

As she left the kitchen, Katie smiled at me with gratitude. "Thanks Jess for helping out. Why don't you start to sweep the floor while I start gathering up the dishes to wash."

"Okay, where's the broom?"

"It's in that utility closet right there."

I went to the closet and began to sweep the floor. It didn't seem very dirty to me, but I swept it anyway. When I finished with that, I took out the trash and joined Katie at the sink. I started to rinse the dishes for her, as we began working together side by side.

She turned to me and smiled. "We make a very good team, don't we?"

"Yeah, we do. Well, except for one thing."

"What's that?"

I pointed at her nose. "Except that, you have a little bit of soap suds on your nose."

She took the back of her hand and rubbed her nose. "I don't have anything on my nose."

With a mischievous smile, I scooped up some subs and placed some on her nose.

"See, right there!"

A look of shock ran across her face. "Jess! I can't believe you just did that!"

I held a pressed smile. "What? I told you that you had suds on your nose."

"You're such a brat!"

She scooped up some suds, then placed some on my nose. "There; how's that!" she said, as if proud of her accomplishment.

"Katie, that's not suds; this is!"

I scooped-up a big bunch of suds and threw them in her face! Shock ran across her face once more, as she grabbed a big handful, and threw some back. Now it was an "all-out war" as we began smashing suds into each other's face and going crazy. We were laughing and throwing suds all over the place in a sort of frenzy, when suddenly Mrs. McCullough walked into the kitchen.

"Katie...!" she shouted at the top of her lungs.

We turned around to face her, as we were covered with suds from head to toe. It was in our hair, clothes, and all over the place. Mrs. McCullough just stood there stunned, and placed her hand over her mouth in disbelief. As she scanned the kitchen covered in suds, she finally spoke up.

"I can't even talk right now—I'm actually speechless."

Katie and I stood biting our lips, knowing we were in big trouble. But at the same time, it was kind of funny, as a little smile creased our lips.

"You think this is funny!" she shouted, as the smiles quickly left our faces.

"No, Mom."

"No, Mrs. McCullough."

She scanned the kitchen once more, and shook her head in disgust.

"I just knew it! I just knew this was a bad idea! I mean, what was I thinking? The two of you alone together, with soap, water, suds... it was a disaster waiting to happen!"

"Sorry, Mom." Katie said sheepishly, like a puppy who had just been scolded.

"I'm sorry too, Katie. I'm sorry I trusted you." She turned her attention toward me. "Jess, I know you were supposed to stay this afternoon, but you are going to have to leave now. Katie and her dad can pick you up later for youth group tonight. But right now, Katherine has a lot of cleaning up to do and I need to have a little talk with her."

"Yes Ma'am," I said, then waved good-bye, saying I would see her later tonight.

When I walked through the door to our house, my mom looked me up and down with an inquisitive stare.

"Jess... why are your clothes all wet? I thought you were going to stay at Katie's until later tonight?"

"Well, it's kind of a long story. I was supposed to stay there, but Katie and I got into a little mischief while washing the dishes. Needless to say, Mrs. McCullough wasn't too happy about it, so she sent me home. Katie and her dad will pick me up later for that youth group thing tonight."

"So let me get this straight. Elizabeth let the two of you wash her dishes—together?"

"Yes."

"Wow... that woman has a lot more faith than I do to let the two of you wash dishes together. I remember last summer when the two of you tried to wash our car for some extra money. I remember it turning into a water-balloon fight. Was it something like that?"

I pressed out a guilty smile. "Yeah, it was something like that. Except this time it didn't involve any soaking wet animals."

"Poor woman, she is probably traumatized—and in her kitchen no less."

About that time the phone rang, so I picked it up quickly to avoid any further discussion on the suds incident. Brian's voice was a welcome distraction.

"Hey, Jess."

"What's up, Brian?"

"Guess what? My dad just bought me a really cool weight set for my birthday. And it's way better than the old set my brother Tim has."

"I didn't know it was your birthday?"

"Actually my birthday isn't until Friday."

"Well happy birthday—just in case I don't see you before Friday."

"Thanks. Now that I have this weight set, we can start working-out like we talked about. We need to start to get ready for freshman football in the fall."

"Yeah, I definitely want to do that."

"Hey… let me know when you can come over and we'll run through a few sets on the weights."

"Okay, that sounds good. Hey Brian… I'd like to talk more, but I need to get something to eat and then get washed up to get ready to go with Katie."

"Where are you going with her this late in the afternoon?"

"Just to some youth group thing with other teens from her church."

"So, are you getting into that church stuff now, or are you just going because she asked you to?"

"I guess a little of both. I mean, I do believe there is a God, but it's not like I'm a born-again Christian or anything like that."

"Not yet Jess, but you keep hanging around them, and you might become one."

"So what's wrong with that? Katie is one, and she's cool."

"Yeah, I guess you're right, she is cool. Alright, have a good time and I'll talk to you later."

"Alright, see you later."

Around six, Katie arrived with her father to pick me up. When I got into the car, I was about to apologize to her father for the suds incident, but he beat me to it.

"So Jess… I heard you and Katie washed our entire kitchen today with dishwashing soap," he said with a bit of whimsy in his voice.

"Yes, Sir, I'm sorry about that."

Katie glanced at her father. "Mom told you we did that, Dad?" she asked with slight embarrassment.

"Of course she did. We don't keep any secrets from one another."

"Am I going to be grounded?"

"No pumpkin, I can remember how it was to have fun at your age. You just got carried away, that's all. Honestly, when I was your age I got into some trouble like that myself. Except in my case it involved starting a fire and burning a spot on my bedroom floor. Just don't do it again, okay pumpkin?"

"I won't, and thanks for not grounding me."

"You're welcome, sweetie."

As I listened to their conversation, it became apparent to me that Katie was "daddy's little girl." I thought it was cool that he wasn't going to ground her, but at the same time he gave her a warning not to do it again. And because I know Katie's character, I knew she would heed his warning and not betray his trust in her.

We arrived at the youth pastor's house, and I was a little nervous as I didn't know what to expect. When we walked into the house the youth pastor came up to us right away with a friendly greeting.

"Hello, Miss Katie… how are you doing today?"

"Just fine, Pastor Tim. I want to introduce you to my friend Jess. He's visiting our youth group for the first time."

He offered his hand. "Hi Jess, I believe I saw you that one Sunday just around summer time, wasn't it?"

"Yes, Katie invited me to church that day."

"Well I am glad you came. This is a lot less formal than on Sunday's, so just relax and have a good time."

"Okay, thanks."

When we were ready to get started, this Pastor Tim guy called everyone into the den and we all sat down on the floor in a circle. He asked us to bow our heads as he said a prayer to open the meeting. Then he introduced me to the whole group, which was a little embarrassing as everyone was just staring at me. Then he grabbed his guitar and they all started singing some songs; which I didn't know any of them. Katie then handed me the words to the songs, prompting me to join in. As I listened to her singing, I found out she has a pretty nice voice. I saw her sing once in glee-club, but when she sang these particular songs, I could tell they meant so much more to her. I tried to sing along very softly, but I don't think I sing very well, so I just kind of whispered it. After that, Pastor Tim; as that is what he asked me to call him, said he had a special announcement for the group.

"I have some exciting news for all of you. This summer our youth group will be making a trip out to Great America!"

When he said that, excitement ran across everyone's face as they turned to each other saying things like, "that's going to be so cool!" and mentioning the different rides they were going to go on.

I leaned into Katie's shoulder. "What's Great America?"

"It's an amusement park near San Jose with rides and everything. It's kind of like a smaller version of Disneyland, except it has more rollercoaster type rides."

Pastor Tim gathered everyone's attention as he continued to give a few more details about the upcoming event. He said it was going to be "Christian Day" where big name Christian music groups were going to be there. He then started to mention a particular group, when a look of excitement rose upon Katie's face. Then this guy named Chris tapped her on the shoulder.

"No way Katie, Sweet Comfort Band! We're going to have to make sure we see them."

I thought to myself, *Hmmm… we're going to have to make sure that we see them?*

When he said that, I gathered that he and Katie must talk quite a bit as they kept going on and on about this band.

After the group settled down from talking about that trip, Pastor Tim started to give his lesson for the evening. He talked to us about how God is always there to hear our prayers, even though he hasn't answered them yet. He quoted some scripture about how God gives an answer to our prayers in his perfect timing. When he said that, I was reminded how that one verse came to me right before the Christmas play. I remembered that the "answer" to my problem came just in the nick of time. He went on to say that in order to grow in the Lord, you must first start slowly. He used the example of a baby that only drinks milk at first, before it is able to eat solid food. He then said you must first have a personal relationship with Jesus Christ. He used that lead-in to ask if there was anyone who might want to accept the Lord as their savior.

As I sat there, I kind of felt like he was directing that question at me. I mean all the other teens in the group were already "saved" and I was the only one who wasn't. I could tell a couple of people glanced my way to see if I was going to do anything. But to be honest, I really didn't feel the need to do anything. I believed there is a God, so I felt that made me a Christian already. I mean, when we used to go to church in Colorado we always went to a Christian church. And I was also baptized when I was a baby in a Christian church. So I felt like I was fine in God's eyes.

After that part ended, he had one of the older girls in the group give some announcements. Then we all went into the kitchen area and got some pizza and sodas. Katie came up to me with a slice of pizza in her hand.

"So Jess, what did you think of the youth service?"

"I liked it; it's pretty cool. I could see myself coming again sometime."

"That's good, I hope you will."

About that time, this guy came over and introduced himself as Moses Martinez.

"Jess, right? Katie tells me you're into video games."

"Yeah I am. I don't play as much as I used to, but I still play."

"So, are you going to Great America at the end of the month?"

Katie interjected before I could answer. "Of course he is, aren't you Jess?"

"Well Moses, I guess the 'boss lady' has spoken, so I guess that means I'm going."

Katie placed her hands on her hips. "I'm not bossy. I'm just trying to be positive and confident."

"Sounds bossy to me, doesn't it Moses?" I countered, as we both laughed.

Katie turned around to leave, acting like she was offended. "I'm going to talk to the girls—you guys are being mean to me!" She said and walked off.

Moses and I got back into our conversation.

"So Jess... do you go to the same school as Katie?"

"Yeah, but I *haven't seen you* at our school. What grade are you in?"

"I'm in the eighth-grade like you, but I go to Calvary Christian Academy. It's ran by our church. It goes up to the 8th grade. A lot of us from the youth group go there; like Chris, Gina and Ryan."

"No wonder I haven't seen you guys in our school."

"Yeah, but we will be going to Fuller Creek High School this coming fall. They don't have a Christian high school in town, but I did hear they might build one in a few years. Hey Jess... it's been cool to meet you, maybe we can hang-out at Great America—that's if you go with us."

"Yeah, that would be pretty cool."

"Well, I better get going, so I'll catch you later."

"Alright, see you later."

In talking to Moses, it seemed like he was a pretty cool guy and we had a lot in common. Well, except for the fact that he's a Raiders fan and I'm a Bronco's fan—but I won't hold that against him.

CHAPTER THREE – WORKING ON "CLUES"

Saturday arrived and Katie was able to come over to my house to work on the case of Rosemary Pullman. When she got there my mother answered the door and invited her in.

"Hi Katie, come on in."

"Thank you, Mrs. Thompson."

"My goodness, Katie! You just seem to get prettier and prettier all the time." She glanced in my direction. "Doesn't she look pretty, Jess?"

"Yeah she's alright," I replied.

"She's alright? Oh these boys, they can never just come out and give a girl a compliment. You know, his father is the same way. It's like trying to pull teeth to get him to say something nice about how I look."

I rolled my eyes. "Mom, we just want to start working on our project, so can we go now?"

"Okay, but you'll have to work on your project up in your room. I'll be cleaning the living room and the vacuum is very noisy."

Katie and I headed upstairs when suddenly panic set in.

Oh my God! I think my room is a total mess! And I hope I don't have any underwear lying around. That would be totally embarrassing!

When we arrived at the top of the stairs I turned with my back against the door.

"Wait here Katie, let me go straighten up a bit. I didn't clean my room today."

"Alright, but I'm sure it's fine, you should see my room sometimes."

I quickly straightened it up a bit, and thank goodness I didn't have any underwear lying around. I opened the door to let her in.

"Okay, I think it's safe now."

She walked in and casually scanned around the room. I have a desk in one corner, so I told her she could sit at the table to write out our investigation notes. She opened her notebook and scanned what we had previously written.

Plan of Action – Notes:
(The search for Rosemary Pullman)

1. Need to find more information on Rose.
2. Need camera
3. Code name: Operation DGC
4. Borrow Becky's badge
5. Cover: doing story on growth of town
6.

"Okay, let's begin with number one," she said. "How are we going to find more information on Rose, and where she might have gone to?"

"Well, I think we need to start at the place where she used to live at the Cedarwood Condos. When we get there, we can look around a bit to see what we can find out."

"Okay, but remember what Mrs. McAllister said. The man in the lobby was rude and wouldn't give them any information."

"I know, but the McAllisters were not there to investigate—*we are*."

"Yeah, you're right. And like you said, maybe an opportunity will come up where we can gather a little information. We might find some filing cabinets with records of where she might have gone to."

I gathered another thought. "What about a phone number for Rose Pullman? I know her old number is now disconnected, but isn't there a forwarding number we can get from the operator?"

"I already asked Mrs. McAllister about that. She said she tried but there wasn't any forwarding number for her."

"Okay, what about number four on our list. What about Becky's Journalism badge?"

"I'll call her this afternoon and get it from her before we go."

"And you're sure it doesn't have her photo on it?"

"Yes, I'm sure. It only has her name and our school logo."

"What happens if we get caught by someone who works there and they don't believe our cover story?"

"Well, I guess we'll have to cross that bridge when we get there."

"Yeah, let's just hope we don't get caught. Oh, what about transportation? How are we going to get there? On our bikes or should we take the bus?"

"I think we should use our bikes. How about we have one of our parents drive us to the mall and drop us off. Then we can go on to Cedarwood from there. It's only about three blocks from the mall."

"Okay, what about number two on our list—the camera. I only have a cheap one. Do you want to bring one, or do you want me to bring mine?"

"I'll bring the one we have at home. It's a 35millimeter, so it takes good pictures."

I scanned over our list. "Well… It looks like we're all set to begin Operation DGC. Now all we need is the day and time to go."

"Let's go on a weekday. How about this Wednesday?"

"Okay, I'll talk to my mom about taking us to the mall that day. Since we got done with this plan pretty quick, I know what we can do. We can brush up on our investigating skills by playing Clue."

"Oh yeah, go get it!"

I went into my closet, which was a total disaster, and finally found the game. We then began to set it up on the floor.

"I know who the murderer is going to be," she said confidently.

"Who's that?"

"It's going to be Miss Scarlet in the dining room with the candle stick."

"You think so, huh? Well I think it's going to be Colonel Mustard in the library with the knife."

She looked off to the side, when suddenly she started laughing.

"What's so funny?"

"I got it Jess; this is the topper... It's going to be Mrs. Weaver, with a cleaver, in our social studies class!"

I busted-up laughing. "You're too much Katie," as I pushed her shoulder and we both fell to the floor laughing. In the midst of our laugher she added, "Weaver, Weaver the pencil cleaver!" which only made us laugh even harder.

As we continued to laugh, she rolled over on her side towards me. At the same time, I rolled over towards her, and my arm feel across her waist. As we were lying next to each other, face to face, our laughter subsided as we gazed into each other's eyes.

Now tell me… why is it when you find yourself in a situation like that, does your sister happens to walk by and see it; as Tami stood in the doorway.

"Whoa…! Did I come at a bad time you two?" she said, with a grin on her face.

I quickly withdrew my hand from Katie's waist, and we separated. Tami laughed and headed downstairs, as Katie got very quiet and started going through some of the game pieces.

"Man…" I said, shaking my head. "That's all I need. As if I needed to give Tami any more reasons to tease me about stuff."

Katie stayed quiet and it was hard to read what she was thinking from the lack of expression on her face. I began to pass out the playing cards, when my mom yelled up to me from the bottom of the stairs.

"Jesse Connor Thompson! Get down here, right now!"

Katie turned to me with a raised brow. "Uh-oh... now it sounds like *you're the one in trouble.* You better get down there and see what she wants; *Connor.*"

I rose from the floor and headed towards the doorway. "See why I never told you my middle name?"

"Actually, I like the name Connor—it's nice."

"I'll be right back."

I started down stairs, when a thought entered my mind.

Oh God... what if Tami told my mom about what she saw up in my bedroom.

I hesitantly walked into the kitchen "You needed me for something, Mom?"

"Jesse, how many times have I told you to make sure that dog's pen is cleaned up? There are ants all in the dog dish."

"Alright, I'll get to it in just a minute."

"No Jess, right now!"

"At least let me tell Katie that I have to do that work."

I walked to the bottom of the stairs. "Katie...!"

She came and stood at the top of the stairs. "What is it, Jess?"

"I need to clean the dog's pen and stuff. It's going to be about fifteen minutes."

"I'll come with you and help."

She came downstairs when my mom saw us walking out the kitchen door.

"Jesse... I don't want Katie doing any of your work. She can shoot baskets or something, but that work is your responsibility."

"Alright, Mom."

We walked out the door and headed around the side of the house when we heard a honk in the front driveway. We walked around to the front and saw that her mother had pulled into our driveway. Katie walked up to the driver's side window.

"Katie honey… I know it's a little early to pick you up, but I need for you to come with me to the grocery store. Your father invited some people over from the church, and I need to hurry and find something to make for this evenings' dinner."

Katie walked over with disappointment. "Jess, I need to go now, my mom needs me to go with her to the store. I guess we can play Clue another time. And don't forget about Wednesday and Operation DGC."

"I won't," I said and saluted her. "We will commence Operation DGC on Wednesday at 0800 hours."

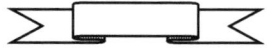

CHAPTER FOUR – "OPERATION DGC"

Wednesday morning I woke up filled with anticipation of what our investigation might bring. After getting dressed my mom drove me over to Katie's, picked her up and then dropped us off in front of the mall. After taking our bikes from the back of the truck, we walked around to the driver's side.

"Thanks for the ride, Mrs. Thompson."

"You're welcome, Katie." My mom then directed her focus to me. "Jess, do you need me to pick you up later?"

"No, we'll ride our bikes home."

"Okay, try to stay inside of the mall. They say it's going to be very hot today."

"Okay, we'll try to stay cool."

I glanced up at the sun and shaded my eyes. "You know, my mom's right. I think it's going to be very hot today. Why don't we get something to drink first? They say you should hydrate yourself on hot days like this. And thinking about that, this will kind of kill two birds with one stone. If we go inside the mall, then technically we won't be lying to her when we said we were going to the mall."

"Okay, that sounds good."

We placed our bikes in the stand and locked them up, then entered the mall. After purchasing a couple of bottles of water, Katie was startled by someone placing their hands over her eyes from behind.

"Guess who?" he said. She turned around to see it was Marc and some of his friends.

"Hey you guys," he greeted. "What are you two doing here?"

"Just hanging out," she replied. "What about you?"

"The same as you; we're just trying to stay cool. They said it's going to get up to 100 degrees today. Hey, do you guys want to hang out with us?"

"No, we can't," Katie said. "We have to do an errand for someone."

"Okay, that's cool. Oh Katie… have you heard they are going to re-open the skating rink in September?"

"You mean that old one a few blocks over from here?"

"Yeah, we heard that some investment company bought the place and is fixing it up. Maybe we can all go when it opens?"

"Sure Marc, I like to skate," she replied.

"Alright we'll plan on doing that. I'll see you guys later."

After walking around the mall for a bit, we decided it was time to head out to the Cedarwood Condos. On our way there, we started to talk about the skating rink.

"So Katie… I assume by what you told Marc that you know how to skate?"

"Yes, I skated a lot when we lived in Carlsbad. They have these beachside walkways that you can skate on, with these great ocean views. They also have all these beautiful bluffs looking over the ocean—it's really nice. So do you skate?"

"Yeah, but I haven't skated for a long time. I guess once you get into riding your bike then you stop roller-skating."

"Maybe when it opens in September we can all go."

"Yeah maybe… I guess that would be alright." I pointed up the street. "Look… there's the Cedarwood Condos on the right side of the street over there."

We turned down this cul-de-sac and rode over towards the entrance of the condos. We got off our bikes and sat by the side of the entrance.

I scanned the building and the surrounding area. "Man... there aren't many cars in the parking lot. I wonder why there aren't that many people living here?"

"Well that's one of the things we need to investigate."

We sat for the next few minutes watching the comings and goings of the complex. On the far side of the buildings we could see a U-Haul truck being loaded.

"Jess, do you see that moving truck over there? They are moving out, not moving in."

"I noticed that too. Let's make a note of that."

She took out her notebook and wrote down a few details on what we observed. She also pulled out her camera and took a picture of the complex and surroundings.

"Okay, now what?" she asked.

"We need to get into the complex itself and look around to see what we can find."

About that time, an older man and woman drove up and started to go through the main entrance. There was a guard at the front doors, who stopped them as they went in.

"Look... that guard is having them sign some kind of book." She commented. "I bet you it's one of those guest books that everyone has to sign before they go in. That's going to make it really hard to get in there."

"Why?"

"Duh, Jess! We don't know anyone in there, so how can we sign that book?" she said, and rolled her eyes.

"Oh yeah, I guess I didn't think about that. Okay Miss Smarty Pants. Then how do we get in there?"

As we sat thinking of way to get in, another car pulled up to the complex. This time it was a couple, like in their late thirties or early forties. Suddenly I got an idea.

"Katie, give me your bottle of water out of your backpack."

"Why? What are you going to do? You better not pour it on me or I'll..."

"Would you stop being paranoid? Just give me your bottle of water and follow my lead."

She warily handed me the bottle. "Jess, what are you doing?"

I directed a sneaky smile. "You'll see..."

I walked up to the man who was exiting his car, and greeted with a welcoming smile.

"Hi Mister... how are you doing today?"

"Hi there young man; I am doing just fine."

I lifted the bottle of water in front of him. "Would you like to buy a couple of bottles of water—it sure is hot out," I said, and swiped my brow for the effect.

"Buy some water?" he questioned, with a confused look on his face.

"Yes, my friend and I are working on a little project. We are selling bottled water to make extra money for it."

With an inquisitive stare, the woman entered our conversation.

"That's an odd item to sell. Usually the kids sell candy bars or cookies for their projects."

"Yes, that's true. But we thought that since its summer, a nice ice-cold bottle of water would be great on a hot smoldering day like today," I said, playing it up.

"Well actually, *I am* rather thirsty," the man said.

"Actually, I am too," the woman agreed. "And besides, the water is already shut off at your father's place. Let's support their project and buy a couple of bottles."

"How much is it?" The man asked.

"One dollar each."

"A dollar each?"

"Yes Sir. Like I said, we do need to make money for our project."

I turned to Katie who gave me a look like she had no idea what I was doing.

"So mister... you said that your father lives here? Maybe we've seen him; what's his name?"

"His name is Samuel Richards. Do you know him?"

"Well, I'm not sure. What is his condo number?"

"A-14, it's on the first floor. So I'm assuming you know someone who lives here too?"

"Well, she used to live here—her name is Rosemary Pullman."

"Oh yes, Mrs. Pullman. She lived in the condo about four doors down from my father. We're here to help him move out today." He reached into his pocket and pulled the money from his wallet. "Here you go young man; here are your two dollars."

I handed him the bottles of water, then scanned the surrounding area.

"So, not very many people are living here anymore; it seems very vacant."

"Yes it is, but I guess that's progress," the man said.

"Yeah I know what you mean—progress."

I said that in order to play along like I knew what was going on, even though I really didn't.

"Yes," The lady added. "I believe they are turning these condos into office spaces."

"Office spaces, huh?"

"Yes, it seems like that investment group is buying up all these old properties around here."

With a flash of acknowledgment in her eyes, Katie finally caught on to what I was doing. She then got into our conversation.

"When you say this investment group is buying old properties, are you talking about old buildings like the skating rink?"

"I'm not sure. My understanding is that this investment group usually tears down and rebuilds these old buildings. I heard the skating rink is being restored. *I do know* this investment group has bought the old market and a few other stores along the west side of Main Street."

I extended my hand. "Well thank you sir, for buying the water from us."

"No problem, I hope you make a lot of money for your project."

"Well, thanks again," I said, giving Katie a telling look. "You have helped us out more than you know."

As we watched them go into the building, they signed in at the front desk, and headed down the left hallway. Katie turned to me in amazement.

"Jess, that was incredible! How did you come up with that idea to gather some information from them?"

"I don't know, I guess I have my moments. I know sometimes I'm a little dense, but then it just came to me. You didn't know what I was doing, did you?"

"No, at first I thought you lost your mind selling our bottles of water."

I playfully pushed her shoulder. "Now who's the 'duh' person, Katie—you are!"

"No I'm not—you are!" she said, and pushed me back.

"Okay, let's call it even."

"Okay, we're even."

With our new found information, we sat down on a grassy area to talk it out. She took out her notebook and started to write down the information we had gathered.

"Okay… we found out that the tenants are moving out because an investment group has bought the property, right?"

"Yeah, except for the fact that *we* didn't find that out, *I* found that out."

"Okay, fine, *you* found that out. But can we get back to business here—I'm trying to be serious."

I rolled my eyes. "Okay, Miss Serious."

"As I was saying... that lady also said this investment group has been buying up older properties and building new structures in its place."

I glanced at the condos, taking note of their age.

"Katie... there's something that doesn't make any sense. Why would Rosemary Pullman sell her condo to this investment group when Mrs. McAllister said she loved it so much? These condos don't seem to be that old, like they are falling apart or anything."

"I don't know, maybe she had to sell when that investment group bought the property."

"Is that how it works? I thought if you owned something it was yours to sell or not to sell."

"I'm not sure. Maybe it doesn't work that way with condos."

I rose to my feet. "Come-on... let's lock our bikes to this fence and go in the complex and look around a bit."

A puzzled expression ran across her face. "Jess, how are we supposed to get in? Don't you remember; you have to sign in at the front desk and we don't know anyone that currently lives here?"

"Yes we do," I said confidently.

"Who do you know that lives here?"

"Samuel Richards! Why do you think I asked that man who his father was?"

Her eyes lit-up with revelation. "Oh yeah, you're pretty smart."

"Yeah, and you're 'Miss Duh' today, Katie. I think the hot sun has fried your brain or something."

"That wasn't very nice; you're being mean to me," she said, pouting her lip.

I placed my hand on her shoulder. "I wasn't being mean to you, I was just kidding."

She smiled. "Okay, but now that you say that, maybe the sun *is* kind of getting to me. I would have drunk some water, *but someone* went and sold it!"

"I know, but at least we now have an owner's name so we can sign-in at the front desk." I looked towards the front doors. "Come-on, it's time to start the next phase of Operation DGC."

We walked through the main entrance and over to where the guard was sitting at the front desk. He glanced up at us, then pointed to the chipboard.

"You need to sign-in if you are here to see a tenant."

Katie picked up the pen to sign us in, when he looked at us with a questioning stare.

"By the way...who are you here to see? There are only a few tenants left, and I can't say I've ever seen you two in here before."

Katie quickly spoke up. "Oh, we're here to see Sam Richards. You probably saw our relatives come in a few minutes ago. We're here to help them with the move."

"Okay, go ahead and sign in. And don't forget to write in the number of his condo."

Katie wrote down A-14, and we headed down the hallway to the left.

"Nice touch, with calling him 'Sam', it made it sound like we now him so well that we call him Sam."

She took a playful bow. "Thank you, I thought it added some realism to it."

We then moved cautiously down the hallway when we saw the lady from the parking lot coming out of a doorway. She gave us a friendly smile, then stacked a box on top of the others and went back inside.

Katie turned to me in a hushed tone. "Jess, whatever were going to do, we better do it quick. That guard might get suspicious if we are found just roaming around."

I looked past her down the hallway. "Come-on... I see some stairs at the end of this hallway."

We made our way to the end of the hallway and took a few steps up the stairs. When we were out of view, we sat down for a moment to think this over.

"Jess, did you see that office near the front entrance?"

"Yeah, what about it?"

"I'm wondering if they have files or records of all the tenants who lived here in that room."

"They probably do, but how are we going to get in there?"

"I saw a man sitting at a desk in that office. Maybe we can try to get a little information out of him, like you did earlier from that couple."

"It's worth a try, but how are you going to approach him?"

"With Becky's Journalism Badge! I'll tell him I am writing a story for the schools newsletter about all the redevelopment in the area. Then I'll ask him if this condo complex is part of that redevelopment."

"Hey, that's a good idea."

"Okay, but first I want to write out a few things of what I'm going to ask him."

"Alright, I'm going up these stairs to the second floor and look around a bit while you work on that."

"Okay, but DGC."

"I'll try not to."

When I got back from looking around, I sat down and looked at the workup sheet she created.

REDEVELOPMENT ARTICLE re: CEDARWOOD CONDOMINUEMS

1. Name of new development company - who now owns property:
2. Name of person I spoke to:
3. What is this complex going to become?

4. What are goals of Investment Company?
5. How did tenants feel about moving out?
6. Can we contact them for their statements? (i.e.: R.P.)
7. Will this impact the environment in any way?
8.

After reading it over, a look of surprise rose upon my face. "Wow! How did you come up with all that in just a few minutes? Man Katie, you're really smart!"

"I'm not that smart, but I am starting to get nervous about doing this."

"I know what you can do. I saw it on an episode of the Brady Bunch. Just imagine that man sitting at his desk in his underwear and you'll feel less nervous."

"Nervous? You mean nauseous! I'm not going to imagine that guy in his underwear—that's just gross!"

"Okay, bad idea. Then just breathe in deeply and try to relax. Besides, I'll be right there by your side, okay?"

"Alright, let's do this."

When we walked to the front lobby, it happened to be great timing. The Richards family had just started out the front door, and the guard was busy helping them with keeping the doors open. We walked over to the office and confidently entered the room. There was a man sitting at a large desk with peppered-grey black hair all slicked back, and wearing an expensive looking suit. He glanced at us with pessimism, as if we were bothering him.

"Can I help you kids with something?"

Katie stretched forth her hand. "Hi mister..."

"It's not mister," he interjected. My name is Ian Thorpe—Dr. Ian Thorpe II. I received my Doctorate in Business at Harvard. What do you kids want? And how did you get in here?"

With his stern greeting, a strand of nervousness ran through my body. I could tell Katie was reluctant to continue, so I quickly tried to help her out.

"Hi Mr. Thorpe, my name is Jesse."

"That's Dr. Thorpe," he said, with irritation in his voice.

"Yes, Dr. Thorpe. To answer your question, we are here helping our relatives, the Richards move out of their condo. In the meantime, we decided to kill two birds with one stone, as they say. You see, my sister is writing an article for her school newspaper about the redevelopment in this area. She thought that while we were here, you could answer a few questions for her. Didn't you sis?"

I glanced at Katie with a telling look, prompting her to start with the questions.

"Oh, right... I do have a few questions for you, Mr. Thorpe."

Once again he started to correct Katie about his name, but she corrected herself first.

"Sorry, I mean Dr. Thorpe." She scanned her list of questions. "Now I have a list of questions to ask you, if you don't mind?"

"Let me see those," he said, then abruptly took the list from her hand.

After looking them over for a moment, he gave the list back to her. "Very well, ask your questions."

"Well the first question..., is I wanted to know if you are the new owner of this complex."

He directed to her a dry stare. "Young lady, what is your name?"

"My name is Ka..." but then she stopped mid-stride and began coughing through her words to cover her mistake.

"Excuse me, I had a tickle in my throat. My name is Becky, Becky Summers."

"Well Miss Summers; that is not the first question on your list. If you plan on being a professional journalist someday, organization and accuracy are a must. So let's start with the first question on your list."

She glanced over at me like, "Oh boy, what did I get myself into here."

She sat up straighter in her seat. "Sorry, Dr. Thorpe. My first question is… what is the name of the development company who now owns this property?"

"We are Equity One Realty Corporation. I am the CEO of the corporation. Do you know what CEO stands for young lady?"

"Like a chairman of the corporation?"

"No!" he snapped. "Now write this down young lady. A CEO means Chief Executive Officer."

As she wrote down the information, I started to scoot my chair closer to see what she was writing down, when this Dr. Thorpe quickly turned to me with a piercing stare.

"Just what do you think you're doing young man? Those chairs are placed in an exact position for a reason. Please leave them where they were."

As I began to move my chair back in its place, this guy actually watched to make sure that the feet of the chair went back into the exact same imprints in the carpet. I thought, *Man, this guy is an organizational wacko!*

Katie then continued. "Dr. Thorpe… is this your main office you work out of?"

He half-laughed with an air of arrogance. "Hardly young lady. I have a corporate office in Sacramento at the Biltmore Building. The only reason I am even here today is my field staff needed my expertise on a few financial matters. You just happened to catch me here."

He straightened out a few papers on his desk, that Katie had accidently moved, then glanced impatiently at his watch.

"So," she continued. "Are you this investment company we've heard about that's been buying up all these properties along Main Street?"

Irritation rose in his voice. "Miss Summers, once again you are not sticking to the questions on your list. Also, we are not a 'company' we are a 'corporation'. Make sure you write that down and get that correct!"

"Sorry Dr. Thorpe," she said, with a quiver in her voice, as she made the correction on her notebook. Flustered, she hesitantly asked her next question.

"So, what are your corporation's goals?"

"Our primary goal is to acquire properties and rebuild them, so it is both financially beneficial to our corporation as well as the community."

As Katie wrote the information in her notebook, this guy was staring at her every move like a hawk. I could tell she was getting nervous with him bearing down on her, so I decided to distract him for a moment.

"So Dr. Thorpe... In other words, your redevelopment goals are to basically tear down the old crap and put up new stuff?"

"A very crude way of putting it young man, but if you must, that is the general idea."

Katie was finished writing, so she bravely plunged forward with her next question.

"Dr. Thorpe... is this going to have an impact on the environment?"

I could tell he got irritated once again because she didn't stay in the order of the questions, but he answered it anyways.

"If you want that kind of information, an Environment Impact Report is public record and you are welcome to research those records yourselves on any of our projects."

"Are you the one who is refurbishing the skating rink?" I asked.

He half-laughed with a tint of sarcasm. "No we are not. A skating rink is not a sound financial investment. That particular project is being funded by an anonymous firm that has been a point of contention to our corporation for some time. Basically, they are in the same business as we are, refurbishing properties in this community. The difference, is they have donated hundreds of thousands of dollars into those projects, without seeking monetary compensation. Imagine that… donating that kind of money without getting anything in return. What kind of a person does that? Apparently a person with no business sense!"

Katie and I looked at each other with the same realization that the "anonymous firm" he was talking about, must be the McAllister's. And in thinking about that, all of this was starting to get very interesting.

Was their some kind of connection or battle going on between this corporation and the McAllister's? And is that why they are having us look into this for them?

As I thought about that, Katie continued with her questions.

"So Dr. Thorpe… how did the people feel about losing their homes? I mean, were they forced to leave when you bought this complex?"

He glanced to the side and gathered his thoughts before answering.

"Miss Summers… none of the tenants living here were forced into selling their homes. The individual owners sold their properties to us voluntarily, and have been well compensated. We have signed agreements with every tenant and everything is well documented."

"Can any of those prior owners be contacted for their statements? For example…there is one person we would like to get in contact with, her name is Rosemary Pullman. We knew Rosemary from coming to see Sam Richards. Do you happen to have her current address so we can visit her?"

When Katie said that, he sat up in his seat and looked at her with suspicion. Once again, he gathered his thoughts carefully before answering.

"In answer to your question, Miss Summers, we do not give out personal information on any current or previous tenants. Besides..., if you were really that close to Rosemary Pullman, then why didn't she give you that information herself?"

Uh oh! I thought. *This guy is starting to ask questions and now seems suspicious of us. I think maybe it's time for an exit plan.*

I placed my hand on her shoulder. "Come on sis, it's time to go," I said with a telling look. "Dad's going to be mad if we are late for that thing."

"Oh yeah, that thing; we don't want to be late for that."

She reached out to shake his hand. "Well Dr. Thorpe... we thank you for your time and information. I'm sure this will make a great article for our schools newsletter."

As we got up to leave, he looked at us suspiciously and watched us closely as we left the building. When we got on our bikes to head home, relief filled our faces at being glad to be out of there.

"Man, Katie. Was that guy a wacko or what?"

"Jess, he was making me so nervous. And then he kept correcting every little thing I said."

"I know, and I felt so bad for you. That's why I distracted him once in a while."

"Well thank you for doing that, my hand was shaking as I tried to write down my notes. And speaking of notes... we need to sit down and go over these notes to figure this thing out. There is definitely something strange going on there—I can feel it."

"Yeah, I feel it too. This Dr. Thorpe is like one of those sleazy business guys, and I don't trust him. And did you hear that comment he made about the 'anonymous firm' being a point of contention for his corporation? I am sure the anonymous firm he was talking about is the McAllisters."

"I think so too. Should we go talk to them and let them know what we have found out so far? I have a feeling that the McAllister's might have a few other secrets that we don't know about."

"I don't know if we should talk to them yet. We still haven't found out where Rose Pullman has gone to. That was the main reason they wanted us to look into this in the first place, and we don't have that information yet."

"Yeah, you're right; we still need to figure that out first."

"Hey, what day is this? Wednesday? How about we get together tomorrow and work on our project then."

"No, let's make it on Friday. I have youth group tomorrow at Pastor Tim's."

"Oh yeah, I forgot."

"Do you want to go with me to youth night again?"

"I don't know; let me think about it."

"Sure, just let me know so I can tell my dad if we need to pick you up."

"So… have you ever invited Becky to go with you to youth night?"

"I did a long time ago, but she made it clear that she likes going to her church and she prefers to go there."

"Okay, I'll call you one way or the other about going to the youth night thing."

"Okay, that sounds good."

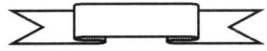

CHAPTER FIVE – JUST A FAN

The following day, I went over to Brian's house to work-out on his new weight set. In gearing up for freshman football next year, we wanted to start lifting weights to be better prepared for the coming season. Brian had grown really big and strong over the past year, and wanted to try out for a linebacker position. I have always been a good wide receiver, thanks to my father playing catch with me in the backyard ever since I was little. I enjoyed spending that time with my dad; although lately, those times seem few and far between. After a vigorous workout, we went to his room to relax.

"Hey Jess… in a few weeks they'll be starting that pre-season work out program for anyone who wants to get ready for tryouts. I want to go to that."

"Yeah, me too. I really need to work on my strength; I feel like I'm still too weak."

"Hey, some of the guys in the neighborhood are having a pick-up game on Friday; do you want to go?"

"Oh really? I wish I could. But I promised Katie I would do something with her that day."

"Katie…? Come on man, no offense to her, but we're about to enter high school where it's going to be filled with tons of hot babes!"

"So. I can check out the babes and still be friends with her."

He placed his hand on my shoulder. "Man, you just don't understand about women. If girls see you hanging around with Katie, they're going to think you guys are a couple, which in turn means you're going to be a lonely man."

"I don't think it will be like that."

"Okay, but I'm just telling you. Do you want a punch in the arm from a friend, or a hot kiss from a high school babe?"

I rolled my eyes. "I don't know about you Brian—you have a one track mind."

That afternoon I gave Katie a call so her father could pick me up to go to the youth group thing again. When we arrived at the youth pastor's house, that guy Moses saw me and right away came up to me.

"Jess, you made it! That's two weeks in a row."

"Yeah, I decided to check it out again."

He lowered his brow with a puzzled expression. "Check it out? Jess, I want to ask you a question. Are you a Christian? I mean have you accepted Christ as your savior?"

"Well, I consider my religion to be Christian, but I haven't done that 'accepting the Lord as your savior' thing."

He glanced to the side, thinking on my statement. "Okay, I was just curious where you stood on that."

As the meeting began, it was pretty much as before, except this time they had a time of prayer requests. Pastor Tim had everyone go around the room to ask for a prayer request or give a testimony. As they went around the group, it finally came time for Katie's turn.

"First of all, I would like to thank God for everyone here. Since I have been coming to this church for the last two years, you have all been such good friends to me. As all of you know, I have asked for many 'unspoken' prayer requests. I just wanted to tell you that one of them is starting to be answered."

As she said that, everyone smiled and then looked my way. That's when I realized that one of those prayer requests must have been about me. As I thought about that, it made me feel good to think she cared enough to ask them to pray for me. Pastor Tim then began his lesson for the evening, which had to do with using your talents for the Lord. He mentioned different types of ministries and said that not all ministries need to be in the 'limelight' so to speak. He said sometimes the most important ministries are never seen, and that something as simple as praying for someone is just as important as preaching from the pulpit. That's about all I got out of it, because to be honest, my mind wandered to the upcoming football tryouts and the aroma of the peperoni pizza coming from the kitchen. When he was done, Pastor Tim once again asked if anyone wanted to accept Christ as their savior. This time it kind of bugged me because I knew I was the only one there he could be talking to. Once again, I blew it off saying to myself that I felt I was a Christian and didn't need to say that 'sinner's prayer' thing.

After it was over we had a time of fellowship, and of course munched down on some pizza. A little later, Katie's dad picked us up and we started to head home. Along the way I began to think about this accepting Christ as your savior thing, so I brought up the subject.

"You know, I don't understand something?"

"What's that, Jess?" Katie asked.

"Why is it such a big deal to have to accept Christ as your savior? I mean, can't I just be a good person and try to do the right things and belong to a Christian church?"

Her father spoke up. "Katie, do you mind if I answer that?"

"No Dad, go ahead."

"Jess, you're into football, right?"

"Yeah."

"Now from what Katie has told me, the Denver Broncos are your favorite team; is that correct?"

"Yeah; they're the best!"

"So you like them for what they stand for, and you like all the players and so forth?"

"Yeah."

"But you're just a fan, right?"

"Yeah, I guess."

"What I mean by that, is you admire them from afar but you're not actually a member of the team, are you?"

"No, I'm not a member of the team. I'm just a fan."

"So let's say the Bronco's make it all the way and win the Super Bowl. But since you are not a member of the team then you can't say that championship trophy is yours, can you?"

"No, I guess not."

"Jess, it's the same way with accepting the Lord as your savior. When you join God's team by accepting Christ, you will be entitled to receive the ultimate prize—to be with the Lord in heaven. But if you stay *just a fan*, then you won't be able to receive the ultimate prize. Fortunately for us, Christ doesn't expect us to be the perfect player or be so good in our own strength in order to make it *on his team*. All he wants is for us to love and accept him as our Savior. What Christ did on the cross qualifies us to be on his team. But if you don't accept him as your savior, you will always remain just a fan and never truly be a member of the team."

I sat silently thinking about what he said, as I had never heard it put that way before. It made me wonder if I was truly a Christian, or was I someone on the outside looking in.

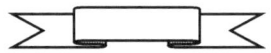

CHAPTER SIX – MORE MCALLISTER SECRETS

On Friday I rode my bike over to Katie's to work some more on the Rosemary Pullman investigation. When I got to the door, Mrs. McCullough answered and let me in.

"Hello Jesse, how are you doing today?"

"I'm doing fine; thanks."

She looked at me with a teasing smile. "Now Jesse… no more soap fights in the kitchen, okay?"

"Uh, no Ma'am; no more soap fights."

Katie entered the room and we went onto the back porch to work on our project. She laid out our investigation folder and opened an envelope with some photos.

"I had Becky develop this film for us of the pictures we took when we were at the Cedarwood Condos."

"How did Becky develop the film for you?"

"Since she's all into photography and journalism, her dad set up a darkroom for her to develop film. I want you to carefully look over these pictures."

"Okay, what am I looking for?"

"In one of these pictures I think I might have found a way to get information on where Rosemary Pullman might have moved to. Take a look and tell me what you see."

I carefully scanned the photos. "I don't know—buildings?"

"No, keep looking."

"Well, I see some trees, bushes, and a few cars in the parking lot. Other than that, I don't see anything out of the ordinary."

"No Jess, the U-Haul truck!"

"So, what about it?"

"Well I was thinking… In order for Rosemary Pullman to move somewhere, she must have used U-Haul or some other company to

157

move her to where she currently lives. I looked in the phone book, and besides U-Haul, there is the only one other moving company in this town."

"Okay, but how is that going to help us get her new address?"

"We're going to get that information from U-Haul. I have an idea, and if I do it right, I might be able to get the person I speak with to volunteer the information we need."

I looked at her with skepticism. "How are you going to do that?"

"Watch, come-err."

As we entered her bedroom she sat on her bed and pulled the telephone next her. She then wrote down the address of the Cedarwood Condos and Mrs. Pullman's condo number which was A-10. Then she wrote down the words; 'about two months ago'.

She looked at me and took in a deep breath. "Okay Jess, wish me luck."

"Okay, I don't know what you're doing, but good luck."

She flipped to the page in the phonebook under moving companies, and dialed the local U-Haul office. After a few rings, one of the employees answered the phone.

"Good afternoon—U-Haul."

She cleared her throat. "Yes, I am calling for my grandma and she believes that your moving company possibly lost her china set with the gold trim—she is very upset!"

"I'm sorry young lady, but did you say that *we moved her?*"

"Yes."

"I believe you are mistaken. We don't move people; people rent our trucks. We are U-Haul as in 'you' drive the truck yourself."

"Oh, sorry, wrong company," she said and quickly hung up the phone.

She let out a grunt of frustration. "I am so dumb!"

"Why?"

The Search for Rosemary Pullman

"I forgot that U-Haul is not a moving company, people only rent their trucks and drive it themselves. I don't think an older woman like Rosemary Pullman would be driving a big truck and moving herself."

"Oh yeah, I didn't think about that either."

Katie crossed U-Haul off her list. "Okay, let me call this other company called Two Brothers Moving Company."

She then dialed the number when a man answered the phone. "Two Brothers... serving all your moving needs. Can I help you?"

"Yes, I'm calling for my Grandma, Rosemary Pullman. She told me to call you because she believes that your company lost her gold-embossed china set when you moved her. She is very upset."

"Who did you say your grandmother is? And can I speak to her, please?"

"Her name is Rosemary Pullman. But she's crying and too upset to talk right now."

Katie covered the phone slightly, and the proceeded to fake like she was talking to someone in the background.

"It'll be okay Grandma; don't cry. We'll find your china set."

She got back on the phone. "Please mister, can you check your records, my Grandma said there were two trucks that moved her, but she doesn't remember seeing them unload her china set."

"Okay, when did she move out, and what was her address?"

Katie covered the phone once more. "Grandma... when was the date you moved out from Cedarwood?" then she paused for the effect, before returning to the phone.

"Okay, mister, my grandmother thinks it was about two months ago, but she's not sure. My grandmother sometimes forgets things."

"Okay, what was the address?"

"It was 100 South Cedar Court, number A-10."

"Okay, hold on while I look up that information for you."

With crossed fingers and a tense smile, she waited with anticipation for the man to return to the phone.

"Okay, here it is. Mrs. Rosemary Pullman 100 South Cedar, #A-10. Our records show that only one truck was dispatched to that address on April 20th. We delivered the contents to 2589 County Line Road, Space #24. Is that your grandmother's address?"

Katie quickly wrote it down. "Yes, that's her address. So there was only one truck that moved her?"

"Yes, just one truck was dispatched to that address."

Then once again Katie called out like she was talking to someone in the background. "What's that Grandma? You did what?"

She returned to the phone. "Oh sorry mister. My grandma just remembered that she gave that china set to Aunt Tilley about two years ago. Like I said, she's a little forgetful. Sorry, thank you for your time."

Katie hung up the phone and rolled over on her bed, then raised her hands in celebration.

"Jess, I got it!"

I sat there utterly amazed. "I can't believe you did that—that was so good!"

"Thanks. My heart was pounding so hard that I thought it was going to leap out of my chest. I was also hoping that man wouldn't ask for a moving receipt or something."

As she lay on the bed catching her breath, her excitement soon faded. She then sat up and looked towards the heavens.

"Sorry, Lord. I know I kind of fibbed a little, but I didn't know any other way of getting that information."

Seeing her sorrowed expression, I placed my hand on her shoulder. "Don't worry about it Katie. At least we didn't go down there and steal records or something. That man voluntarily gave you that info."

A tinge of consolation resonated from her voice. "Yeah, I guess so."

Seeing how she felt bad about it, I quickly moved on.

"You know, County Line Road is off of Hwy 49 about 30 miles from here."

"I know. And since the address has a space number that usually means it's a mobile home park. I bet you it's that one you see right there off Hwy 49 going towards Newcastle."

"Yeah, I was thinking the same thing."

She smiled with a sense of resolve. "Okay good. Now we can go back to the McAllister's and let them know that our search is over—we have found Rosemary Pullman."

*****

The next day we called the McAllister's and made an appointment to see them. When we arrived at their house, we told them we found an address for Rosemary Pullman. Mrs. McAllister seemed relieved, but as Katie went over all the information we obtained at Cedarwood, a look of concern grew upon on Mr. McAllister's face. When we mentioned the name Ian Thorpe, he seemed to be even more concerned, and I could tell a million thoughts were swirling in his mind. After Katie finished reading all the information, Mr. McAllister rose from his chair and just stared out the window. He then turned and commented as if he really wasn't surprised to hear that Ian Thorpe was involved.

"So, the development company who bought Cedarwood is Ian Thorpe and Equity One."

Katie and I glanced at one another when he said that. This seemed to confirm our suspicions about the connection between them.

"What is this all about, Mr. McAllister?" I asked "This Ian Thorpe made a comment about an "anonymous firm" being a point of contention for him. He also said this anonymous firm has been donating hundreds of thousands of dollars into this town. Was he talking about you?"

Mr. McAllister glanced at Mrs. McAllister with a telling look and then cleared his throat.

"Jesse... I wish I could go into more detail with you about this, but for now, I feel it would be best not too. It's not that I don't trust you and Katie, but I want for us to talk to Rosemary before we get any deeper into this."

Katie and I glanced at one another, wondering what other secrets the McAllister's had that they weren't telling us. Mr. McAllister then smiled in appreciation.

"Thank you so much for getting that address for us. We had confidence that the two of you would be able to find Rosemary. What I would like, is for the both of you to come with Emma and I when we go to see Rosemary."

"Sure," we both said.

Mr. McAllister looked at the calendar on the kitchen wall. "Tomorrow is Sunday and we don't want to do anything on the Lord's Day. How about we make it this coming Monday—is that alright?"

We nodded our heads in agreement. "Yes," Katie said. "Monday should be fine. I don't see a problem in our parents letting us go with you."

"Jess, Katie... before you go, Emma and I want to thank you for all you've done. That was very impressive investigative work the two of you did. Thank you so much."

"You're welcome," we both said.

As we left their house, I couldn't help but wonder what this was all about. Mr. McAllister seemed to be holding on to some kind of secret where this simple favor of finding Rosemary had suddenly taken a strange twist.

*****

Come Monday morning, I rode my bike over to Katie's, as that was where the McAllister's said they would pick us up. We then drove to the mobile home park off of Hwy 49, where Mr. McAllister parked his big ole' Cadillac in front of the Space 24, and we exited the car. We walked up the steps to the mobile home and knocked on the door.

A few moments later the door opened and this elderly woman stood in the doorway.

"Rose!" Mrs. McAllister greeted with excitement.

"Ruth, Harold…, my goodness; come on in."

We entered the mobile home, and sat down on flower-patterned couches in the living room. Mr. McAllister then began the introductions.

"Rose, I would like you to meet a couple of youngsters that mean so much to us—they are like our adopted grandchildren. This young man here is Jesse, and this beautiful young lady is Katie."

We cordially shook her hand. "Nice to finally meet you, Rosemary," I said.

"Nice to meet you too," she said. She then returned her focus to Mr. and Mrs. McAllister. "Harold, Ruth…, what are you doing here?"

"We hadn't heard from you for some time. And when we went to your Condo at Cedarwood, they told us you moved out."

"Yes, I moved away; I don't live there anymore."

"But Rose, why did you move? You loved that place," Mrs. McAllister asked with concern.

"Oh, I just needed to move, so I'm living here now."

Rose swallowed her emotions, got up and walked into the kitchen. Mr. McAllister spoke towards the kitchen.

"Rose… what is it that you're not telling us? What's the matter?"

"Nothing Harold, just leave it be."

Mr. and Mrs. McAllister looked at each other with growing concern. Rose then spoke from the kitchen.

"I have some tea and cookies, would you like some?"

Mrs. McAllister got up from the couch and went into the kitchen for a few moments. When she returned, she leaned close to us and spoke in a hushed tone.

"She won't talk to me about what happened. I tried again in the kitchen, but she seems to be afraid of something."

Katie then turned to Mrs. McAllister. "Can I try? Sometimes it's easier to open up to a stranger than those closest to us."

"Sure honey, give it a try."

Katie then asked if she could have some time alone with Rose; just the two of them. Mr. McAllister then spoke towards the kitchen.

"Rose… we are going to take a walk and have a look around at your mobile home park. Young Katie is going to stay with you and help you with the tea."

When all of us left, Katie entered the kitchen to talk to her.

"Hi Mrs. Pullman, can I help with anything?"

"Yes dear, you can get the teacups out of that cupboard right there. And please call me Rose."

Katie opened the cupboard and arranged the cups and saucers on a serving tray. She then walked over to where Rose who was standing near the stove, waiting for the tea kettle to boil. She placed her hand on Rose, and caringly rubbed her back.

"It's alright Rose, just let it out," she said, hugging her close to her side.

Immediately the tears began to flow, as Rose broke down and fell into Katie's waiting arms.

Katie held her close to her side. "Come on Rose, let's go and sit down on the couch."

She guided her over to the couch, as Katie placed her arm around her.

"You never wanted to leave your home at Cedarwood, did you?"

"No," she said, through her tears.

"It's okay Rose; tell me… Were you forced to leave your home at Cedarwood?"

Rose continued to weep, but did not answer. Katie once again rubbed her back as Rose began to melt with Katie's touch. Then suddenly, it all came bursting out.

"Yes! They forced me and they threatened me!" she said, then crumbled into Katie's arms.

About that time, we came back into the mobile home, and saw Rose weeping in Katie's arms. Katie looked up at us with a nod of her head, as if to say, "She's okay, she's letting it out."

Mrs. McAllister got a tissue and handed it to Rose. After a minute, Rose composed herself and started to tell the whole story of what happened.

"I can't remember all the details as I am getting so forgetful lately. But this all started some months back when a group of men wanted to have a meeting with all the owners at Cedarwood. They told us they were there to possibly purchase the property, and gave us all kinds of papers showing what they were proposing. We were told us that basically our building had all this structural damage and our complex needed repairs that would cost us thousands and thousands of dollars. They explained something about new codes that required us to get this work done, and that all the expenses of this work would fall on us, the owners, unless we were willing to sell to them. The way they explained it to us, it was almost like we didn't have a choice. After they left, about half of the people wanted to take their offer, but myself and others did not. However, as time went on, more and more owners were signing agreements to sell their condos. I was talking with Mr. Richards, who lived down the hall from me, and we both agreed we did not want to sell. Oh, I almost forgot to mention that this investment company needed for all of us homeowners to agree to sell, otherwise they couldn't buy the property from us. Getting back to my story, one day some man from that company came to visit me about selling. I told the man I was not going to sell. This man seemed to get very upset with me and kept insisting it was going to cost me so much more to stay and do those repairs to the building. I told him firmly I was not going to sell and then he left. The next day this same man came back and asked me again if I would agree to sell. I told him, no, that there were others besides me who did not want to sell either. The following day he came back once more, but this time he had with him a man named Mr. Thorpe, or Doctor, or something like that. I am getting so bad at remembering names. When they came into my house they sat down next to me, one on each side of me. This Mr. Thorpe said he was there to make me a higher offer to buy my condo—I believe it was ten thousand dollars more. After I kept saying no, he got angry and I was starting to get frightened, as the both of them were staring at me with these awful looks. Then this Mr. Thorpe said, 'Mrs. Pullman... you seem to be confused about what is going on. Perhaps you do not fully understand what's at stake here. Do you have any family, Mrs. Pullman?' he asked. I told him no, that I only have a sister who is in a rest home in Arkansas, but that is all the family I have. Then he said to me in a threatening tone, 'Mrs. Pullman, I would hate to have to put you into a mental institution. You seem like you are mentally unstable and we can have one of our corporate physiologists declare you as being mentally unfit! In fact, we know of a nice home called Sun Country Mental Institution in Las Cruses, New Mexico.' After he said that they were just staring at me so horribly. Then that Mr. Thorpe placed some papers in front of me and said, 'This can all go away Rose, as long as you sign these papers.' I was so afraid of being put in a mental institution that I signed the papers. A few days later the two of you (referring to Mr. and Mrs. McAllister) came over to visit me, but I was afraid to say anything about what happened. It was about two weeks later that I moved out of Cedarwood."

Mr. McAllister rose to his feet in anger and looked out the front door. He then turned abruptly—visibly upset.

"Rose... this is not right what they did to you! Maybe there is something we can do about this."

"No Harold, please just leave it be. These people seem to be very powerful and could cause problems for all of us," she said, and wiped a tear from her eye.

"Okay Rose, for now we won't do anything. But in a few days, after I have looked into this further, we are going to come visit with you again, alright?"

"Yes, that's fine—I do miss having you visit with me." She then turned her focus on Katie. "Will young Katie be coming also?"

By the warmth in her voice, I could tell she got attached to Katie right away. Katie hugged her to the side.

"Of course I will, Rose. I will come over to visit anytime you like."

While we were on our way home, I could see by Katie's expression that she was just fuming about what happened to Rose. Then it finally came bursting out.

"Mr. and Mrs. McAllister... this just isn't right! They threatened her! Isn't that against the law?"

I added. "Yeah, can't we do something about this?"

Mr. McAllister looked at us the rearview mirror. "*Emma and I* can't do anything about it, but *the two of you* may be able to do something. I know of a certain public interest law firm called, The American League for Law and Justice. They might be able to help us by taking on a case like this. Jess, Katie... before I go into a few details about our families business dealings, I need to explain something to you. If we are going to pursue some type of legal action on behalf of Rose, then you must understand a few things first. One...; it has to be the two of you helping Rose pursue an action through this law firm. Second...; Emma and I cannot be a part of this lawsuit, other than our financial support with legal costs. Also, you must know one thing... if we pursue this, then we will have to go all the way or not do it at all."

"What do you mean, Mr. McAllister?"

"Jess, accusing a corporation of fraud, and or coercion is a serious matter. It requires enough evidence in order for a legal firm to undertake such a case. It also might get pretty ugly as this corporation is known to get down and dirty whenever others have tried to pursue legal action against them. I know of others who have tried to take them to court and lost. This Ian Thorpe and his lawyers are very sharp, and they cover their bases very well. They do very detailed investigations into those who try to pursue action against them, digging up all of their 'skeletons in the closet' and discredit them before the judge and the court. This is the reason why Emma and I cannot be a part of this. If they were to find out we were part of pursuing this, it would open the door for them to investigate the details of our lives. Then they could subpoena records and get information on us that would reveal who we really are. Because of that, we cannot be involved in this. They could also claim that we have a vested interest in this matter because we have competed with them on different projects in our community. You see... my firm has been in battle with them over building permits and county ordinances in the past. Ian Thorpe and his legal team seem to know certain people in 'high places' if you know what I mean, and he has them in his back pocket."

"In his back pocket?" I questioned. "What does that mean?"

"It means he may be paying them off to get past the red tape regarding permits to get what he wants."

I didn't completely understand all of the terms that Mr. McAllister was saying. I was also surprised how suddenly he seemed to be way sharper than I had thought. To me he was ole' Mr. McAllister sitting there chewing his tobacco and watching the world go by on his front porch. But now, all of a sudden he seemed to be this intelligent businessman.

"Mr. McAllister... what is this subpoena thing you talked about?"

"A subpoena is legal order that requires someone to show up in court or to produce documents that the other person is requesting."

Katie and I looked at each other amazed at how much he knew about all this. He then continued.

"There is something else I think you should know as to why I do not like Ian Thorpe and this corporation. During the last few years our economy has been in a recession. We are just starting to get out of it, so now is the time that companies try to invest before property values start to go back up again. When the two of you found that chest of gold up at the house and we agreed on building the Burger King, we ran up against Ian Thorpe and his corporation fighting for permits. There are only so many building permits that can be issued per-year, per square mile in this town. All the permits have to adhere to county ordinances and be approved by the town's building department."

"I understand a little about that Mr. McAllister," Katie interjected. "My father works in the permit section of the Building Department."

"Yes Katie, I know."

"You do?"

"Yes, my executor knows your father very well. In fact he tries to deal with your father on permit issues. Your father is a by-the-book kind of man that has integrity and will not let something slide by. He makes sure that everything is on the up and up."

"I didn't realize how important my dad's job was."

"It's very important. You see, what this Equity One Corporation does, is they buy up property really cheap and then tear it down or rebuild it for investment purposes only. Then they turn around and lease out the buildings to other investors. The problem with that, is they still own the land but they do not follow up on the upkeep of the properties. Most of the new investors don't care either, so these properties go downhill really fast and eventually become eyesores in the community. When our firm donates funds to have something built, we have the Town Counsel sign an agreement that they will always maintain these properties. My father founded this town and we have helped maintain it all these years. We do not want investors like Ian Thorpe to come in and ruin what we have worked so hard to do."

A look of amazement drew upon our faces, as all of this was a bit overwhelming.

"Gee Mr. McAllister, I guess Katie and I never realized how complicated all of this was. I guess when you told us that you donated money to this town, I had this image of you simply writing out a check and that was it. There is a lot more business stuff that we didn't realize you were involved with."

"Yes, there really is. Now… if you decide you still want to pursue this, I will give you the name and phone number of that law firm I told you about. But I think the two of you should take a couple of days to consider this very seriously. There is nothing more I would like to see than to have someone catch Ian Thorpe and his suspicious business practices. But be warned… If you decide to go up against a big corporation like Equity One, you will be in for a battle."

After Mr. and Mrs. McAllister dropped us off at Katie's house, we sat on the porch steps to talk it through.

"I don't know Katie; this sounds like stuff for grownups, not teens like us."

"I know, and I'm not sure what to do about this. Jess, if you could have seen the hurt Rose was feeling inside. As I hugged her, it was if I could feel her pain; she was really hurt by all of this. Let's think about this for a few days. I need to pray about it and we have that trip to Great America coming up. After that, we'll talk about what we are going to do about this."

"Yeah, that's sounds like a good idea."

CHAPTER SEVEN – THE GREAT AMERICA ADVENTURE

The day came when we would be leaving to go on our adventure at Great America. Everyone who was going was to meet at the church parking lot at six in the morning. The drive would take about two hours, so we made sure we left early to get there right when it opened. When I arrived at the church Katie was not there yet, and so I began talking with Moses.

"Hey Moses... have you ever been to Great America before?"

"No, this is my first time, but I heard there are some pretty good rides to go on, like the Demon. I hear it's a pretty fast."

Just then Chris approached us. "Hi Moses, hey Jess. There's going to be some good music groups there. Like the Imperials and Sweet Comfort Band. Katie and I can't wait to see Sweet Comfort Band." He then scanned around the parking lot. "By the way... have you guys seen her?"

"No," I quickly said. "But I talked to her this morning. I reminded her that we shouldn't wear our matching cross-necklaces because we might lose them on the rides."

As I thought about my response, I had to honestly question my motives.

Why did I say that in front of him? Was I jealous because he made that comment about Katie and that band? Did I mention the necklaces to show him that I have a connection with her too?

I shrugged off those thoughts and then turned to Moses. "So... whatever happened with you and Gina? Are you guys going to hang around together today?"

"No, she said she would go on a couple of rides with me, but she didn't want it to be like a date or anything. She's only in the seventh-grade and her dad doesn't want her to be with a guy like that. I can understand because of her age."

I gave him a friendly pat on the shoulder. "Hey, at least she didn't tell you to get lost or anything."

"Yeah, really."

Just then Katie arrived and Pastor Tim called the group together to pray.

"Dear Lord, we are thankful for the opportunity you have given us to enjoy this time of fellowship together. Keep us from any harm on the roads, and let us always remember who we are as Christians and show that in our behavior, Amen."

Everyone entered the bus and Katie and I sat together. Moses sat behind me with this other guy named Ryan, and Chris sat in front of us. As we got on our way, everyone began talking about which rides they wanted to go on, or other activities to do while we were there. Pastor Tim had previously told us that we could split-off into different groups, but he wanted everyone to check in at twelve-noon by the large fountain in the middle of the park. He also told us we would be leaving at five o'clock.

During our drive to the park, Katie and I saw large numbers of buses from other churches that were apparently on their way to the park also. We started to play a little game of naming them along the way.

"Look Katie… that must be a really big church, they have two large buses. They're from Faith Fellowship in Modesto."

"And look at that one Jess; it must be a Spanish church—Templo-Elim from San Jose."

We travelled a little ways further when I spotted something on the side of the road.

"Uh oh, that's not good."

"What's that?" she said, while stretching across me to look out the window.

"That bus is broken down on the side of the road, and it looks like their engine is on fire."

As we passed by, you could see flames and smoke coming from the engine while the fire-fighters were dousing it with their hoses.

"Oh Lord, I hope nobody got hurt," Katie said with concern.

As we slowed passed the broken-down bus, we read the name on the side of the bus which said Grace Community Church. About that time, Chris leaned over the top of the seat.

"Katie… which concerts are we going to see? I have a schedule of events, and it says that the Imperials are having concerts at 10 am and 4 pm. Sweet Comfort is going to have theirs at 1 and 6."

"Chris, how about we go to the Imperials at 10 and Sweet Comfort at 1 pm. Pastor Tim said we were not going to stay until closing, so I think we need to see Sweet Comfort at the first showing."

"Alright, sounds good. Hey… do you think they are going to play a lot of their songs off of Cutting Edge?"

"I hope so; I have all their albums. I really like that song 'I loved you with my life' off of the album, Breakin' the Ice."

"Yeah me too, I also like 'Searching for Love' off of that same album. Speaking of searching… remember how Mandy left the church because she wanted to search and see what the world had to offer her? Well guess what? She came back last Sunday night and rededicated her life back to the Lord."

"Really, that's great! I was worried about Mandy; I really like her a lot."

"Yeah, me too."

As I sat there listening to them talk, I didn't understand half of what they were saying. I didn't know any of these music groups they were talking about, much less this rededicating your life stuff and all that 'Christianees' talk. That's one thing that bugs me about Christians. They use all this religious language and you can't understand what they're saying. At that point I felt kind of left out of the conversation, so I decided to turn my attention to Moses the rest of the way there.

When we arrived at Great America we walked to the main entrance and got in line to get our tickets. When they finally opened the doors, all of us rushed through the gates. Some of the older teens, like the juniors and seniors, went in one group, while the rest of us went together in another group. In our particular group were me and Katie, Moses, Chris, Gina, Ryan and Lindsey. I think Pastor Tim had Lindsey go with our group because she is a little older and could keep an eye on us. We all decided to go on a few rides that were closer to the entrance since we were right there. On the first ride Katie and I got on together, but on the next one she rode with Chris. After going on a few more rides, we played some of those games where you can try to win a stuffed animal. Chris won a stuffed kangaroo on that ping pong thing that you toss into a glass of water and gave it to Katie. Of course he won it on a game that requires no skill whatsoever—lucky shot.

About nine-thirty we came to the place where one of the Christian groups was going to be having a concert. As we walked closer to the area, there was already a lot of people waiting to get in. Chris noted the huge line forming.

"Katie… look at that big line. We better get in line if we're going to see the Imperials."

"Yeah, we probably should."

She turned to get my attention. "Jess… we're getting in line for this concert, okay?"

"Who is this for?"

"The Imperials. You like the Eagles and they sort of have that type of sound. I want you to see them."

I shrugged my shoulders with a hint of negativity. "Alright, I guess that's fine."

As we stood there in line, once again Chris and Katie were going on and on about Christian groups and all these other singers. Once again I felt like an outsider so I turned to Moses once more.

"Hey Moses... do you know this group we're going to see?"

"Yeah, I have one of their tapes. They're not my favorite group, but they're alright."

Lindsey was standing nearby and commented, "I wish Petra or Rez Band were here—now that's Christian rock music!"

I smiled to Lindsey's comment, then looked around the area. "Do you really want to see this concert?" I asked Moses.

"Why? What did you want to do?"

"I don't know, you mentioned there was a pretty cool arcade in the park. Do you want to go there instead?"

He perked up with interest. "Yeah, let's do that."

I turned my focus to Lindsey, Gina and Ryan, and asked them if they wanted to go with us to the arcade, but they wanted to stay and watch the concert. I turned to Katie to let her know I was leaving with Moses.

"Katie..., Katie...!" I shouted, as I finally got her attention away from Chris.

"Moses and I are going to the arcade. We'll be back when your concert lets out, okay?"

A look of concern drew upon her face, as she came and pulled me to the side.

"Jess, why are you going? I wanted you to see this group."

"You're too busy with Chris—I don't think you'll miss me."

"Why are you being like this?"

"Just go with Chris. We're going to play a few games, so I'll see you later."

"But Jess...."

As I started to walk off, I could see the hurt in her eyes. But I was hurt too. I thought she invited me so we could hang around together, but all she has done is talk to Chris. As Moses and I walked away, I thought about turning back to look at her, but I knew once I looked at those eyes of hers I would fold and go back to the concert; so I just kept walking.

When Moses and I got to the arcade, we started to play some games. We played for a while by ourselves, and then played a couple of games together. I found out he's a pretty good video game player, and he also found out how good I was.

"Wow, Jess. Katie wasn't kidding about how good you are."

"Thanks. I just wish I was as good at figuring out girls as I am at playing video games."

"Well, since you brought up the subject of girls, let's finish this game and then we'll go over to the snack bar and talk."

After we finished the game, he bought us a couple of cokes and we sat down.

"So Jess... I know we haven't known each other that long, but I feel like we can talk pretty good. You were there when I needed to talk to someone about Gina, so I want to be there for you too."

I wasn't quite sure why I trusted him, but I guess I needed someone to talk to and he seemed to know it.

"Well Moses, it's kind of a long story. But Katie and I have been friends since the seventh-grade. We just seemed to hit it off from the beginning, and we have spent a lot of time doing things together. I guess what's bothering me, is that she invited me to come here and all she has done is talk to Chris. I guess I thought we were going to be hanging around together, but she seems to be ignoring me."

"Well, I don't know about her ignoring you, but I do know one thing: Katie cares about you a lot. Do you know that when she first started coming to our church that practically every time we had prayer requests she would bring you up? She would say, 'Can you pray for my best friend Jess, it's an unspoken request.'"

"What's an unspoken request?"

"It's when someone wants the group to pray about something, but they don't want to give details because it's usually personal."

"Really?"

"Yeah. And every time Pastor Tim would ask for prayer requests, we usually knew Katie was going to bring up your name. Then when you finally came to youth group for the first time, all of us looked at each other like, 'wow we finally get to meet Jess; the one Katie has been asking prayer for.'"

"I guess I didn't realize I needed that much prayer," I said jokingly.

"We all need prayer, but I think that Katie had particular things in mind. Now as far as Chris is concerned, honestly I think he does have a little crush on her. But I don't think that Katie was talking to him because she's interested in him. Chris is going through a rough time right now since his parents have recently separated. His father doesn't want anything to do with church, and that's one of the reasons for the separation. Chris is really having a hard time of it right now, and that's why Katie is spending time with him. In the short amount of time Katie has been a part of our church, she's has gotten the nickname of 'Caregiver Katie.' When she senses that someone is feeling down or needs comfort, she comes and gives them a hug to make them feel better—especially some of the senior citizens in our church."

As I sat there listening to all that he was saying, my heart began to stir with regret.

"Moses, I am so messed up. I just said something mean to her because I thought that she was ignoring me."

"That's alright. You have the rest of the day to make it up her."

"Yeah, I guess so. Thanks man, for having this talk with me—you helped me a lot."

"Hey, that's what friends are for, right? I mean we are starting to be friends, aren't we?"

"Yeah, of course. You know, it's kind of strange, I seem to be able to open up to you, yet with my other friend Brian, I have trouble talking to him about certain subjects."

"Well, I'm glad I can be here for you. You know sometimes God puts people in our lives for a reason."

"Well, thanks again, but I guess we better go back. I want to be there when Katie gets out of that concert."

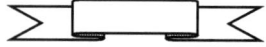

CHAPTER EIGHT – THE UNEXPECTED "ROADIE" AHEAD

The concert had ended, and Katie and the rest of the group came out and walked over towards us. Katie seemed excited as she talked with Gina, apparently about what went on at the concert. However, once she laid eyes on me, that excitement drained from her face and she quickly looked away from me. Lindsey then spoke up and told the group that we needed to check in with Pastor Tim at the large fountain in the middle of the park by noon. There was one of those "skyway" tram rides nearby, so we all decided to take it over to the other side of the park. Chris and Katie started to walk with Lindsay in the direction of the tram, while the rest of us followed. As we got near the tram, I guess Moses decided to take matters into his own hands.

"Hey Chris!" he called out. "Let's ride together on the skyway tram. I want to talk to you about something."

Chris slowed his pace, when suddenly, Moses shoved me in the back towards Katie. I quickly caught up and began walking alongside her.

"Can I ride with you?" I asked hesitantly.

She shrugged her shoulders. "I guess if you want to."

We got on the tram and started on our way. She began to look around at all the sites, except directly at me.

"Are you mad at me, Katie?"

She turned to me with a solemn expression. "No, I'm not mad at you; I'm disappointed. Jess, I wasn't ignoring you. Chris needed someone to talk to about some personal things, and I wanted to be there for him. Jess, we are together all the time. We hang out before school, after school, during lunch sometimes, and even during summer vacation. I spend more time with you than anyone else. Yet you couldn't just give me a couple hours with someone else?"

When she put it that way; it made me sound like a real jerk.

"I'm sorry…I didn't mean it to come out like I was trying to have you all to myself. I think part of the reason I got upset, was that you and Chris were talking all your 'Christianees' talk and I felt left out. That's what bugs me about Christians. They sit there and talk in their spiritual language like you guys think you're better than other people."

She turned and directed a questioning stare. "Is that what you think about me and other Christians? That just because we talk about spiritual things that we think we're better than other people? We talk about spiritual things because we have that in common, not because we think we are better than anyone else." She paused for a moment, gathering a thought. "And what about you Jess? You do the same thing to me."

"How? When do I do that to you?"

"When you and your dad are watching football. You guys start talking in all those football terms and I feel left out also. All those football terms are like a foreign language to me, just like you feel our spiritual talk is foreign to you. You start talking about the players being in certain formations and all that safely blitzing stuff."

"It's called a safety blitz."

"See…! I don't know all those terms about football, just like you don't know all the terms that Christians use. Should I assume that you and your dad think you are better than me just because you understand football and I don't?"

"No, of course not."

"Then you shouldn't think that way about Christians either."

I thought about her statement for a moment and realized she was right.

"Gee Katie, you sure know how to make a point. I guess I never looked at it that way." I directed an apologetic smile. "I'm so sorry for acting the way I did. Will you forgive me for being such a jerk?"

"Of course I will. Jess... some of the things you don't understand in Christianity are because you don't have God's spirit in you to help you understand them. That's why a person needs to accept Christ as their savior and be born again. When you receive God's spirit into your life, then you will be able to see spiritual things from a different perspective. I wish you would have come with us to the concert. The lead singer always gives a brief message at the end of their concerts and I was hoping..."

"You were hoping what?"

"Oh nothing... I just wished you would have gone."

We changed the subject and began looking at the sites below from the view of the tramway. I happened to notice a couple of vans pulling some trailers on the other side of the park barrier wall. I looked a little closer and saw the initials, "SCB" printed on the sides of the vans.

"Look!" I said, and pointed beyond the barrier wall. "That van says SCB on the side of it. Do you think they belong to that group you like—that Sweet Comfort Band?"

"Where?" she asked with interest, and quickly sat up to get a better look.

"Right there, on the other side of that green wall."

She focused to where I had pointed. "Oh my God, it's the band! They always us the initials SCB on their albums. I wonder if they are just getting here, because if they are, then they're really late. Their first concert starts in less than an hour."

I pointed to something below. "Look over there!"

"Look at what?"

"Oh, you missed it. I saw a gate with a chain that looked pretty loose. How would you like to go meet those guys from that band?"

"Are you crazy? We can't just go over there and meet the band—I'm so sure."

"Seriously, wouldn't you want to meet them? I mean the way you go on about them, wouldn't that be neat to meet them in person?"

"How are we going to do that?"

"We can go through that gap in the fence where that chain is loose. Then we will casually walk by them, as if we work for Great America. We'll just say something like, 'Good to have you with us.' And then shake their hands."

Initially a look of skepticism crossed her face. But then she got that twinkle in her eyes of another daring adventure.

"I don't know, Jess. I'd like to meet them, but we also need to check in with Pastor Tim, remember?"

As we sat there deciding to go on our adventure, the tram ride ended so we headed towards the rest of the group.

Suddenly an idea flashed in my mind. "I know… I'll tell Moses to check-in for us. Moses can tell Pastor Tim that we had something to do, and we'll join them at the concert. What do you say?"

She glanced to the side in thought. "Okay, but I can't believe I'm going to do this."

As we approached the group, I called Moses over to where we were standing.

"Hey Moses, can you do us a favor? Can you tell Pastor Tim that we needed to do something first, and we'll meet up with the group later."

"Why? What are you going to do?"

"Katie and I are going on a little adventure, but we need time to do it."

"Alright. But what about the concert? Are you guys going to make it back on time?"

"Yeah, we shouldn't be too long. Tell Pastor Tim we'll catch up to you guys and see you there at the concert."

"Alright, I'll tell him."

He started to walk off, when I called out to him. "Hey Moses!"

He turned around. "Yeah..."

I nodded my head and smiled, "Thanks for the favor."

"No problem, Jess. But you owe me one."

"Actually I owe you two. One for the favor, and one for the shove in the back."

After we left the group, we took off towards the area where I saw that gate in the green wall. When we got near the gate, Katie suddenly stopped with a look of introspection on her face.

"Wait Jess...What am I doing? Here I am a *Christian,* at a *Christian* Day event with our *Christian* youth group, and I'm about to sneak into another 'unauthorized area.' You would think after the repercussions of sneaking into that secret room at the museum that I would have learned my lesson. What kind of Christian example am I setting? What is wrong with me?"

I placed my hand caringly on her shoulder. "Don't feel bad, it was my idea. You were just going along with it. Now I feel bad for trying to make you do something that you knew was wrong. Well look at it this way... *you have* learned your lesson. At least you caught yourself before you actually did it."

She pressed out a smile. "Yes, I guess that's a little consolation."

"Come on; let's head back to meet up with our group at the concert."

Just then, this guy approached the gate and called us over. As we approached, he unlocked the gate and swung it open. When Katie focused in on him, a strange look ran across her face.

The man scanned us up and down. "Are you Glenn and Bobby?"

"No, we're not," I replied. "I'm Jess and this is my friend Katie."

"Oh, I'm looking for a couple of guys from Grace Community Church that were supposed to be our set-up roadies for the concert today. They were to meet us here at this gate, but since we're so late, maybe they decided to take off. I thought that maybe you might be them since the name Bobby can also be a girl's name. Oh, by the way... I'm Randy Thomas," he said.

With growing excitement, Katie took a hold of his hand. "I know who you are. You're with the band, you're with..."

"Yes I am young lady. I'm with Sweet Comfort Band."

A look of awe ran across her face. Then she finally composed herself.

"Did you say those guys were supposed to be from Grace Community Church?"

"Yes, Grace Community was to provide us with a couple of set-up roadies."

"Well, I don't think they are coming, Mr. Thomas. Jess and I saw a broken down bus on the side of the highway and it was from Grace Community Church."

"Well that's too bad about them breaking down like that. In fact, that's probably the accident that caused the backup on the freeway, which is why we're late."

He looked at us with a questioning stare and placed his hand under his chin. "Hmmm... how would the two of you like to be our set-up roadies?"

Excitement ran across our faces. Katie could hardly contain her excitement.

"Really? Yeah, we'll do it!"

"Great. I'll pay you twenty-five dollars apiece and you can watch the concert from the side of the stage if you like." He extended his hand to us. "Oh, and call me Randy."

He led us through the gate and locked it behind us. We hurried over to where the other band members were starting to open up the trailers to set up.

"Okay you two, we need to move fast because we only have about an hour to get ready. What we need for you to do is to start pulling out all the equipment from both of those trailers. Then bring it over to us so we can begin to set up. But first, let me introduce you to the rest of the guys."

He first walked us over to these other two guys who were already starting to set things up.

"As you can probably tell by the resemblance, these two guys are brothers. That's Kevin and that's Rick. Guys…, this is Jess and Katie. They are going to be our set-up roadies today. The other ones couldn't make it."

As both of these guys shook our hands, I thought about the irony of our situation.

Well how about that... Katie got to meet these guys after all, and we didn't even have to break-in or lie or anything.

Randy then pointed to this other guy who was leaning against one of the vans.

"You see that crazy little guy over there with a cup of coffee in his hand? Well that's Bryan—Mr. Duncan."

As we walked over to meet this guy, Katie gazed upon him like she was star-struck or something. When she went to shake his hand, this Bryan guy commented to the other guys from the band.

"Hey guys… at least the roadies are getting better looking, aren't they?" Katie's face flushed red by his little compliment.

Randy then pointed to the trailers. "Okay roadies, are you ready?"

"Yes we are," we said with enthusiasm.

"Okay, anything that is for keyboards goes to Bryan. Guitar stuff will go to me, the equipment for the bass guitar goes to Kevin, and the equipment for the drums goes to Rick."

As we started to unload the equipment we couldn't tell what some of the items were, because they were inside the cases. Realizing our dilemma, Randy began to direct us on where they should go.

185

"Katie, those two cases are the toms for the drums. Jess, that's a part of Bryan's foot pedals for his keyboards. Just set them in his area."

After a while it seemed like the three of us had gotten into a rhythm.

"Katie, snare drum. Jess, microphone stand for Rick. Katie, crash-cymbal stands for drums. Jess, left stage speaker."

Then Katie was about to grab this big-ole' case out of the trailer when Randy stopped her.

"Wait Katie, that's the bass drum. Let me get that for you sweetie; it's pretty heavy."

I don't know if it was that Katie's adrenalin was pumping or the fact that he called her "sweetie," insinuating that she was too weak as a girl. But she pulled that case from the trailer, picked it up like it was nothing, and carried it over to where he was standing. As she held it in her arms, she said with a confident smile, "Where do you want it?"

All of the guys in the group looked at each other and started busting-up laughing.

"Oh my God!" Randy said. "That must weigh more than she does! Wow, we have a little wonder woman here!"

As she walked back to the trailer in confidence, a proud feeling rushed over me and I couldn't help but think, *Yep, that's my spunky little girl!* Well, I know she's not *my girl*, but you know what I mean.

After we got the equipment out of the trailers, we helped them set up microphones and lead cables, and got everything ready for the sound check. As they started to go through a practice song, I soon realized they were a really polished group, and I looked forward to this concert. When everything was just about set up, Randy came over to thank us.

"You know, we have used set-up roadies before, but I don't think I have ever had a better pair than the two of you. You just did the job and did not mess around. Here's the twenty-five dollars apiece I promised you."

As he handed Katie the money she took it with a smile of appreciation.

"Thank you for the money, but for me it was a special experience just meeting all of you. You guys are my favorite group, and we had a lot of fun helping you."

"Well enjoy the concert. There are a couple of chairs setup to the side of the stage just for the two of you."

I held out my hand. "Thanks for letting us help out. I enjoyed helping you guys set up and stuff."

"You're welcome, Jess. Now just sit back and enjoy the concert. Oh and Jess... see this girl standing here by your side," he said glancing at Katie. "She's a keeper."

I glanced at Katie with a look of admiration. "Yeah, I think *I will* keep her."

She playfully punched me in the arm. "You better keep me!"

As the crowd gathered in the seating area, we saw our youth-group come in and take their seats. Suddenly, Gina pointed in our direction as the others looked our way. With puzzled expressions, they saw us sitting in an area normally reserved for only family and friends. As soon as the crowd got settled, some guy came up on stage, said a little prayer, and introduced the band. We all clapped as the band came on stage and took their places. As they started to play their first song, Katie began to sing along—knowing every word. After the first song ended, Randy introduced Kevin, Rick and Bryan, as I have come to know them. Then to our surprise, he turned in our direction.

"I would also like to introduce a couple of special guests who really saved us today. I would like for Jess and Katie to stand up. Give these two a round of applause. Without them, we might not have had been able to make this first concert."

The people in the audience clapped, as our youth-group looked at us in total amazement—it was kind of cool. The band then played a few more fast songs and then started to play a soft intro to their next song. Upon hearing the intro, Katie quickly turned with excitement.

"Oh Jess, this is my favorite song! I hoped they would play it!"

They started to play a song called "I love you with my life," and I could tell right away that it really meant a lot to her. She closed her eyes and raised her hands in worship to God. As I saw her totally lost in worship, I felt a yearning in my heart like I was missing something. Something that I couldn't describe, but I knew was real because I have seen it so vividly in her life. I knew that I believed in God to a point, but it wasn't real like it was with her. My mind began to battle with my heart as to what I believed. And for some reason, I just knew I needed to make a decision of whether or not to accept Christ as my savior. However, I was scared. Scared of how it might change me. Scared of what people might think of me—my family and my friends. My thoughts coursed through recent events where I had seen God do some pretty miraculous things in our lives. And now, as I sat here at this concert, I knew I had a choice to make on what I believed.

Do I really believe in this? Christ dying on the cross for us—for me? Was there someone really out there? A God who really cares about me? Was it true like Mr. McCullough said, that I needed to stop being a fan and join God's team?

As these thoughts swirled in my mind, the song ended and Randy began to speak to the crowd.

"Normally we would finish with a couple of songs from our latest album. But right now I am being led to sing a song from one of our older albums. The song we are going to play tonight is called, 'When I was Alone.' As we play this song, I would like for you to evaluate where you stand with the Lord this afternoon. If you don't know Christ as your personal savior, then come up to the front area and stand here. Don't worry about the person next to you; this is your decision to make. I pray that you make that decision today."

As I listened to the lyrics of the song, it was if they mirrored what I was feeling inside. *I did* feel alone, and knew I needed something to fill that loneliness inside. Not of being physically alone, because I had a loving family and friends, but a spiritual loneliness that I knew only God could fill. As I stood there, a warm sensation rested over me—one that I can't explain. I held my face in my hands, as I fought the tears that were building inside me. As I sat there, I could feel my heart pounding as to what to do. Katie had helped me to this point in my life, but just like the title of that song, I knew I was alone. Alone to make this decision of whether to accept him or not. Alone to decide if I wanted this personal relationship with God, and all that came with it. And alone to make the biggest decision in my life.

Katie could see the emotional state I was in, and placed her arm around me. "Jess, are you okay?"

I shook my head back and forth. "I don't know… I just don't know."

As the chorus repeated, "Jesus…, I love you." I felt that warm sensation come over me once again. I began to sing softly along with the lyrics when I uttered the words, "Yes Jesus, *I do* love you."

When I said that, it was if something released inside of me, and all those tears I had been suppressing came bursting out. Katie once again held me close, as the tears were streaming down my face. I turned to her as the emotions reflected in my voice.

"It's time Katie—it's *my time*."

I rose from my seat and walked around the stage barrier to the front and stood there. Katie came with me and I could tell she motioned someone over from our youth group. As I stood there, I could feel all this stuff releasing inside me. At one point I felt like I couldn't stand anymore, so I got down on my knees. Suddenly, I felt a hand on my shoulder and realized it was Moses, who started to pray over me. A few of the girls from the group came and placed their hands on Katie as well. After a few moments she fell to her knees also, and I heard her weeping deeply. I felt another hand on my other shoulder and saw it was Pastor Tim. He leaned in close to me.

"Jess… do you want to accept the Christ as your savior?"

I nodded my head, "Yes, I do."

He then led me in the sinner's prayer. A prayer in which I had heard many times before. However, this time it was real. This time it meant more to me than just a bunch of words to repeat. And this time, I knew those words would change me for the rest of my life.

After we prayed, both Moses and Pastor Tim gave me a caring hug.

"Welcome to the Lord's family," Pastor Tim said. "You are now a child of God."

About that time, the girls who were praying with Katie helped her up, and I could tell she was emotionally drained. She turned to me with a warm, caring hug, and we both started crying again. I'm normally not much of a crier, especially in public, but I couldn't help it. I felt clean inside, like all of my past sins were forgiven and the hurts in my life were now washed away.

After it was over, Pastor Tim gathered everyone together and told us he was going to treat us to pizza. As we ate our pizza, most of the youth gathered around me and Katie. A lot of them wanted to know how we knew the band and how it came about that we were their roadies. Others came and gave me a hug or shook my hand, saying how happy they were that I accepted Christ into my life. Moses then came over and started to talk to me, one on one.

"Jess… this is so neat that you have become a true Christian. I say 'true Christian' because like you said yourself, you were a Christian by name only." He glanced over at Katie and then back to me. "You know, I think another one of Katie's prayer requests has just been answered."

I looked her way and smiled. "You know Moses... I have a feeling that a lot of *my prayers* were answered the day I met her."

About that time the group decided to go on a few more rides. Then we played some more games, trying to win stuffed animals while others went to buy souvenirs before we left for home.

When it was time to leave the park, we took our seats in the bus and talked about the fun-filled day we had at Great America. It was really neat to see everyone getting along, like one big family. At one point we started to sing a couple of songs which we sing in youth group. I say "we" because I now felt like I was a part of this new family. As we rode home, my thoughts reflected on my life. How I knew things were going to be much different than they were in the past. It's not like I thought my life would be perfect, because believe me... I knew from watching Katie, that life as a Christian is just as hard as anyone else's—maybe even harder. Christians try to live a pure life in a world that is trying to pull them down and is getting worse all the time. One thing that brought comfort to me was the knowledge that I had people around me to help with being a new Christian. Like my new friend Moses who seemed to come into my life at the right time.

After a while, things settled down to a murmur, as everyone was tired from being out all day. Katie then turned to me and spoke in a hushed tone.

"So, how do you feel?"

"It feels good—really good. I never thought you could actually feel God's spirit rest upon you. You also feel so clean inside—it's hard to describe."

"All your sins are now forgiven, that's why you feel so clean."

"You know, when I used to hear people talk about being 'saved' and saying you could feel it inside, I didn't believe them. But it's real, and I have you to thank for that."

"I only helped, but thank you for saying that. I have been praying for you for a long time and now God has answered my prayer. You know sometimes we think that God is not listening to our prayers, but God knows his perfect timing. And apparently your time was to come on our adventure at Great America."

After we talked a little more, the wear of the day hit us, and we laid our heads on the back of the seat. As Katie fell asleep, her head happened to fall on my shoulder. My head was facing her, so when her head fell on my shoulder, some of her hair fell in my face.

Now… I know this might sound dumb, but her hair smelled so good to me. I had never had a girl close enough to me to smell her hair, so this was a first for me. As I took in a breath of her sweet smelling hair, I didn't want to stop. However, feeling somehow it wasn't right with her being asleep and all, I pulled away. She then turned her head the other way, and it wasn't long before I must have fallen asleep myself.

When we arrived at the church, Katie's dad was waiting for us in the parking lot. When we got into the van he asked about our day.

"So, how did it go you two?"

"Good, Dad… very good!"

"Yes Mr. McCullough," I added. "We had a really great time. And guess what? You are now going to have a new person joining your church on regular basis."

"Really, Jess. Who's that?"

"Me!"

"Really?"

Katie interjected. "Yeah, Dad. Jess gave his life to the Lord today at the Sweet Comfort Band concert—it was awesome!"

Mr. McCullough glanced in the rearview mirror. "Really, Jess?"

"Yes Mr. McCullough. And like you told me the other day. Before I was just a fan, but now I'm a member of the team…"

CHAPTER NINE – THE PURSUIT OF JUSTICE

The following afternoon Becky called Katie, who invited her over to the house. When Becky arrived, the two of them went to hang-out in Katie's room. They were both sitting on the bed when Becky opened the conversation.

"So, how are you doing? When we were talking on the phone your voice sounded lower for some reason."

"My voice gets like this when I'm really tired. We didn't get back until late last night and then my parents were talking to me about the trip."

"So, how did it go at Great America? Did you and Jess go on another one of your adventures?"

"Actually, we did, but it was a different kind of an adventure."

"So what happened?"

Katie glanced to the side to gather her thoughts. "Well let's see… on the way there we saw a bus that caught on fire. Jess got mad at me, so he and Moses ditched us. At the Imperials concert, Chris was trying to flirt with me. Jess and I became set-up roadies for a Christian band. Jess accepted the Lord as his savior at the concert. Oh yeah… and on the way home, Jess was smelling my hair. I think that just about covers it."

"What? No way…! Come on Katie, tell me what *really* happened?"

"I'm telling you the truth. And in just about in that order."

"Okay, you're going to have to start at the beginning—and slowly."

"Becks, I'm really tired, so I'm going to have to give you the condensed version, okay?"

"Oh, alright." Becky said with a slight disappointment.

"Well, on the way to Great America, we saw a bus that had broken down on the side of the road. There were some people on that bus that were supposed to be set-up roadies for that group I like—Sweet Comfort Band. Jess and I had thoughts of sneaking in through a side gate to meet the band, when one of the band members came looking for those guys that were supposed to help them set up. He then asked us if we wanted to help, and that's how we became roadies for a Christian band. Earlier in the day, Jess got mad at me because he thought I was ignoring him, so he and Moses ditched us and went to play games at some arcade. Then at the concert that Jess didn't go to, Chris was trying to tickle me at times and kept calling me angel eyes. Then he started hinting about me and him going to another concert—just the two of us. The best thing that happened, was that Jess accepted the Lord at the concert. Well anyway, that's what happened."

"Okay, but you're forgetting the last part. What was this thing about Jess smelling your hair?"

"Oh, it was nothing—just forget it."

"No, it's not nothing! Katie, why do you always do that? When you have these little moments with Jess, you keep it to yourself."

"There's nothing to keep. It was just something that happened; it was innocent."

"Come on girl, I want details!"

"Okay, fine… On the way home, I guess I must have fallen asleep, and my head apparently fell on Jess' shoulder. Then I must have fallen back asleep again, and when I woke up, my hair was in his face. That's when I noticed he was smelling my hair. Like I said, it was innocent."

"Okay, back up a minute. You said that after you woke up, you knew your head fell on Jess's shoulder. So why did you leave it there?"

"I don't know, it just felt comfortable; that's all."

"I don't know, Katie. You have that same secretive smile on our face as you did last week. And as I recall, you said you were with Jess earlier in the day. I think you said the two of you were playing that game, Clue. Did something else happen that day too?"

Katie glanced to the side, trying to suppress her smile. "No... not really."

"Oh my God, look at you! You're blushing! Something did happen, didn't it?"

"I'm not saying anything—it was nothing."

"Well your *nothings* are a lot better than my *somethings*. You get to go on this great trip to an amusement park; get to meet a rock band, become the band's roadies, and now you have two guys that like you. I don't even have Jason anymore."

"I don't have two guys that like me. Jess and I are just friends."

"I don't know, my life is dull compared to yours. And here I thought that born-again Christians never have any fun."

"It's not *all good*. Now I have to deal with Chris. I don't know what to do about him."

Becky directed a teasing smile. "Oh poor little Katie... she has to worry about all these guys that like her."

Katie slapped her shoulder, "Would you stop!"

"Okay, but I would sure like to have some of *your* problems. So anyway, what's this thing with this Chris guy? Do you like him?"

"He's nice and all, but like I told you before, I'm not sure I want to be boyfriend and girlfriend with anyone yet."

"Why not? You just had a birthday; you're fourteen years old now."

"I know, but I'm just not ready. Besides, my dad won't let me officially date until I'm sixteen."

"Well, just wait. There's going to be a lot more guys to choose from in high school."

"We'll see... Anyways, we better start to get ready if we're going to the mall."

"Okay, I'll just sit and wait for you to finish getting dressed—me and my boring life."

"Well, if you think it's so boring, why don't you come to our youth group meetings? I know you said you are comfortable at your church, but we do a lot of fun activities—like that trip to Great America."

"I know, but I like things more structured not with all that clapping and singing fast songs."

"Okay, but the invitation is always open."

"I know, thanks."

*****

After our trip to Great America, things were a little different at home. My parents didn't seem to mind me going to church because I was doing things differently in my life. When a certain decision would come up, there was now this voice inside telling me the right decision to make. Because of that, I guess I was a better son to them. However, my new found faith did not please my sister Tami, and for some reason she seemed to resent it.

The following Monday we were all in the kitchen eating breakfast, when Tami wasted no time in showing her displeasure.

"So Jess…what's this I hear about you becoming a Christian?"

"Yeah, I did. At this concert at Great America." I turned my attention to my mom. "Hey Mom, I'm going over to Katie's today, is that alright?"

"Sure honey, but when are you going? I want you to make sure you do your chores first."

"I've already done them all, including cleaning the dog's pen. I just need to take out the trash and I'll be all finished."

"Really? Wow. You are really taking responsibility in helping out around the house. I am very proud of you."

"Thanks, Mom."

Then Tami interjected with her usual sarcasm. "So squirt... you and Katie going to have a Bible study today?"

"No, we don't have Bible studies all the time. Besides, I don't know why you have to make sarcastic comments like that anyways."

She half-laughed. "We'll see..."

"What do you mean by that?"

"I mean, we'll see if this is all for real or not."

"It's for real. I just don't know why you have such a problem with it."

"I have a problem with it because most Christians are a bunch of phonies. I have seen a lot of people who say they got 'saved,' but a few months later, they are back to acting the way they were before—sometimes even worse."

"You say it like you are hoping that will happen to me."

"No, I'm just saying, that people get all emotional when they become Christians. But when they come down from that emotional high, they realize it's not for real."

I would normally just brushed off her comments, but for some reason her words pierced me deep. Usually I would have some kind of harsh comeback, but I just sat silent. Hurt by her comments, I gathered my emotions and changed the subject.

"Anyway... how are your cheerleading tryouts going?"

"Fine. Cheryl and I have been working on a routine for the tryout this coming Friday. I think we will make the squad."

"Well, that's good. I hope you do."

I said that to encourage her, but in my mind I really didn't think she would make the squad. Tami just isn't very good when it comes to athletic activities. I went back upstairs and decided to read a little from the Bible. Pastor Tim said it would be good for me to read a little bit every day. The youth group was in the book of Proverbs, so I opened it up and started to read. I read about half a page, when this one verse seemed to jump out at me. Proverbs 18:5: *"It is not good to be partial to the wicked or to deprive the innocent of justice." (NIV)*

I thought it was kind of strange how I happened to read that particular verse. In the past few days I had been thinking about Rosemary Pullman and what we were going to do about her. At this point, I had pretty much decided we were too young and didn't know enough about the law to go up against a giant like Ian Thorpe and his corporation. However, after reading that scripture about not depriving the innocent of justice, I started to rethink us taking on the case.

Later in the day my mom was going to the store, so I asked her to drop me off at Katie's. She pulled into the driveway, and I took my bike and placed it on the porch. Katie greeted me at the door and we went inside.

"So Jess… have you been thinking about what we are going to do about Rose?"

"Actually, I was just thinking about it earlier this morning. I had been thinking we shouldn't do it because we're too young. But then I read a scripture about how we should never deprive the innocent of justice. So now I'm wondering if we should do it after all. How about you?"

"I was kind of like you. I wasn't sure we should do it either. But then I started to think how David defeated Goliath, and yet he was just a young teen like us. We might not have all the big weapons like Ian Thorpe and his lawyers will have, but we have God on our side. I think we should look into taking on this case for Rose."

"I think we should too. I guess we need to call Mr. McAllister about getting the phone number of that law firm, then make an appointment to go talk to them."

"Okay, I'll go call Mr. McAllister right now."

Katie called Mr. McAllister and told him we wanted to pursue the lawsuit on behalf of Rose. After giving us the name and phone number of the law firm, we made an appointment to meet with them. We knew at that point we were now fully into this, so we knew we had to tell our parents. That evening we got them together at our house to explain what we wanted to do. Katie stood in front of them and began to explain.

"Well, the reason we wanted to talk to you is to tell you about something that Jess and I want to do. But we need to make sure it will be alright with you guys first."

"What is it honey?" Mrs. McCullough asked.

"Well it's kind of a long story. But basically, Mr. and Mrs. McAllister asked us to do them a favor by finding this woman named Rosemary Pullman. That was the day they invited us over for blueberry pancakes. As it turned out, this big corporation pressured and even threatened Rosemary into signing an agreement to sell her condo. We also think they pressured others to do the same thing. For reasons I cannot go into, Mr. and Mrs. McAllister cannot be involved in pursuing an action against this company. However, they will help us with the money for all the court costs."

Mrs. McCullough sat up straighter in her seat. "Court costs? Pursuing an action? Katie what are you talking about?"

"We are talking about filing a lawsuit against a man named Ian Thorpe and his company called Equity One Realty Corporation."

As the name of the corporation lingered in the air, an inquisitive look drew upon Mr. McCullough's face.

"That's strange, where have I heard that name before?"

"Dad, you probably heard that name while at your job. I believe you might know this corporation from dealing with them at the building department."

"Oh yes, now that you say that I think I have dealt with them before."

Katie returned her focus to her mother. "Anyway Mom, Mr. McAllister gave us the name of this law firm that helps people like

Rose and others who have been discriminated against. They take on cases to help those who are elderly, or to defend people for their religious rights."

"So you mean to tell me that the two of you are bringing a lawsuit against a big corporation?"

"Not us, but we will be pursuing this on behalf of Rosemary along with this law firm."

"But you're just kids, Katie, what can you do?"

"Mom, I don't want to go into all the details, but Jess and I are pretty good at investigating into things. We are very good at finding clues and figuring things out. Besides, wasn't David just a teen like us when he went up against Goliath in the Bible?"

Concern ran across her face. "Yes Katie, but a lawsuit? We need to talk about this."

Mr. and Mrs. McCullough rose from the couch to discuss the matter and entered into the kitchen to talk privately.

"Babe," Mr. McCullough said. "I know you're a little worried about this, but I don't think anything will come of this. You need all kinds of evidence to pursue a lawsuit. I am sure this law firm will not take their little case seriously. But in the meantime, I think this could be a good learning experience for them, so let them do it."

"Okay, but this worries me. You know how they are—they're like bloodhounds. They get the scent of the slightest little thing and won't stop till they find it."

Mr. McCullough gently placed his hand on her shoulder. "It'll be alright. I'll keep an eye on them, okay?"

"Okay, I'll go tell them they can do this investigation."

They walked into the room, as Katie and I waited in anticipation.

"You can do your little investigation, as long as it's alright with John and Cindy," she said, and turned to them for their approval.

"It's alright with us," my dad said. "I don't want to discourage them from trying to do something nice for someone."

"Really?" we said with excitement.

"Yes, as long as you two don't get into any trouble. And pay attention to the McAllister's with whatever they want you to do."

"Oh, we will," Katie answered. "Jess and I will be on our best behavior."

Mr. McCullough turned to his wife with a wary eye. "Yes, where have we heard that before."

*****

The next day we went to the office building where the law firm was located and looked for the suite that said The American League for Law and Justice. When we walked in the door the woman at the front desk asked if she could help us. I stood up straight and tried to sound as professional as possible.

"Yes ma'am. I am Jesse Thompson and this is Katie McCullough. We have an appointment to see Dan Nelson."

The woman scanned us up and down with a questioning stare. Probably because we were teens.

"Okay, if you say you have an appointment, I will let him know you're here."

The receptionist let him know we were here through an intercom. Katie's mom stayed in the lobby while the secretary escorted us to his office. When we got inside, Mr. Nelson told us to have a seat.

"So... what can I do for the two of you today?"

With a quick glance, I let Katie know I wanted her to do the talking. I think she speaks better than I do when dealing with professional matters like this.

"Mr. Nelson... Jess and I were told from a friend of ours, Mr. Harold McAllister, that you might be able to help us."

"So Harold sent you? He is one of our best contributors; he has been very generous with his donations. We are a fairly new organization and people like Mr. McAllister have helped us tremendously. So explain to me what you are looking to do."

Katie went through the whole story, explaining every detail of what happened to Rose.

"And so that's the whole story Mr. Nelson. This is why we want to pursue some kind of action against Ian Thorpe and his corporation. We want to try to get Rosemary Pullman's condo back for her and others who probably feel the same way she does."

Mr. Nelson sat deep in thought, tapping his finger on his desk. Then he pulled a pen from his desk drawer and began to write down a list of things on a pad of paper. After a few moments he began to address a few things with us.

"First of all, let me explain how filing an action against someone works. The first step is to obtain documented evidence to support your claim, otherwise the court will throw it out. Secondly, that supporting evidence must violate some kind of law or ordinance. For example; from what you told me, this Rosemary Pullman was threatened and coerced into signing that real estate transaction. In order to pursue that, we would need her to sign an affidavit saying under penalty of perjury that she was threatened, and or coerced into signing that agreement under duress."

"What's an affidavit?" I asked.

"It's a legal document, signed under penalty of perjury, of her statement regarding what happened. It will be presented before the judge and Rosemary would need to testify to the facts of her statements. Now… there is something else on these lines. Since the two of you are the only witnesses to her making those statements, you yourselves would also have to take the stand and testify. Additionally, we are going to need more evidence than that in order to pursue this case. If you are going to try to pursue misrepresentation, then you need evidence that shows the homeowners were lied to, or made to believe that they needed to sell their properties. One of the obstacles we are going run into, is we are still a small law firm and do not have the manpower to be investigating and gathering evidence. The two of you will have to do the leg work on this case. This in turn, means you would also have to testify as 'Investigating Witnesses' regarding the evidence you discover. In the matter of fraud, we might be able to prove it, if there was *intent to defraud*. In other words, you would have to gather evidence that either shows this corporation deliberately lied to the owners, or knew what they told the owners was in fact, false."

Mr. Nelson leaned forward in his seat, as his face revealed the seriousness of the moment.

"Now… after hearing all of this, do you still want to try to pursue this case against Ian Thorpe and Equity One Realty Corporation?"

Katie and I glanced at one another contemplating the question. And although overwhelmed by all of this, we nodded our heads in agreement.

"Yes," she said. "We want to pursue this."

"Very well, I can see your firm resolve in pursuing this—that's good. Now, what I am going to do is to make you a case file. I will enclose the list of things we talked about in order to pursue this case. Then I will draft up some notes and have my secretary type it up for you. When it's ready in a couple of days, you can come back into my office to pick it up."

As we rose from our chairs to leave his office, Mr. Nelson shook our hands with admiration.

"You know, I do not meet many teens your age trying to do something nice for someone like a Rosemary Pullman. I don't know if you are aware of this, but we are a Christian based organization. Are the two of you Christians?"

"Yes we are. I have been a Christian most of my life, and Jess accepted the Lord about a week ago."

"Very good, I thought there was something different about you two. Actually, this is exactly the type of case we like, when an elderly person's rights have been violated or their religious rights are being taking away from them. I hope you can come up with the evidence needed to pursue this."

I offered a question. "Mr. Nelson… someone told us that if you want to get documents, that you have to do a subpoena to get them? Usually Katie and I just kind of get the evidence by our own ways."

He lowered his brow. "By your own ways? I don't like the sound of that. I was going to go over subpoenas when you came to pick up your case file, but basically any and all evidence has to be obtained legally. If you don't obtain it by legal methods, such as a subpoena, then the evidence will be thrown out by the judge and you look bad before the court. I'll go over the proper procedures the next time we meet. There is one other thing… we can provide the legal counsel, meaning a lawyer if this goes to a hearing. But there will also be many court costs in dealing with this case. Do you or Mrs. Pullman have that kind of money to pursue a case like this?"

"Yes we do. Jess and I have someone who will back us with all the money we need."

"Very good, I will see you in a few days."

"Okay, we'll see you then."

CHAPTER TEN – A GATHERING OF EVIDENCE

After we left his office we talked to the McAllister's about the status of the case. Mr. McAllister offered us any money we needed, and told us he felt we should try to gather the evidence before talking to Rose. He said he wanted the evidence first, in order to convince her we had a chance of winning the case.

A few days later, Katie and I got a call from Dan Nelson's office that our case file was ready to pick up. As we sat down with him, he went over the list of things we would need. He told us that since we knew the situation and the people involved, we would have to figure out what evidence we would need to pursue to prove the violations of the law.

When we arrived back at Katie's house, we looked over the package and began making a plan to gather the evidence. We sat down at the dining room table and she opened her notebook.

"Jess, let's talk this out like we do. That seems to work for us."

"Okay, you start first."

"Wait, before we start I need some sugar. My brain works better with a little sugar rush."

"Some Starburst?"

"No, not this time. My mom is making some brownies and I can smell then in the kitchen. Let's go and see if they're ready yet."

We walked into the kitchen, where the aroma of baking brownies made our mouths water. We sat at the kitchen table and eyed a batch of brownies she had just placed on a cooling rack.

"Okay you two, I see you eyeing those brownies. I thought you were busy working on that little investigation of yours?"

"We were, but then I realized I needed a sugar rush. Can we have a brownie?"

"Sure honey, but it worries me how you need so much sugar sometimes."

"I know, but I start to feel weak and light-headed if I don't have something sweet."

"It sounds like you might have Hypoglycemia."

"What's that?" she question, and took a bite of a brownie.

"It's kind of the opposite of Diabetes. You're body burns sugar very rapidly and the sugar level in your blood gets low. That's why you feel the need to eat something with sugar in it."

I glanced at her with a teasing smile. "Yeah Katie, that's why you're so skinny. You burn-off all those sugar calories. I mean just look at you—you look like a Twiggy!"

"What about you, Jess? It seems like you're the opposite. Maybe you shouldn't have any brownies at all, seeing how fat you're getting!"

I rolled my shirt-sleeve back and flexed my bicep muscle. "That's not fat, that's pure muscle!"

She laughed. "Pure muscle? You mean pure baby-fat!"

"Hey, I'm trying. Brian and I are working out for the upcoming football season."

"You're going out for football?"

"Sure am."

"What position are you going to play—fullback? I think that's the perfect position for you, considering that *your backside* is getting pretty full!"

Mrs. McCullough snapped sharply. "Katie…! That wasn't a very nice thing to say."

"We're just playing around, Mom. We always tease each other like this."

She shook her head. "I don't know about you two."

With Katie now pumped with a little sugar, we took our work into the den. She glanced to the side deep in thought before beginning.

"Do you know what I think we should do before we begin this whole lawsuit?"

"Pray?"

"Exactly…We need to have the Lord helping us with this. If he is not a part of this, then we will be doing this on our own strength."

We held hands and she said a prayer for God's hand to be upon us.

Over the next half hour, we talked the whole thing out about what evidence we would need. And although I was still a little unsure about this whole thing, I think we had a pretty good plan to gather the evidence.

Evidence for Rosemary Pullman Case
Re: Lawsuit to prove fraud, misrepresentation and coercion.

1. Contract Evidence: Need to make copies of Rose's contract and attachments

2. Any other Documents: Need to make copies of paperwork that said that all homeowners would be responsible to pay thousands of dollars for repairs.

3. Affidavit: Need Rose to sign statement that she was coerced and threatened.

4. Other statements from other Owners: Others who feel they were coerced too. Get Affidavits. (Mr. Richards, etc.)

5. Proving Fraud: Find a way to prove that Equity One Realty Corporation deliberately misled the owners about the building needing all that work.

6. Other: Witnesses. See which homeowners are willing to testify at a hearing.

"Katie, I think the first thing we should do is talk to the other homeowners and get some of their statements. I mean if Rosemary is the only one willing to say they were coerced into signing those contracts, then we won't have much of a case."

"I think you're right. And I know just the person who we can get all the names of the homeowners at Cedarwood?"

"From who?"

"From Ian Thorpe."

Shock ran across my face. "What!"

"Yes, Mr. Nelson told us that anytime we need to subpoena some records to call his office and they would have one served. We can serve Ian Thorpe with a subpoena to have him give us the names of all the homeowners at Cedarwood. From there we can contact them and get their statements."

"Oh yeah; that's good thinking. I'm sure Ian Thorpe has all that information in his files somewhere. Why don't we make a list of all the things we need, and we can do a subpoena all at once."

As she chewed on her pen-cap, her eyes suddenly sparkled with revelation.

"Jess, I have an idea. We should get a copy of the sign-in log sheet at Cedarwood."

"Why do we need the log-in sheet?"

"Remember when Rose was telling her story? She said those men from the Equity One came three times to her condo to try to force her to sign. That sign-in log sheet will help prove that they kept pressuring her to sign. It will go to show they were harassing her; especially if those records show that Ian Thorpe himself signed in. I mean, why would the CEO of a big corporation need to go see little ole' Rose about something."

I looked at her in admiration. "That's really smart. I'm glad I have you as my partner."

She smiled. "Me too Jess, me too."

*****

The next day we made an appointment to see Dan Nelson and showed him our plan to obtain the evidence for the case.

"Jess, Katie…, this is very impressive work for young people your age. However, I need to caution you before we issue out subpoenas. The minute you do that, it puts the other party on the alert and we don't want to do that at this point. Get me the Affidavit signed by Rose and any other individuals who are willing to testify that they were misled and or coerced into signing those agreements. You also need evidence that contradicts the statements that Equity One made to the owners about their complex having all this structural damage. Once we have that, then we can think about serving subpoenas. I wish I could give you more legal counsel right now, but all of my lawyers are tied up with other cases. You're going to have to try to muddle through this on your own. But if you have a question that you're not sure about, give me a call."

We left his office and decided to talk with Katie's father at the building department. Katie had an idea of how to get some of the evidence we needed. When we arrived she asked the clerk at the front counter to speak to him. A few moments later he greeted us with a look of surprise.

"Hey there you two. What are you doing here?"

"Dad, I don't know if you can do this, but can you get records on the property at Cedarwood?"

"Why pumpkin? What are you looking for?"

Katie motioned with her finger for him to lean-in closer. "Dad, maybe you shouldn't call me pumpkin in public while I'm conducting an investigation."

"Sure, I didn't think about the two of you being 'big time' investigators."

"Dad, what we're looking for is anything like an inspection report that might show that those condos were not in as bad of a condition as Equity One told those owners it was."

"That's not a problem. Any inspection report that comes into our office is a public record."

"Oh, that's good."

"However, I'll have to get it for you later since I'm pretty busy right now. But I'll make you a copy and bring it home with me, okay?"

"Okay, thanks Dad; we really appreciate it."

As we stood talking about the case, her dad turned to my mom. "So, how is it going with these two?"

"Oh you know them; the minute they get together they're like an unstoppable force."

"Yes, I know. But at least they are involved in something like this instead of getting into trouble like other kids their age."

"Yes, that's true."

Just then Katie remembered something. "Mom… we need to go back to Mr. Nelson's office. We forget to get the Affidavit forms from the secretary."

"Okay we'll go back, but after that, no more investigating for the day."

We picked up the forms from Dan Nelson's office and on the way home we started talking more about the case.

"Jess… maybe on Thursday before youth night we can go visit the McAllister's and let them know what's going on with the case."

I turned to my mom for her approval. "Is that okay, Mom? Can I do that on Thursday?"

"Sure honey, but it sounds like this is getting very serious and I'm getting a little worried about it. I didn't think it would go this far."

"What do you mean by that?"

"Come on Jess, the two of you are just kids. You don't really think you are going to pursue a lawsuit against a big corporation, do you?"

The way my mom said that hurt my feelings. I knew we were 'just kids' or teens, but I could tell she thought this was all a big joke. Katie glanced at me, and I could tell it discouraged her too.

*****

On Thursday, I rode my bike to Katie's. We went into the den and she laid out the documents on the table. Based upon my mom's recent comments, I wasn't feeling very confident about pursuing the case.

"So, do you think my mom is right? That we're just a couple of stupid kids, and this is all a big joke?"

"I don't think so," she said with confidence. "I think we are just doing what we feel is right. Oh, by the way... my dad was finally able to get those records on the property at Cedarwood. And guess what? We found a few things that were very interesting."

"Really?"

"Yes, my dad said he thinks there is something fishy going on. You need to take a look at these records. This is an inspection report they did on the Cedarwood complex in 1980, just three years ago. This report was requested by the prior owners of Cedarwood, a company called Sherman Investments out of Sacramento. The reason why they did that inspection was the result of some cracks in a couple of the lower units of the complex. It turned out these cracks were just 'surface cracks' and the report says nothing about there being any structural damage at all. The report shows that a few things need to be brought up to the new earthquake standards. However, the work needed to bring it up to these new standards doesn't need to be completed until January 1, 1988. That's five years from now! My dad also said there does not appear to be anything that Equity One could say the complex had all this structural damage. My dad then ran an estimate to bring the complex up to earthquake code and it would cost about $40,000.00 total. If you break that down between the 40 homeowners, it would only cost them $1,000.00 apiece."

My face lit-up with excitement. "Really? Then that means we have the evidence to prove the violation of misrepresentation. By Equity One telling the owners it was going to cost thousands of dollars, they misrepresented the facts."

"Yeah, and since this inspection report is public record, it means that Equity One knew about it. Which proves they deliberately misled those homeowners, which in turn means we have the evidence to prove the fraud violation."

"That's right! Now all we need is get a copy of that paperwork that Rose has, and have her sign that Affidavit. I also think we should talk to this Sherman Investments who were the prior owners. Maybe they have some information as to why they were selling the complex to Equity One in the first place."

"Good idea, Jess. I think we are really on a roll in gathering the evidence."

*****

The following day we had an appointment with the vice-president of Sherman Investments. We went into work with my dad, since his job is only a few blocks from their office. He dropped us off in front of the building and gave us some money to get something to eat afterwards. We walked into Sherman Investments and sat down with a man who introduced himself as Ralph Wheeler, Vice-President for the company.

I extended my hand. "Mr. Wheeler, my name is Jesse Thompson and this is Katie McCullough."

"Nice to meet you Jesse, Katie. How can I help you?"

I started to explain the story about what happened to Rose, when he interrupted me.

"I'm sorry, Jesse. Are you saying that the homeowners at Cedarwood were forced and possibly threatened to sell their condo's to Equity One?"

"Yes, sir, that's part of what we are trying to prove. That's why we wanted to know any information you could give us on the agreement you had with Equity One to sell the property."

"Jesse, if what you are saying is true then I will do everything I can to help you. I had no idea any of this was going on." He then glanced off to the side, deep in thought. "You know, come to think of it, when this file came by my desk, something told me I should look at it a little closer, but I didn't. We had a new person working for us in our Property Acquisitions and Sales Unit, and he was the one who handled this transaction. I thought it was awfully strange that all of the co-ops would want to sell."

An inquisitive look drew upon Katie face. "What do you mean that all of the co-ops would want to sell?"

"Well the way a Cooperative works, is that the homeowners don't actually own their condos, but lease the unit they live in. However, they can receive equity if the property or unit increases in value, and in turn they receive money if they sell their condo. We own the land and make our money by leasing out the units. Because we own the land, it was far less expensive for the buyers to lease their condos than to purchase the units. Because of that, we don't charge any association fees which is far better for the owners. However, the only way we can sell the property, is if all of the homeowners sign an agreement that they are willing to relinquish their leases to the new buyer. Let me take a look in the file because there is usually a time frame that all the owners must sign that agreement for the contract to be valid."

Mr. Wheeler went into another room and came back with the file. He began flipping through the paperwork.

"Let me see... here it is; September 1, 1983. That is the final date of closing on this purchase agreement."

Katie took the paperwork and looked it over. "Mr. Wheeler... are you saying that if Equity One does not get all of the homeowners to sign agreements to sell, then this deal does not go through?"

"Well yes, but according to the file, we did get signed agreements from all of the owners. The only thing we are waiting for is the closing date of September 1st."

"Mr. Wheeler, if we can bring you a person that does not want to sell, will this stop this transaction from going through?"

"No, I'm afraid not Miss McCullough—that's not how it works. Since we already have their signed agreements and Escrow has opened, there is nothing we can do to stop it."

"What if we could prove in a court of law that the owners were misled and coerced into signing these agreements? Would that stop the deal?"

"If you could get a court order or an adjudicated decision saying that Equity One was in violation, then yes that would make this deal null and void. The property would go back to us, and the condos would go back to the original owners."

"Mr. Wheeler, we are going to need copies of those signed agreements from your file so we can contact some of these owners to be our witnesses. Because of that, we will need to subpoena those records from you."

"That won't be necessary. Now that I am looking at this file I can tell there is something very wrong here. In fact, I always felt there was something suspicious about that person we had in our Property Acquisitions and Sales Department. He was just too eager to work on this particular file. At the time, I just thought he was a go-getter trying to make a good impression on us. Now that I think about it, I wouldn't put it past Equity One to plant someone in our office. Come to think about it, he quit just a few days after he filed this transaction into Escrow. This really upsets me that this was going on and I didn't catch it. I'll have my secretary make copies of all the files you want. By the way... if you do file that lawsuit against Equity One, I will be more than happy to testify for you."

"Thank you very much, Mr. Wheeler. You have been very helpful."

"No problem. And good luck you two."

"Thanks," I said. "We're going to need it."

*****

The next couple of days Katie and I spent most of the time gathering evidence. We obtained the contract documents from Rosemary Pullman, and had her sign the Affidavit. Based on the information we got off of the documents that Mr. Wheeler gave us, we began to make some calls to the homeowners of Cedarwood. We thought they would be happy to hear they might get their condos back, but after many calls we soon found that not to be the case. Katie then dialed the next person on our list.

"Mrs. Simpson…"

"Yes."

"My name is Katie McCullough. And we are looking into possibly pursuing a lawsuit against Equity One Realty Corporation. We believe they committed fraud and possibly forced you into signing your agreement with them. I was wondering if you would be willing…"

The phone then made a resounding, "CLICK," as she abruptly hung up.

"Another hang-up, Jess. Now I know what phone solicitors must feel like."

"I don't understand why they don't want to talk to us. We are just trying to help them."

"I know, but so far all we have is Samuel Richards who said he was also pressured into selling his condo. The only other person who is willing to testify, is that dirty-ole' man, Mr. Peterson, who said I have a sexy voice and kept calling me cutie pie."

"Do you think the homeowners are all scared to testify against Equity One?"

"Maybe, but this is very discouraging. I hope that Mr. Nelson thinks we have enough evidence to file the law suit."

"Well, I guess we'll see tomorrow."

*****

The next day, we took all the evidence we had gathered and took it to Mr. Nelson's office. He looked over the file, then got up from his desk and said he would be right back. With our nerves fluttering in our stomachs, we waited in anticipation of his return. On the one hand… we were nervous for fear of not having enough evidence to file the lawsuit. On the other hand… if he did think we had enough, then that meant we were going to court. A few minutes later he returned with another man by his side and began the introductions.

"David… I would like to introduce a couple of fine young investigators. This young man is Jesse Thompson, and this young lady is Katie McCullough. Jess and Katie… I would like you to meet David Johnson. He will be your lead counsel in representing the case of Rosemary Pullman vs. Equity One Realty Corporation."

Our eyes filled with excitement. "So you're taking our case?"

He nodded his head in the affirmative. "Yes, Miss McCullough, we are."

Then David turned his attention towards us. "Well you two, we have a lot for work before we can actually file this case. Come with me to my office so we can discuss a few things about the case."

We followed him into his office, where he told us to have a seat.

"Now before we begin, I want to know the reason you are pursuing this case? You do know this case has no monetary benefits to you, right?"

Katie sat up straighter in her seat. "Yes, we know we won't get any money out of it. But the reason why Jess and I want to pursue this case is to help Rosemary Pullman get her condo back. I guess it's the injustice of it all. I don't like to see people, especially elderly people, get pushed around and taken advantage of. It just gets me so mad!"

Mr. Johnson raised his brow, taking note of the fire in her eyes.

"Wow young lady, I can see there's a passion burning inside you about this."

"Yes sir, there is."

"Okay, good; that's all I needed to hear. Let's get started."

*****

Over the next several days we were very busy. Mr. Johnson worked on the case, issuing out subpoenas for records, and was coaching us on courtroom procedures and stuff like that. We didn't realize how many different motions and procedures you had to know. Katie seemed to catch on much quicker than I did, but I was still learning a lot. He interviewed Rosemary Pullman and Samuel Richards for their statements. He also interviewed that person who Katie said was a dirty-ole' man and had called her cutie pie. David determined that the dirty-ole' man, Thomas "Buck" Petersen, was not a good witness so we took him off our list. Basically this Buck Petersen thought the lawsuit was going to get him some money. So when he found out there was no money in it for him, he told David to forget it. David decided that considering the circumstances, we needed to 'protect our main witness.' He said that Rose shouldn't stay by herself, fearing that Equity One might try to threaten her some more. We decided it would be best if she stayed with Katie, since she seemed to take a liking to her. David also put Katie's father on the witness list to testify about the records from the building department. We filed the lawsuit on August 7th, hoping it would be enough time be completed before September 1st, the date the contract agreement between Equity One and Sherman Investments would be considered final and binding. Katie and I also had a special interest in the lawsuit being settled by that date, because on September 3rd, we had to start the ninth-grade.

A few days after we filed the suit we received a Notice to Appear for what they call an Arraignment. When I got my notice in the mail, suddenly it became very real to our families—especially for my mother.

"Jesse, please don't do this! Just say you cannot be a part of this!" she said, with tears welling in her eyes.

"Mom, I have to. I'm going to be one of the witnesses to our investigation. They need me to be there."

Tami was standing nearby and interjected. "Yeah, Mom, let the squirt go to court. Maybe they'll sentence him to jail!"

"Tami, don't you say that!" My mom snapped. "Up to your room—now!"

"To my room? How old do you think I am? I hate that everything in this house revolves around Jess! I can't wait till I graduate so I can get the heck out of this place!"

I knew there was something bugging Tami. So after talking with my mom and calming her fears about the upcoming trial, I went upstairs and knocked on my sister's door.

"Tami?"

"Leave me alone, Jess."

"Can I come in?"

"Whatever... it's a free country."

I walked in her room to find her just lying on her bed reading a magazine.

"Tami, what's the matter? Why are so upset with us all of a sudden?"

She kept her focus on the magazine. "You wouldn't understand."

"Come on, try me."

She lowered the magazine. "Well, while you were off playing 'investigator' with your little girlfriend, some things have not gone too good for me—but what do you care."

"*I do* care; I've just been busy."

"Do you see anything different in my room?"

I looked around her room. "No, it's looks the same to me."

"Notice the pictures on my walls?"

I glanced at her walls once more. "I don't know; I never really paid attention to your pictures."

"Notice how you don't see Cheryl or the other girl's pictures on my walls? Well those pictures are off my walls, because my so-called friends are out of my life!"

"What?"

"Yeah, I didn't make the cheerleading squad. So since I'm not a cheerleader like they are, they don't want anything to do with me. They make up excuses when I call and don't want to hang around me anymore."

Tears began to form in her eyes, so she lifted the magazine trying to cover the hurt.

"That's so messed up, Tami. But if that's how they are treating you, then they weren't your friends in the first place."

"Jess, spare me the 'you deserve better' speech, okay?"

"Tami, why don't you start to go to church with me? They have a lot of girls your age there. You can make new friends—better friends."

"Church? Give me a break. If there was really a God out there, he would have never made this world so messed up, or allow all this pain and suffering!"

I had never seen Tami like this before and it worried me. I didn't want to push the issue, so I backed off.

"Things will get better, Tami—you'll see."

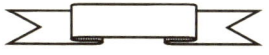

CHAPTER ELEVEN – THE TRIAL BEGINS

It was now August 7th, and we all met at the courthouse and waited for the Arraignment to start. When we walked into the courtroom it was empty except for this woman who I was told was the court reporter. She is there to type out every single word that is being said during the trial. There was also a uniformed officer standing to the side of the judge's platform, which added to the seriousness of what we were about to undertake. As we sat down, Katie nervously bit on her pen-cap.

"I'm a little anxious," she said, glancing around the courtroom.

"Don't be Katie," David reassured her. "This is only a formality."

About that time, we saw Ian Thorpe and a whole bunch of guys dressed in these fancy suits walk in the room. As he passed by where we were sitting, he directed a glaring stare and shook his head back and forth. I have to admit at that point I wasn't sure what we had gotten ourselves into.

Just then the officer of the court stood up and said, "Would you all rise for the honorable Judge Harold Wilson Sr."

We all stood up, as the judge began to address the court.

"I have read the case file before me. Who is the assigned legal counsel on behalf of the Plaintiff, Mrs. Rosemary Pullman?"

David stood up. "I am, your Honor. I am David Johnson from the legal firm of The American League for Law and Justice."

The judge turned to Ian Thorpe and his lawyer. "Who is representing the Defendant, Dr. Ian Thorpe II, CEO of Equity One Realty Corporation?"

"I am your honor. I am Mason Richardson from the legal team of Richardson, Ryan and Associates."

The judge cleared his throat. "Mr. Mason, I have read the allegations and charges against your client. There is one count of Misrepresentation, one count of Fraud and/or Intent to commit Fraud, and two counts of Coercion. How does your client plead?"

"Not guilty, your Honor, on all counts," Mr. Mason replied.

"Very well, a bench trial will be set for August the 12th, beginning at 8:00 am. We will begin proceedings at that time. All parties will be notified as to the assigned venue. This proceeding is adjourned."

The officer of the court stood up, "Would you all rise as the judge leaves. You are dismissed."

David began to put things back in his briefcase. I glanced around the room with a questioning stare.

"What? It that it?" I asked.

"Jesse... this is all an Arraignment is. The defendant and his attorney hear the formal charges being brought against him, and he pleads guilty or not guilty."

"So what did it mean by a bench trial?"

Katie turned to answer. "A bench trial means that this case is only going to be heard before this judge, not before people on a Jury—right David?"

"Very good Katie, that's exactly right."

"Well, that first part of this Arraignment was easy," I commented.

"You're right, Jesse," David said. "Now the hard part begins."

*****

On August 12th, we all showed up for the start of the trial. The courtroom was filled with a lot more people than were at the Arraignment. There was even a local newspaper reporter on hand to report on the happenings of the trial. Both of our parents came, as well as Mr. and Mrs. McAllister who sat way in the back of the courtroom. The officer of the court once again told us to rise, as the judge entered and took his seat. Rosemary Pullman was sitting next to David at the plaintiff's desk, while Katie and I sat behind them in the first row of bench seats. The judge then hit his gavel to call the proceedings to order.

"Mr. Johnson… would you please call your first witness for direct examination."

Direct examination meant that he would be asking questions of the witnesses for our side.

"Yes, your Honor," David replied. "I would like to call to the stand, Mr. James McCullough, Senior Building Inspector for the Town of Fuller Creek Building Department."

Katie's dad walked up to the stand, as the officer of the court made him raise his right hand and give an oath.

"Do you promise to tell the truth and nothing but the truth, so help you God?"

"Yes," Mr. McCullough said.

David then began his examination.

"Mr. McCullough… you are the Senior Inspector for the Town of Fuller Creek Building Department. Do you recognize this document known as Exhibit #7?"

Mr. McCullough took the document in hand and looked it over. "Yes I do."

"Can you explain to us what this document is and how it relates to the structural condition of the property at Cedarwood?"

"Yes, this is an inspection report dated April 6th, 1980. It was requested by Sherman Investments due to concerns over some cracks on interior walls on a couple of the units in the complex. After a thorough inspection, it was revealed the cracks were only surface cracks and there were no signs of any structural damage."

"Now Mr. McCullough… statements have been made by Equity One Realty Corporation to the owners at Cedarwood saying their complex needed 'urgent repairs' of extensive earthquake retrofitting to bring the complex up to earthquake codes. Can you explain how these statements relate to the findings of this report?"

"Yes, the new earthquake standards were not established until last year and require that all buildings in the Town of Fuller Creek be brought up to code standards by January 1st, 1988. This means the owners at Cedarwood would have approximately five years to bring the property up to those standards. Five years does not indicate to me an 'urgency' to bring it up to code."

Mr. Mason rose to his feet. "Objection, your Honor! Mr. McCullough is giving his personal opinion as to the 'urgency' of these repairs."

"Objection sustained. Mr. McCullough, please stick to the facts and findings of the report only."

"Yes, your Honor."

David then continued. "Mr. McCullough... as Senior Building Inspector with twenty years of experience, in your professional opinion, how much would it cost to bring Cedarwood up to earthquake standards, and in turn, cost each owner personally?"

"I did a work up based on current constructions costs, permits, etc. and came up with a total cost of approximately $40,000.00. When you divide that between the 40 owners, it comes out to a cost of only $1,000.00 each."

"Thank you, Mr. McCullough. No further questions, your Honor."

The judge then turned to the defense. "Mr. Mason... do you have cross examination for this witness?"

"No, your honor; not at this time. But we reserve the right to cross examine this witness at a later time."

"Very well, we will take a 20 minute recess and reconvene at that time."

I found out that "reconvene" simply meant that we would return back to the court after taking a break. I didn't understand why they had to use all that fancy language. I mean why they couldn't just talk in plain English is beyond me. Anyway..., we went outside and started talking with David on how he felt the trial was going.

"Well, I think things are going pretty good so far. The fact that their defense lawyer, Mr. Mason, did not want to cross examine Katie's father was a good thing. Usually it means that the evidence we brought up was good and they don't want to touch it."

"So what's next?" I asked.

"Well, Equity One has a couple of homeowners from Cedarwood that are going to testify on their behalf. I don't know the woman they have set to testify, but the other one is not a very credible witness."

When we went returned to the courtroom, the judge asked the defense lawyer, Mr. Mason, to call up his first witness.

"Yes, your Honor. I would like to call to the stand, Mrs. Lucinda Sanchez."

This woman, who spoke in broken English, rose from her seat and took the stand. Mr. Mason walked up confidently and stood next to the witness stand.

"Mrs. Sanchez... when the men from Equity One came to talk to you about selling your condo, did you feel they pressured you in any way or threatened to sell your home?"

"Oh no, they are good people. They made me a good offer to buy my home."

"Now, when you were told that the cost for repairs could be a lot of money, how did you feel about that?"

"I was afraid because I no have money for repairs. I have only a small retirement check each month."

"So what you are saying Mrs. Sanchez, is that even if the repairs were $1,000, which is a questionable estimate which can be disputed. Is the amount still too much for you come up with?"

"Oh yes, too much money for me."

As this woman was giving her testimony, I could see David quickly write some things in his notebook. He then began to run some numbers on his calculator. After Mrs. Sanchez was finished answering the questions, the judge asked David for his cross-examination of this witness. David rose from his seat and began his examination.

"Mrs. Sanchez... you stated to Mr. Mason that $1,000.00 is a lot of money. And to look at coming up with a $1,000.00 dollars all at once, it does seem like a lot of money, doesn't it?"

"Oh yes, very much money."

"Mrs. Sanchez... do you always cook your dinner and other meals at home."

"No, not every day. I have family, and we go out to eat at restaurants sometimes."

"Where do you like to eat at Mrs. Sanchez?"

"I like to go to the Sizzler."

"Yes, so do I; I like their Malibu Chicken. Now... how many times per month would you say you go out to eat?"

Mr. Mason rose to his feet. "Objection, your Honor! I don't see the relevance in this line of questioning. What does Mrs. Sanchez's eating habits have to do with this case?"

David countered. "Your Honor, my line of questioning is leading to a relevant question."

"Objection overruled. But Counselor, please get to the question."

"Yes, your Honor. Now Mrs. Sanchez... how many times per month would you say you go out to eat?"

"I think about four times a month."

"And how much would you say on an average, does your meal cost you—say at the Sizzler?"

"For everything? Drink and tip?"

"Yes, everything."

"I think fifteen or sixteen dollars."

"Do you think that's a lot of money?"

"No, not a lot of money."

"Mrs. Sanchez... do you know how much, $16.50 times 60 months equals?"

"No, I'm no good at math."

"It equals to about $1,000.00. Which means, if you simply saved the money of only one meal per month for the next five years, you would have saved enough money for your part of those repairs on your building. Now…, does that seem like a lot of money to save towards those repairs?"

"No, I don't think that's too much money to save. I'm getting too fat anyways; I cannot eat at Sizzler once a month."

"Thank you, Mrs. Sanchez. No further questions, your Honor."

Katie and I looked at each other like, "Yes! We won that one!"

I glanced over to the defense lawyer and Ian Thorpe, and they were not happy with what just happened to their witness on the stand, which was good for us.

After Mrs. Sanchez left the stand, the judge asked for the next witness to be called. Mr. Mason stood to this feet and prompted his next witness.

"I would like to call to the stand, Mr. Thomas "Buck" Petersen."

When Katie heard his name, she perked up with interest. She recalled the name as being the dirty-ole' man that called her "cutie pie" on the phone. Mr. Petersen said his oath, as Mr. Mason began his examination.

"Mr. Peterson…"

"You can call me Buck."

"Okay, Buck. When you were approached by Equity One about selling your condo, how did they treat you in your dealings with them?"

"These people from Equity One made me a right-good offer, and I jumped at the chance to get out that place! I knew that building was falling apart. I worked in construction for some forty-years, and they are crazy when they say that those cracks were not structural."

"Now… did anyone from Equity One ever pressure you to sell your property?"

"No, sir. They were very generous with their offer to buy me out of my lease, and they paid me a handsome sum of money for the appreciation of the property."

"Thank you, Mr. Petersen. No further questions, your Honor."

David then leaned over to us and whispered, "Sounds like this guy rehearsed everything he said. I wonder how much they paid him to say that."

The judge pounded his gavel. "Counselor! Do you have something to say or would you like to make a motion?"

"No, your Honor. I apologize for the interruption."

"Very well. Since we are approaching lunchtime, we will take an hour break and reconvene then."

We were all dismissed from the courtroom and headed to the cafeteria. My mom and dad, as well as Katie's parents came along with us.

"It looks pretty good so far, wouldn't you say?" my dad commented to David.

"Yes, but we have a long way to go. I have a feeling these guys have something up their sleeves, but we will have to wait and see. Now in regards to our cross examination of Buck Petersen, it may not get us anywhere. I think this guy has been paid-off to say what they want him to say. Do you remember when I asked him to be our witness? The minute he found out we were not going to pay him any money, he said to forget it—that he wasn't going to do something for nothing. Anyway, I'll question him, but it's probably going to be a waste of time."

After we ate our lunch, our party was asked to move from the cafeteria so the defense team with Ian Thorpe, Mr. Mason, and his witnesses, could now eat. As we were leaving the cafeteria we passed by their party, when Katie quickly turned to me with a disgusted look on her face.

"Oh my God, that was totally gross!"

"What Katie? What's gross?"

"That dirty-ole' man Buck Petersen. As we were passing by, he looked me up and down and then he pushed his lips at me, like to kiss me or something."

"That's gross—the pervert!"

As we made our way back through the hallway, I could tell Katie was deep in thought. She then pulled David aside and they began discussing something among themselves. When they were done, David replied, "Sure Katie, I can make a motion for that. Now you're not on the list, but we can try."

When the hearing reconvened, David rose from his seat to make a motion.

"Your Honor… I would like to make a request to have Miss Katie McCullough be assigned as co-counsel to cross-examine this particular witness."

Mr. Mason quickly rose to his feet. "Objection! Miss McCullough was not on the original list of authorized assigned counsel."

I leaned over the bench seat and called out in his direction. "Hey Mason! What's the matter? You afraid of a fourteen year old girl!"

The pounding of the judge's gavel resounded throughout the courtroom.

"Mr. Thompson! You are out of order! Sit down and refrain from any further outburst. And Counselor… please keep your witnesses under control."

"Yes, your Honor," David said, and then gave me a glaring stare.

I could tell David was very upset with me, but my little plan worked like I wanted. Mr. Mason then turned and looked straight at me while addressing the judge.

"Your Honor, I have no objection to Miss McCullough acting as co-counsel."

"Very well. Miss McCullough, you may precede."

Katie then walked up and stood in front of Mr. Petersen. The judge reminded Mr. Petersen that he was still under oath.

Katie approached the witness in a care-free manner. "Hi Mr. Petersen..."

He eyed her up and down. "You can call me Buck, there sweetie."

"You know Buck, we have met before."

"Before today? I think I would have remembered *you*," he said, raising his eyebrows at her—the pervert!

"Yes, don't you remember? We spoke on the phone a few weeks ago. I believe you called me cutie-pie."

"Objection, your Honor!" Mr. Mason shouted. "What does this ridiculous banter have to do with anything?"

"Objection sustained... Miss McCullough, please try to stick to questions for the witness."

"Yes, your Honor. Now Mr. Buck... in that conversation I had with you, at first you said you would be a witness for our side. So why did you change your mind?"

"Well sweetie, I got to thinking about things differently—that's all."

"Well that's too bad, because I wish you would have been a witness *for our side*," she said in a flirting way.

"Well, you got my full attention now, sweetie—I'm all yours," he said with a smile. Which was so gross because he had half his teeth missing.

At this point, I could tell she had this guy all tied up in knots, and was playing him like a fiddle. She then edged in closer to the witness stand, and gave that cute little pout of hers.

"Well that's too bad, Buck. Because I would have liked for you to be *my witness*," she said with a flirtatious flip of her hair.

He quickly sat up straighter in his seat. "Oh sweetie! It's not that I didn't *want you*. It's just that your side couldn't pay me enough money to be your witness."

His words lingered in the air and fell heavy on the courtroom. Everyone looked around as they realized what he had just admitted. Katie then turned confidently to the judge.

"I think this witness is done, don't you? No further questions, your Honor."

Ian Thorpe and Mr. Mason shook their heads in disgust, as Katie had torn apart this guy's credibility. At that point the judge decided it was getting late and he said we would continue with the hearing the following Monday.

As we began to walk out of the courthouse, David told Katie how good she did in getting Buck Petersen to show his true character and discredited himself as a witness. I also saw a side of Katie that I had never seen before, in that flirty kind of way. I have to admit, it kind of intrigued me.

CHAPTER TWELVE – PLAYING WITH THE "BIG BOYS"

The weekend passed quickly, and we were back in court the following Monday. The judge called everyone to order and told Mr. Mason to call up his first witness for the day.

"Yes, I would like to call to the stand, Norman Dietz from the Town of Fuller Creek Building Department."

Upon hearing his name, a look of surprised and concern ran across Mr. McCullough's face. Mr. Dietz walked up and took the witness stand.

"Mr. Dietz… you are an employee for the Town of Fuller Creek Building Department and your current position is the Assistant Clerk in the records department. Is this correct?"

"Yes, I am."

"Now Mr. Dietz… I understand you have with you an inspection report done on the subject property at Cedarwood, dated August 15, 1981."

"Yes, that is correct."

"How did you come to have this inspection report in your possession?"

"I received a subpoena for records regarding any and all inspection reports on the subject property. What I found in the file were two inspection reports. The one which Mr. McCullough presented to the court the other day, and the one that is being presented at this time."

David rose to his feet. "Objection, your Honor! This person was not on the witness list. There were no Rights of Discovery given to us regarding this new evidence that is being brought before this court."

I could tell this whole thing caught David off guard and he was not happy about it by his stern objection. The judge thought on it for a moment, before giving his answer.

"I hear your objection, Counselor. However, for the time being I am going to allow it until it is determined what bearing, if any, it will have on this case."

David shook his head in disagreement over the judge allowing this evidence to be presented at this time. Mr. Mason then continued with his examination.

"Now Mr. Dietz... what can you tell me about this inspection report?"

"When I received the subpoena for these records, I went to the back room and saw the file we had on the property at Cedarwood. In the file was the inspection report from 1980, which Mr. McCullough testified to. However, I also found another inspection report that seemed to be pushed way in the back of the cabinet—almost like someone was trying to hide it."

David rose to his feet. "Objection, your Honor! I would like to know just what Mr. Dietz is implying. Is he saying that that Senior Building Inspector James McCullough deliberately withheld another report?"

"Objection sustained. Mr. Dietz, please reframe from personal opinions and stick to the facts."

"Yes, your Honor. Anyway, as I was saying... when I looked at this other report, it was dated *after* the report that Mr. McCullough presented to the court. What this report basically says, is that there is *in fact* structural damage to the complex, with a cost to repair at a minimum of $500,000."

David rose to his feet. "Your Honor, I would like a ten minute recess to confer with my witnesses. I feel this time should be granted considering this new evidence was brought before this court without us having Right of Discovery."

The judge pounded his gavel. "Granted... We will break for ten minutes."

We walked into the hallway as David gathered us together to discuss the report. David asked Katie's dad about this Mr. Dietz and this other report.

"That report has to be a false." Mr. McCullough said. "This Mr. Dietz is just the kind of shady guy that I could easily see Equity One paying off to make up a phony report."

"Mr. McCullough, I am going to put you back on the stand. But first we are going to request to have a look at this *so-called* other report."

When we returned to the courtroom, David and Mr. McCullough were allowed to examine the other report. Mr. McCullough was put back on the stand, as David began his examination.

"Mr. McCullough... you have now examined this other inspection report. Have you ever seen this inspection report before today?"

"No, I have never seen it before. And upon inspection of this report, I have seen a few things that would bring its validity into question."

"What things are you referring to, Mr. McCullough?"

"First of all, the paper that it's printed on appears to very new. It is not faded or dog-eared like a document that has been handled a lot. Also, as Senior Building Inspector, any and all inspection reports have to go through my desk for my signature. My signature is not on this report."

"Thank you, Mr. McCullough. That is all the questions I have."

The Judge turned to Mr. Mason and asked him if he wanted to cross examine.

"Yes, your Honor, I do."

Mr. Mason walked up to the witness stand. "Mr. McCullough... you testified a few minutes ago that the paper this report was printed on appeared to be new. Therefore you were doubting its validity. Now Mr. McCullough… are you an 'expert' in paper processing?"

"No, but…"

Mr. Mason interrupted. "Just answer the question, Mr. McCullough. Are you an expert to determine the age of paper or methods of paper processing?"

"Well, no."

"No, I didn't think so," he said, with a tinge of sarcasm.

Katie and I looked at each other and just shook are heads. I was starting to get a bad feeling in my stomach.

"Now Mr. McCullough… you also testified that this report was not valid because it did not have your signature on it. Mr. McCullough, what is your anniversary date of being married with your wife."

"I don't see what that has to do with anything, but it's August 15th".

"Now isn't it true that you always take that day off to celebrate your anniversary with your wife?"

"Yes, I do."

"Well then Mr. McCullough… if you took that day off, then how could you be at your desk to sign this particular inspection report? You weren't even in the office that day!"

Katie's dad, David, and all of us, knew we were in trouble. And just when we thought things couldn't get worse—they did.

"Now Mr. McCullough… isn't it true that you have a daughter by the name of Katie McCullough who has now been assigned as co-counsel of behalf of the Plaintiff Rosemary Pullman?"

"Yes, she's my daughter."

"Well it seems to me that you would probably do anything for your own daughter. Like trying to hide evidence from this court!"

David abruptly stood to his feet. "Objection, your Honor! Counselor is making unfounded accusations and is badgering the witness."

"Objection sustained. Counselor, please reframe from such commentary."

"Your Honor, I would like to make a motion, as there appears to be a conflict of interest between this witness and his daughter. Since she is now assigned as co-counsel, it is a conflict of interest for her father to be a witness on behalf of the Plaintiff. I move to have Mr. McCullough's testimony removed and stricken from the record."

The Judge thought about it for a few moments, before making his decision.

"I would have to agree with Mr. Mason that there appears to be a conflict of interest in this case. I also determine that this other inspection report brought before this court by Mr. Norman Dietz, be declared invalid based on the fact that the proper Rights of Discovery were not allowed. Both of these inspection reports and testimonies will be thrown out. We will now break for lunch and return at 1 p.m."

As we left the courtroom, you could see the dejection draped across our faces. This was the first time things didn't go our way, and we could tell that David was starting to get worried. As we were eating lunch, we began to discuss what had transpired in the courtroom. Katie's dad opened the conversation.

"I'm sorry, David. I didn't even think that being her father would be a conflict of interest."

"Actually, it wouldn't have if I had not assigned Katie as co-counsel. It's not your fault, Mr. McCullough, I slipped up."

"But how did they know when my anniversary is to be able to put that date on that false inspection report?"

"These guys are slick and they have the resources to make all kinds of things suddenly appear. Looks like our case for Misrepresentation is gone. We will have to focus on the count of Coercion. Katie… I think I will put you on the stand as being a witness to the statements by Rosemary Pullman. You were the primary person who Rosemary told the story to of how she was threatened and coerced into signing that agreement."

"Okay, no problem."

When we returned to the courtroom, David put Katie on the stand. She began to tell the story of her conversation with Rosemary.

"It all started when some friends of ours, asked Jesse Thompson and me to do them a favor by locating Rosemary Pullman. When we found her, Rose began to tell me the story of her dealings with Equity One. She told me that Mr. Ian Thorpe and another man had threatened her into signing that agreement. Rose said they also threatened to send her to a mental institution, and that is why she sold her condo to Mr. Thorpe and his corporation."

"Thank you, Miss McCullough. I have no further questions, your Honor."

The Judge turned to the defense. "Mr. Mason... you may proceed with your cross examination of the witness."

"Miss McCullough… you mentioned in your testimony that you did a favor for some friends of yours to locate Rosemary Pullman. Just who were these friends of yours and why aren't they here to be witnesses for Mrs. Pullman?"

Oh God. I thought. *Katie can't tell who these friends are, because they are the McAllister's.*

She hesitated for a moment, and glanced towards the back of the courtroom, before returning her focus to Mr. Mason.

"I can't say who those friends are. They wish to remain anonymous."

"Why do they wish to remain anonymous? Is it because they heard something different than what you are testifying to!" he said, raising his voice.

"Objection, your Honor!" David said. "Counselor is putting words in the witnesses' mouth."

"Objection sustained. Move on Counselor."

"Yes, your Honor. Now Miss McCullough… I understand that you and Jesse Thompson have gotten yourselves into quite a bit of trouble over the years."

A questioning look grew on her face. "I don't know what you mean, Mr. Mason."

"Well, I have a pretty large file here which shows that you and Mr. Thompson have gotten yourselves into quite a bit of trouble—including with the law!"

David rose to his feet. "Objection, your Honor! We were not given Right of Discovery of this 'file' that Mr. Mason is bringing before this court."

Mr. Mason interjected. "Your Honor, the reason there was no Right of Discovery, is because we did not have time to give one. We just obtained these records late yesterday afternoon. And the reason we felt the need to obtain this information, is because Miss McCullough was assigned as co-counsel. We wanted to find out a little more about her and her background. Since we were not given prior notice when Miss McCullough was assigned as co-counsel, I feel this court should give us that same consideration in allowing this information with no prior notice as well."

The Judge thought it over a moment. "I will allow it."

David started to object, but the judge held up his hand. "Your objection is noted Mr. Johnson, but I am going to allow it."

I could see the concern on both David's and Katie's face, and I knew we were in trouble. Mr. Mason smiled confidently as he walked back to the witness stand to continue his examination.

"Now Miss McCullough… I have evidence in this file that I would like to bring to the court's attention. First of all, I have a report from the Fuller Creek Police Department which shows that you and Jesse Thompson were found to be 'Trespassing' on private property. And although no charges were filed, there is still a formal report on file. Also, we found another report from the Sherriff's Department in the County of Coconino in Arizona. In that report you 'alleged' to have seen a homicide site where you 'claim' to have seen a pair of skeletons. Yet when this was further investigated, your claims could not be proven. Also, there is a report with the Fuller Creek School District that you received a 'Warning' for once again trespassing in an 'unauthorized area' of the Museum of Natural History in Sacramento. And in the process of doing that, you lied to an official from the museum where you and Mr. Thompson fled from the scene after being told not to move from those premises. Furthermore, Dr. Ian Thorpe can testify to the fact that you misrepresented yourself to be a 'Becky Summers' gathering information for your case. It seems to me, that you and your partner, Jesse Thompson, have a long history of making up stories and lying to the authorities. So tell me Miss McCullough... isn't this just another one of your 'little adventures' making up this whole story about Rosemary Pullman being threatened? I mean, how can we trust a single word you are saying, when you have lied about so many things in the past!"

I could see Katie starting to get emotional, as Mr. Mason pounded away at her. As the tears began to well in her eyes, I finally had enough and stood to my feet.

"Leave her alone! If you want to question someone, question me, you jerk!"

The judge pounded his gavel. "Mr. Thompson! One more outburst like that and I will have you removed from this courtroom!"

Katie then swallowed her emotions and tried to answer the accusations which Mr. Mason had brought against her.

"Yes, Mr. Mason, Jess and I have done those things. But not in the way you are making it out to be. Jess and I *have* made a few mistakes. But I'm not lying about Rosemary Pullman, so don't try to make it out like I am, because I'm telling the truth!"

Mr. Masons smirked and shook his head. "The truth? I'm not so sure you even know what that means," he muttered, walking away from the witness stand.

As Katie got off the stand, I knew we were in trouble. Mr. Mason had torn down our integrity as witnesses, and so her testimony was discredited. The judge then decided to call it a day and dismissed us. As we began to walk out of the courtroom, Katie and I happened to pass by Ian Thorpe and his legal team. As we passed by, he turned to us with a smirk on his face and a few departing words.

"And that's what it's like to play with the big boys, kiddies!"

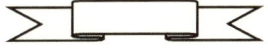

CHAPTER THIRTEEN – DAVID AND GOLIATH

When we arrived home from a very bad day in court, Katie and I sat dejected on the couch. Mr. McCullough tried to give us some words of encouragement.

"Don't feel bad you two. No matter what happens tomorrow, I am so proud of you for trying to defend Rosemary."

My dad added. "I am very proud of you also. These high-priced 'suits' have had to resort to cheating in order to win this case. That's pretty impressive that you have pushed them into having to do that."

"Thanks for saying that," I said. "But I guess all of our 'little adventures' that Katie and I have gone on, have probably cost us this case."

Mr. McCullough placed his hand on my shoulder. "Jesse... by way you and Katie live your lives, you are experiencing things that most of us would only dare to dream of. The two of you have such a sense of adventure—don't ever lose that."

As our parents came and hugged us, it felt good to feel their support. But on the other hand, it was going to take a lot more than their support, to win this case.

*****

It was the final day in court. David met us at the front of the courthouse just before 8am and pulled our team to the side. The discouraged look on his face spoke volumes.

"I have some more bad news. Samuel Richards petitioned the judge last night to be removed from our list of witnesses. Apparently Ian Thorpe and his high-priced lawyers got to him too. I tried to call him last night when I was notified of this, but when he heard my voice he hung up on me. I have to say, it's not looking good right now. All we have left is Rosemary's testimony, and I hope she holds up."

As we took our seats in the courtroom, the judge started the proceedings by asking David to call his next witness.

"Yes, your Honor... I would like to call to the stand, Mrs. Rosemary Pullman."

Rosemary made her way to the stand and said her oath. With the knowledge of her being a little nervous, David approached her with a calm and reassuring voice.

"Good morning Rosemary. I'm going to ask you a few questions, so just relax and answer them as best you can. What I would like you to do, is describe in your own words your understanding of the purchase agreement to sell your condo. Also, please explain to us your dealings with Ian Thorpe or any other person employed by Equity One Realty Corporation."

Rosemary looked nervous being on the stand. Her voice quivered as she began to tell her story.

"All of us at Cedarwood were asked to have a meeting with this company, Equity One Realty Corporation. They showed us all kinds of documents, most of which we did not understand because it was in legal terms. One of the men from their company explained they were there to possibly buy the property from us. They said they had inspected our complex and it was not safe—saying something about structure damage. They told us in order to do these repairs, it would cost thousands of dollars for each homeowner. They told us they would be contacting each of us to discuss selling our condos, and they would make us very good offers above market value."

"Thank you, Rosemary. Now tell us the part about how Equity One pressured you into signing that agreement with them."

"Objection, your Honor!" Mr. Mason shouted. "Counselor is putting words in the witness' mouth. Saying that Equity One pressured her into signing the agreement."

"Objection sustained... Mr. Johnson, please re-phrase the question."

"Yes, your Honor. Rosemary… would you please tell us about your dealings with Equity One and any problems you might have encountered with them."

"One day a man from Equity One came to my door and spoke to me about selling my condo. I told him I didn't want to sell, but he told me to think it over and he would leave the contract with me. A few days later, well…, I think it was a few days later, he came back and tried to convince me to sell again. He kept saying if I didn't sell that it would cost me more money because then all of those repairs would fall on me and anyone who did not want to sell either. The next day he came back again, but this time he had Mr. Thorpe with him. They tried to get me to sell my condo, but once again I told them, no, that I did not want to sell. Then this Mr. Thorpe offered me ten-thousand dollars more if I would sell to him. I told him that I still wasn't interested in selling. This is when they sat down next to me and started to pressure me. Then Mr. Thorpe threatened me by saying that I was mentally unstable and that he would put me in a mental institution. I was so scared, I was shaking. Because they were threatening me, I went ahead and signed the agreement even though I didn't want to."

David reached out and gently placed his hand on her shoulder. "Thank you, Rosemary. I know this was hard for you." He turned to the judge. "I have no further questions, your Honor."

The judge turned to the defense. "Counselor… you may cross examine the witness."

Mr. Mason walked towards Rosemary like a lion ready to pounce upon a wounded lamb. I could tell by the fearful look on her face, that she was deathly afraid of him.

"Mrs. Pullman… do you remember when you were first given the original contract agreement to sell your condo?"

"No, I can't remember the exact date, but sometime in late March, I believe."

"And do you remember who gave you that contract?"

"Well… there was a man who came to my condo and gave it to me. But I don't remember his name."

"So let me get this straight. You testified in detail that a man came to your condo twice, and that Dr. Thorpe himself came to your condo and offered you more money to buy your condo. It just seems odd that you remember that part in such detail, yet you can't even remember the name of the person who gave you the contract in the first place?"

Panic and confusion rose upon her face. "Well, sometimes I can be forgetful, so I don't remember his name."

"Perhaps, Mrs. Pullman you were coached on what to say before this court!"

David rose to his feet. "Objection, your Honor! Counselor is stating his opinions before this court."

"Objection sustained. Counselor, please refrain from your personal opinions." The judge glanced towards the court reporter. "Mr. Mason's comments will be stricken from the records."

Mr. Mason continued his examination.

"Mrs. Pullman… please listen to this very carefully so you can understand this. Why did you first sign the contract agreeing to sell your condo, and then turn around and sign another document saying you never wanted to sell?"

Mrs. Pullman lowered her brow in confusion. "I don't remember that second document you are talking about?"

"Objection, your Honor." David said. "Mr. Mason is being vague in order try to confuse the witness."

"Yes, Mr. Mason. Please make your questions straight forward. Objection sustained."

"The document I am referring to is the Affidavit given to you by your Attorney, David Johnson. In that Affidavit you signed, you attested to the fact that you never wanted to sell your condo."

"Oh yes, he wanted me to sign it because I didn't want to leave my home at Cedarwood."

"He *wanted you* to sign it?"

"Yes, he said I needed to sign it for the case."

"So are you saying he pressured you into signing it? Like you are claiming that Mr. Taylor and Dr. Thorpe pressured you too?"

David rose to his feet. "Objection, your Honor. Counselors statement is argumentative."

"Objection sustained. Mr. Mason, please rephrase your question."

"Yes, your Honor. Now Mrs. Pullman… did you completely understand what you were signing when he gave you the Affidavit?"

"I don't know… Mr. Johnson explained it at the time, but I don't remember all that he said."

"So Mrs. Pullman… if you can't even remember something that happened only a few weeks ago when Mr. Johnson had you sign that Affidavit, then how can you remember details of a conversation that happened months ago when you said that Dr. Thorpe threatened you? Perhaps you are at a stage in your life where you don't have the mental capacity to accurately remember conversations you had. Or maybe someone else put these things in your mind that you were threatened and that you were going to be placed in a mental institution. Well Mrs. Pullman, can you remember anything—anything at all!"

Rosemary began to crumble right before our very eyes. Her hands began to tremble and her eyes began to well with tears. As Mr. Mason repeated the question over and over, she was overwhelmed with emotion.

"No!" she cried out. "I just don't remember anymore!"

Katie could not bear to see this go on any longer. She jumped out of her seat and rushed to Rosemary's side.

"Stop!" she said, and waved Mr. Mason off. "Leave her alone!" as Katie held Rosemary in her arms.

Mr. Mason turned to the judge with a smirk on his face. "I'm done with this witness, your Honor."

The judge ordered a short recess in order for Rosemary to compose herself. We all went into the hallway, as Katie sat Rose down who was trembling in her arms. She looked at Katie with tear-filled eyes.

"Katie, please don't make me go back! I can't, I just can't anymore!"

Katie looked our way and waved us off, like saying; "No more, she can't handle any more of this—it's over."

Katie motioned for her mother to come sit with Rose for a moment. David gathered us together to discuss where we stood on the case.

"Well, I think it's over. I guess it looks like David is going to lose to Goliath this time."

As we sat dejected, Katie got up and walked-off by herself and began staring out the windows of the courthouse. After a moment, I went to her side and placed my hand on her shoulder.

"Hey, we tried, Katie."

"I know. But why should those who lie and threaten people get away with it—it's just not fair!"

Seeing how upset she was, I tried to cheer her up by saying something funny.

"Well, it's still early. Maybe Mrs. McAllister can make us some of her famous blueberry pancakes."

Katie looked off to the side, deep in thought. Suddenly those big beautiful eyes of hers began to fill with a glimmer of hope.

"That's it, Jess—blueberry pancakes!"

She quickly ran over to David and pulled him to the side. Then I heard David say, "Well it's worth a try Katie—we have nothing to lose."

They began to walk towards the courtroom, when I asked her what she and David were talking about.

"Jess, in the Bible, David took down Goliath with just a single stone. Do you know why? Because God allowed that stone to hit Goliath in the only vulnerable spot he had. I'm going to take down *our Goliath* at his weakest spot!"

Katie walked into that courtroom with a look in her eyes that I had never seen before. I had no idea what she was going to do. But whoever she was going after—they were in for a battle!

When we returned to the courtroom, David advised the judge that Katie was going to be calling one of defendants to the stand. The judge told Katie the floor was hers, and that she could proceed with the next witness.

"I would like to call to the stand, Mr. Ian Thorpe, CEO of Equity One Realty Corporation."

Shock ran across both Ian Thorpe and Mr. Mason's face. I think they were surprised he was being called to the stand at this time, since he had not been called him to testify before this.

The judge told him to raise his right hand and say his oath. But to me, that was a big joke. I knew this guy was not going to be saying "the whole truth and nothing but the truth."

Katie walked over to where David was sitting, and he handed her a file folder of exhibits. Katie walked up to the witness stand and then handed Ian Thorpe one of the documents from the exhibits folder. She then began her examination of the witness.

"Mr. Thorpe."

"Dr. Thorpe, please."

"Okay, Dr. Thorpe… I have handed you one of the exhibits in this case. Can you please tell the court what this document is?"

"Certainly, young lady. It is the sign-in log sheet from the Cedarwood Condominium complex."

"Now Dr. Thorpe… if you look at the date of April 6th, you will see it has your associate, Mr. Taylor going to see Rosemary Pullman in condo #A-10 on that date."

"Yes, young lady. That is when he gave her a written offer to purchase her condo."

"Now the log also shows that he came back two days later. Why did he do that?"

"Well, that is when he came back to see if she was going to accept the offer."

"Yes, but why would he need to do that when she told him in their first meeting that she wasn't interested in selling her condo?"

"Well sometimes people change their minds. We wanted to give her the opportunity to think about it."

"Wouldn't that be considered a type of harassment when she already told him no?"

"No it is not!" he snapped. "Mr. Taylor was merely trying to convince her that it was in her best interest to sell. I do not consider that to be harassment, young lady."

"It's Miss McCullough, thank you—not young lady!" Katie said with sarcasm.

"Fine, Miss McCullough," he countered with irritation of *her* correcting *him*.

"Now, Dr. Thorpe... After that second offer where she still refused to sell, then why did you yourself go to see her?"

"I don't recall that."

"So are you're saying you didn't go to see her on that date?"

"If you recall, Miss McCullough, that was Rosemary Pullman's testimony, not mine. I never made a statement about going to her condo and threatening her. That was her statement."

"Well maybe this will help refresh your memory?" she said, and pointed to the sign-in log sheet once more. "See right there. It shows you signed-in on April 9th going to the condo of Rosemary Pullman."

As Ian Thorpe scanned the document, his face flushed red with anger. He took the glass of water that was on the stand, and took a drink to gather his thoughts.

"Okay, now that I'm thinking about it, I did go to see her. And the reason I went to see her, was to offer her a larger sum of money for her condo."

"Well then Dr. Thorpe, it appears that you made a mistake right now in recalling the facts, didn't you?"

"No I did not! I had momentarily forgotten about that meeting with her."

"Hmm… you and Mr. Mason talk about Mrs. Pullman being forgetful; seems like somebody else is a little forgetful too!" she said sarcastically.

Mr. Mason stood to his feet. "Objection, your Honor!"

"Sustained... Miss McCullough, will you please refrain from your personal opinions."

"Yes, your Honor."

Ian Thorpe then sat up straighter in his seat, taking a defensive posture. Katie had him on the defense and I could tell by the fire in her eyes that she was ready to take him down!

"Now Dr. Thorpe… isn't it true that you told Rosemary Pullman that you were going to send her to a mental institution if she did not sign the contract?"

Mr. Mason stood to his feet once more. "Objection, your Honor; Counselor is leading the witness."

"Sustained... Miss McCullough, please rephrase your question."

"Yes, your Honor. Dr. Thorpe… did you tell Rosemary Pullman that you were going to send her to a mental institution?"

"I did not! That conversation never happened. I merely offered her more money for her condo."

"So Dr. Thorpe… you never told her you were going to send her to a mental institution in Las Vegas, Nevada?" As she said that, she turned to me with a strange telling look.

"No I did not," he replied. "Like I said before, that conversation never took place."

I thought about Katie's prior statement, coupled with the strange look she gave me. Suddenly, the light came on as to what she was doing, so I stood up and addressed the judge.

"Your Honor, may I approach the floor to confer with Miss McCullough? I believe she has made a statement to the court that I feel was incorrect."

"Very well, Mr. Thompson."

I walked over to where she was standing and began to tell her about the mistake.

"Katie, you made a mistake. You said that Dr. Thorpe told Rosemary that he was going to send her to a mental institution in Las Vegas, Nevada. It was Las Cruses, New Mexico."

"No Jess, I remember she said it was Las Vegas."

"No Katie, it was Las Cruses."

"No Jess, it was Las Vegas!" she said, and raised her voice.

"No, it was Las Cruses!" I countered, and raised my voice to be heard above hers.

Mr. Mason rose to his feet. "Objection, your Honor! This is ridiculous. Now the two of them can't even get *this story* straight."

"Miss McCullough… can make a decision about this issue, so we can continue," the judge urged.

"Yes, your Honor, but Jess is wrong. We need to get this exactly correct. I mean these statements are going down in the official records. Aren't they your Honor?"

"Yes Miss McCullough, it will be made a part of your official examination."

Ian Thorpe took out his handkerchief and wiped his brow. Then he looked over at the court reporter who was typing every word that was being spoken. This is when Katie and I got out our slingshots and started to fling our stones at Goliath!

Katie took hold of Ian Thorpe's pen and waved it in my face. "Jess, you're wrong. It was Las Vegas, Nevada."

Then she set the pen back down, but laid it sideways. Ian Thorpe then moved the pen perfectly back in place like he had it before. I then placed my hand on his glass of water and moved it slightly.

"Come on Katie, get it right. It was Las Cruses, New Mexico!"

Katie took hold of his pen once more. "No Jess, I remember it was Las Vegas because my aunt likes to call Las Vegas—Lost Wages." Then she laid the pen back down sideways.

Once again Ian Thorpe put the pen back in its place

"No Katie, it was Las Cruses, New Mexico!" I said, and moved the glass of water once more.

Then we got into this rhythm as she would grab his pen, set it down sideways and say, "Las Vegas!" Then I would move Ian Thorpe's glass of water and say, "Las Cruses!" Each time we did that, Ian Thorpe would move the pen and the glass of water back to its original spot. With each movement, his face began to flush with frustration, seeing this display in front of him.

"Las Vegas!", "Las Cruses!", "Las Vegas!" Las Cruses!", "Las Vegas!", "Las Cruses!"

Mr. Mason finally had enough and rose to this feet. "Objection your Honor! How long are we going to have to listen to this nonsense?"

The judge then pounded his gavel with authority, in order get Katie and I to stop.

"Miss McCullough and Mr. Thompson! If you do not stop this right now, I am going to hold the two of you in contempt of court!"

Katie turned to the judge. "Okay, your Honor, I guess I am going to have to make a final decision about this. I mean, I don't want to make a mistake and be inaccurate. After all, the court reporter is putting this down in the official records to be sealed up for all of time, as a fact!"

Ian Thorpe was now beside himself. He pulled his handkerchief from his pocket and wiped his brow which was beading with sweat.

Then he looked to the court reporter and then back to Katie, in anticipation of what she was going to say. Katie took in a deep breathe, and gave her final decision.

"Okay, here we go for the record... What Rosemary Pullman heard Dr. Ian Thorpe say, was that he was going to send her to a mental institution in..., Las Vegas, Nevada."

Upon hearing the final decision, anger and disbelief rose upon Ian Thorpe's face. He stood to his feet and pounded his fist on the stand. "NO YOU IDIOTS..., IT WAS LAS CRUSES, NEW MEXICO!"

The courtroom fell silent. As Dr. Ian Thorpe II stood trembling with his eyes bulging-out and mumbling to himself. Apparently having a nervous breakdown right there in the courtroom. David then turned to the judge to make a motion.

"Your Honor... I move that based upon Dr. Ian Thorpe's own admission, that he and Equity One Corporation be found guilty of Fraud, Misrepresentation and Coercion. I also move that the original contract between Sherman Investments and Equity One be considered null and void. Furthermore, that all homeowners, including my client Rosemary Pullman, be allowed to return to their homes at Cedarwood."

Judge Harold Wilson then addressed the courtroom.

"Based upon this confession of Dr. Ian Thorpe, I rule in favor of the Plaintiff, Rosemary Pullman. The contract between Equity One Realty Corporation and Sherman Investment is hereby declared null and void." He turned his focus towards Rosemary. "Mrs. Pullman... you may return to your home at Cedarwood. Court is adjourned."

"YES!" We shouted, and congratulated each other with a swarm of hugs.

After a few moments of celebrating, Judge Wilson approached Katie and me with a warm handshake.

"Very impressive work, Miss McCullough. You might make a fine lawyer someday. You and your partner make a very good team."

"Thank you, Judge Wilson. Jess and I *do* make a very good team. In regards to what you said about me becoming a lawyer, we will have to wait and see. I just know that my calling from God is to help people that are being taken advantage of, like Rosemary Pullman."

I turned to the Judge with a knowing smile. "So Judge Wilson… how long were you going to let us continue with that display, in order to get Ian Thorpe to say the mental institution was in Las Cruses, New Mexico?"

"You should know better than that. A judge in my position would never do such a thing." Then he gave us a little wink, and left the courtroom.

After more celebrating and hugs from our parents, David came over to give his congratulations.

"Well, we did it! Or shall I say, the both of you did it—especially you Katie."

"Well David, once I figured out where his weak spot was, Jess and I flung our stones at Goliath and left the rest up to God."

I playfully squeezed her bicep. "She's a lot stronger than she looks. Believe me, I have the bruises on my arms to prove it!"

"Jess, I can't believe you said that!" as she reared back and slugged me.

I rubbed my shoulder. "See what I mean, David?"

He laughed, and then continued with his praise.

"I am so impressed by the two of you. Other than a few outbursts in there, you both were amazing. Perhaps in the future we might be able to work something out and have you do a little investigative work for our firm. It would have to be after you turn sixteen because of labor laws, but I will keep the two of you in mind. And Katie… you have a gift to work with the elderly and a talent in presenting evidence with poise and a professional presence. Perhaps you might consider that direction in the future."

"Thank you, David. I think I may be heading in that direction."

As David walked off, we headed out to meet our parents who were waiting for us in the parking lot. As we made our way, I turned to her with a question that was pressing on my mind.

"So Katie… what made you think of going after Ian Thorpe and his weakness of having to be correct, accurate, and obsessive like he is?"

"Blueberry Pancakes!" she said with a beaming smile.

"What?"

"Yeah. Remember when you were trying to make me feel better by saying your little joke about blueberry pancakes? Well that reminded me of Mrs. McAllister being a neat-freak. Which in turn reminded me that Ian Thorpe had a real problem with accuracy and having to be correct all the time. That's when I realized what his weakness was."

I looked at her with admiration. "Wow Katie, you are really something, you know that?"

"Thank you for saying that. But I know it's God who helps me to be that something."

Before heading out, our parents gave us the choice of where we wanted to go to eat. They suggested a fancy restaurant, but we had other plans—no not Burger-King.

Katie and I decided we wanted to just order-in a good tasting pizza. When we arrived at her house we went in the den, while we waited for the pizza to arrive. After talking a bit more about the case, I stared at her in amazement.

"What Jess? Why are you looking at me that way?"

"I don't know; you never cease to amaze me."

She shyly turned away. "Stop it, you're going to make me blush."

"No really… you looked different up there in that courtroom. It was like you were growing-up right before my very eyes; from just a kid to a young lady."

She reached out and felt my forehead. "Are you okay? You're not tripping out or anything, are you?"

"No, I'm being serious. I am just so proud of you."

"Stop it; you're going to make me cry."

"No, don't do that. The pizza just arrived and I don't want it to get all soggy!"

She shook her head and rolled her eyes. "Jess, you're such a brat."

"I'm a brat? I thought you said I was your investigating partner."

"You're both. A brat, and my investigating partner."

I rose to my feet and helped her up. "Okay partner… now that our pizza has arrived, are you ready to celebrate our winning that case in court today?"

She smiled confidently. "Yes I am. But the real winner of that case, was Rosemary Pullman."

THE CONCLUSION

Later that evening, I lay in my bed thinking about the many changes happening in my life. Becoming a Christian was already changing the way I looked at things, as I began to listen to that voice inside me. I found out that sometimes you have people praying for you when you don't even realize it. And although sometimes it seems like it's taking a long time for those prayers to be answered, God knows exactly when to answer them. I also found out that coming to know the Lord as your savior is all about His perfect timing. Not only does the opportunity need to be there, but your heart needs to be ready to receive it. Too many times people repeat the sinner's prayer because someone asked them to. However, if those words are only coming from your mouth and not your heart, then you are not really making a true commitment. It's kind of funny how I had many other opportunities to make that decision, but "my time" ended up coming at a Christian concert at Great America.

Our search to find Rosemary Pullman only confirmed to me that God does in fact have a plan for our lives. I also believe what happened in that courtroom was just the beginning of a path which Katie and I were now on. A path which, in the near future would find us investigating something else that would turn up missing.

I also learned how we have a responsibility to try to pursue justice, and help those who cannot help themselves. Also, for us to never think that just because we are too young that we cannot be used of God; like when David was used to defeat Goliath.

I recently read a scripture verse that said, *"God hath chosen the weak things of the world to confound the things which are mighty."* He proved that in a great way, as we watched the "Goliath" in our lives fall by the hands of a fourteen year old girl!

There are times in our lives when we do not understand the path that God has set before us. Had Katie and I not been willing to do a small favor for the McAllister's, we would have never seen how mightily God can work in our lives. As it turned out, we not only helped a woman in great need, but defeated a giant corporation in the process.

So as we look ahead to the future, we need to be open to the path which God has set before us. And you never know when God will choose to use you on the next path you take. Like the path which lead us on our search… for Rosemary Pullman.

The saga continues in Episode Five of the series...

A message to my readers.

I hope you enjoyed the second book in this exciting series! To obtain the next book in the series, please visit my website at www.dcreyesauthor.com and follow the links to purchase. If the next book is not yet available, please link to my Contact page and mark, "Yes" that you wish to be notified when the next book is released. All books are available wherever books are sold. Besides the aforementioned series, I have other available titles as well!

David C. Reyes

***

Acknowledgments:

Thanks: To my lovely wife Linda, whose support and encouragement has been immeasurable. Without her by my side, all the hard work and timeless hours spent on writing my books, would have no meaning.

Editing: Jack Minor, JM Publications
http://www.jmpublications.com/

***

Book Cover Design Element Credits:
Front Cover: Wolf - Shuterstock Image_254862
http://www.shutterstock.com/

Back Cover: Gavel and clipboard with space for messages. Shutterstock Image_4073200.
http://www.shutterstock.com/pic.mhtml?id=4073200&src=id

Manufactured by Amazon.ca
Bolton, ON